BREAKUP, MAKEUP

BREAKUP, MAKEUP

STACEY ANTHONY

RP | TEENS
PHILADELPHIA

Running Press Teens
Hachette Book Group
1290 Avenue of the Americas, New York, NY 10104
www.runningpress.com/rpkids
@runningpresskids

Printed in the United States of America

First Edition: May 2023

Published by Running Press Kids, an imprint of Perseus Books, LLC,
a subsidiary of Hachette Book Group, Inc. The Running Press Kids name and
logo are trademarks of the Hachette Book Group.

The Hachette Speakers Bureau provides a wide range of authors for speaking events.
To find out more, go to www.hachettespeakersbureau.com
or email HachetteSpeakers@hbgusa.com.

Running Press books may be purchased in bulk for business, educational, or promotional
use. For more information, please contact your local bookseller or the Hachette Book
Group Special Markets Department at Special.Markets@hbgusa.com.

The publisher is not responsible for websites (or their content)
that are not owned by the publisher.

Print book cover and interior design by Mary Boyer

Library of Congress Cataloging-in-Publication Data: Name: Anthony, Stacey, author.
Title: Breakup, makeup / Stacey Anthony. Description: First edition. | New York, NY:
Running Press Kids, 2023. | Audience: Ages 13–99. | Audience: Grades 10–12. Identifiers:
LCCN 2022027526 | ISBN 9780762481637 (hardcover) | ISBN 9780762481651 (ebook)
Subjects: CYAC: Gender identity—Fiction. | LGBTQ+ people—Fiction. | Cosmetics—
Fiction. | Competition—Fiction. | Interpersonal relations—Fiction. | LCGFT: Novels.
Classification: LCC PZ7.1.A597 Br 2023 | DDC [Fic]—dc23 LC record available at
https://lccn.loc.gov/2022027526

ISBNs: 9780762481637 (hardcover), 9780762481651 (ebook)

LSC-C

Printing 1, 2023

For the anime club presidents, theater kids, dungeon masters, gay besties, and wild dreamers—you deserve everything and beyond

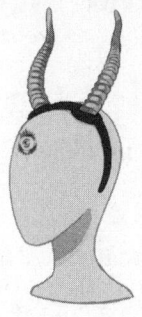

CHAPTER ONE

Los Angeles-FaeCon

"FORTUNE FAVORS THE BRAVE," ELI WHISPERED TO THEIR reflection.

They folded their upper half over a paint-speckled hotel sink and tipped their head from side to side, inspecting their work. The person staring back at them was in the last stage of metamorphosis, familiarity stripped away, new features sculpted in their place. Makeup had the power to do that—bury any uncertainties beneath a perfectly rendered likeness of an otherworldly somebody. Like this, with their shorn golden hair sprayed white and dusted with metallic glitter and their freckled cheeks lifted high, accentuated by two silicone prostheses, Eli became royal and mythical and *changed.*

The Hyatt staff wouldn't know what to do with a mess like this. A bottle of liquid latex sat untouched next to colorful ribbon trimmings, a palette of Ben Nye body paint, and blue-stained sponges. Glitter shimmered in the shallow sink, and a popsicle stick coated with half-dried Pros-Aide, a medical-grade adhesive, dangled from the lip of the nearby trash can.

An acrylic eyeball, created with a handmade mold Eli had debuted on their Weblog channel last week, rested in the soap dish. Their "Castor for FaeCon" video had raked in their highest numbers yet: twenty thousand views, fifteen thousand likes, and three hundred individual comments. They kind of wanted to kick themself for choosing to bust out the most difficult cosplay they'd ever created at a convention they'd never attended before, but a new convention meant new photographers, new cosplayers, new artists, and more exposure. And if Eli wanted to land another sponsorship, they needed to make a splash. They swallowed hard, then plucked the eyeball out of the dish. Difficulty aside, they were going to pull off this hard-as-hell cosplay even if it meant missing the shuttle to the convention center.

They'd walked three miles in head-to-toe makeup before, and they'd walk three miles in head-to-toe makeup again if they had to. Horns, tail, hooves, and all.

Carefully, Eli pressed the delicate eyeball into a glob of Spirit Gum and held it in place. One wrong move could potentially ruin their almost finished design, and unlike the gorgeously grotesque creations horror artists and Haunt Masters produced for scare-fests during Halloween, Eli couldn't fix a mistake with a splatter of fake blood. They groaned when their phone buzzed, clattering atop a closed eyeshadow palette. They tapped the screen, but their fake talons wouldn't register. "Jesus . . . *Christ* . . . C'mon," they grumbled, then hit the speaker icon with their knuckle. "Yeah?"

"Where the hell are you?" Eli's screen was instantly filled with the image of their best friend. Ghostly white contact lenses bleached Bodhi's brown eyes, a stark contrast to her copper skin. She bared her fake fangs in a grin and leaned closer to her phone. "Damn, son. That third eye, though."

Eli glanced at their reflection and cautiously lifted two fingers away from the pale blue eyeball, ringed in gold and framed by fake lashes. *There.* With their face shaped by prostheses, a third eye glued to their forehead, and two antelope horns attached to their temples, Eli had become King of the Northern Fae, Castor Iceheart, a character from one of the most popular tabletop role-playing podcasts out there right now.

Bodhi cleared her throat. "Eli, seriously. Come *on.*"

Three hours of work and no time to appreciate it. They huffed, a little annoyed but a lot excited. "All right, okay, I'll be down in two minutes. I just need my boots. Don't let them leave!" Eli screwed the Spirit Gum tube shut and dusted their brows with teal glitter.

"Yeah, sure, I'll just lay in front of the bus. Hurry your ass up," Bodhi barked. Her black-painted mouth crowded the screen. "And do *not* forget your badge!"

"Yes, yeah, okay," they mumbled and ended the Face-Time, tucking their phone into the hidden bag clipped around their waist.

Their hotel room was in disarray. A pink wig waterfalled over the edge of the nightstand, while tall leather boots slouched against the closet doors, and abandoned clothing littered the floor. Eli hunted for their staff—*There, next to the TV*—and their boot coverings, which were stashed in a suitcase. *Okay, done, ready to—*

They almost knocked one of their horns loose as they reached through the half-closed door to snatch their purple lanyard, which was weighed down by enamel pins, colorful buttons, and their pro badge, from the coat rack. *Two minutes to make the shuttle.* The door closed with a loud click as they darted down the hall, holding their floor-length robe off the ground in one hand and six-foot staff in the other, trying not to trip as they hurried into the lobby. Bodhi waved from outside, waiting half on the sidewalk, half in the bus.

"They're coming! Yes, right there! They're *right there*," Bodhi snapped, whipping back and forth between the driver and Eli.

Eli climbed into the bus, trying to catch their breath. Wearing a heavy cosplay *and* a half-tank binder didn't make it easy. "Hi, I'm here—I'm so sorry."

The driver, a balding man with a thick mustache, gave them a once-over. "I gather you don't get anywhere quick in those get-ups, huh?"

They heaved a sigh. Their chest strained against restrictive fabric. "Definitely not."

From the back of the bus, someone cosplaying Casual Castor, dressed in jeans, a hoodie, and much smaller horns, hollered, "What's up, Castor!" Eli laughed in response, waving two clawed fingers as they shuffled down the aisle.

Bodhi squeezed past them and shoved her backpack aside, making room for Eli to sit beside her. "Always late, always—"

"I know, okay? But the paint had to dry between layers or I'd look like a giant blue mess. Can you help me buckle these things?" They gestured to their feet, then poked Bodhi's knee, wrapped in shiny black vinyl. She was dressed as Valeria the Vengeful, a minor but popular vampire–turned–vampire hunter from *Chaos Reign*, the same podcast responsible for Castor. "You look awesome, by the way."

"I better look awesome after squeezing myself into this bodysuit," she said before blowing a breath and clasping Eli's hooves around their ankles, concealing their black combat boots. "Anyway, do we have a plan? Courtyard first, Hall A second, or ... ?"

"I really wanna make it to the Fears, Queers, and Other Monster Makers panel," Eli said, leaning back in their seat.

"You do know panels are in Hall C, right? Which is, like, a hop, skip, and a jump away from the Exhibitor Hall? We won't get ten feet through the door."

"We can try," they assured her and held their phone at arm's length. "Flash your fangs, Valeria."

Bodhi adjusted her long brunette curls and then gave a fake hiss for the camera. Eli opened Instagram and started typing the caption:

> Castor and Val are on the move. See you at West Coast FaeCon! Snap a pic with us and tag #EliSFX for a chance to win a Night Life Palette!

Then they posted the goofy picture. Not even a millisecond later, notifications popped up in their feed.

Being a makeup influencer wasn't what Eli had pictured for their first out-of-the-nest job, but they couldn't complain. Their name and social media handles—Eli Peterson, @EliSFX, and Makeup by Eli—brought in half the rent for their newly acquired five-hundred-square-foot apartment and covered a few bills. Honestly, the free products alone made the gig worthwhile. Makeup companies sent them palettes, glues, glitters, and concept sheets to feature on their platforms in exchange for a tag beneath a photo or a mention in their videos. Granted, Eli typically used household materials and affordable brands, but having the opportunity to play with the *good shit* made the job more fun.

They frowned at their phone.

HecateCosmetics liked your photo 32s.

"Oh, please," Eli scoffed, tilting the screen toward Bodhi. "Can you believe this shit? I've been begging them to let me test their product since sophomore year."

"Oof, yeah, they're high end, though. Don't they stock the Haunt Masters for Universal Horror Nights?"

"Yeah, but still. It's rude to ghost my emails and then like my posts."

"True."

Eli wanted to be the real deal: to walk on set for a multimillion-dollar movie and see their makeup on the big screen. But that, just like everything else, was a fantasy. High school was over, the end of their gap year and college were looming on the horizon, and being an influencer paid *half* the bills. Working at Denny's paid the rest. Anything they had left over went straight into the YEET THESE TEETS savings account they'd created halfway through senior year. Top surgery wasn't cheap, and neither was living in Los Angeles, but that's where the special effects makeup scene thrived, so LA would always be home.

Bodhi craned to look out the window as the bus cruised by lines of people hustling toward a red sign labeled BADGE PICKUP.

"Damn, it's packed," she said with a sigh. "You ready? Need any eye drops?"

Midnight-black contact lenses darkened the whites of Eli's eyes and their indigo irises. They couldn't wear them for long, but they'd last a few hours. "Nah, I'm good. You?"

"I'm good, too."

The bus halted in front of the Los Angeles Convention Center, and people whooped and cheered as the doors swung open. Convention-goers filled the sidewalk, some dressed in street clothes, others showing off their cosplay skills in over-the-top costumes or more subtle nods to their favorite characters. Eli adjusted the wooden buttons on their high-necked tunic and straightened the white faux-fur collar on their navy cape.

"Tail?" they asked.

"Looks fine. It's supposed to drag, right?"

"Yeah, it's painted foam. Horns?"

"Pointy. Fangs?" Bodhi hissed again.

"Also pointy."

Bodhi took a deep breath. "Ready?"

Eli nodded. "Ready."

They both stepped off the bus and made it exactly twenty feet before being stopped by a group of photographers. "Castor!" one of them called. "Val! Hey, can we get you two in a battle pose?"

"We're on our way to a panel, so just a couple," Eli said.

They spun their staff, squared their shoulders, and lifted their chin. A practiced sweep of their leg sent the robe billowing behind them. Next to them, Bodhi sank into a crouch, clutching a fake stake, and bared her fangs. After a few other photographers rushed in for a picture, some people pulled out their phones, snapping selfies and candid shots while Eli and Bodhi adjusted their poses. It had only been a few minutes, but Bodhi nudged Eli's foot and tipped her head toward the double doors.

Eli cleared their throat. "We'll be on the stairs for the *Chaos Reign* meetup this afternoon," they said, loud enough to be heard over the bustle of the crowd. "Thanks, everyone! Yep, yeah, thank you. Oh, hey, sure—" Eli paused to snap a selfie with someone. "Yeah, that's me. No space between 'Eli' and 'SFX.' Have a good con!"

Bodhi impatiently tugged their wrist. "You know we're never gonna make it to that panel."

"Just . . . walk, like, speed walk. Smile and nod."

"Yeah, yeah, I hear you."

The convention center courtyard was packed with cosplayers, photographers, and con-goers. Mecha suits flexed for flashing cameras. Popular comic-book heroes and villains pretended to duke it out next to a pretzel cart. Other *Chaos Reign* cosplayers nodded to them as Bodhi pulled Eli through the crowd, but before they could make it to Hall C, a princess in a yellow ball gown twirled in front of them.

"Pardon me," she said in a singsong voice and continued to spin through the room.

Before Eli could dip around a Sherlock and Holmes and keep moving, two younger cosplayers inched closer with their phones raised. Eli shot Bodhi an apologetic smile. Looking at those kids, their bright grins and eager eyes, made Eli hungry for a time they'd left behind. Waiting in online queues for tickets to conventions; attempting a zombie makeup with toilet paper, a glue stick, red food coloring, and gelatin; filling notebooks during panels with tips and tricks from the best in the industry.

It all started when they were fifteen, walking into a convention hall holding Zach's hand, coming face-to-face with impeccable cosplays. Now, almost four years later, on the cusp of choosing a college and a future they had no interest in, Eli desperately wanted to go back. Back to uncomplicated. Back to late-night makeup practices in Zach's bedroom. Back to everything they'd walked away from.

Bodhi sighed through her smile. "It's two *thirty*."

Eli covered their flinch with a smile as the two took their picture. "Thanks, guys! Have a good one!"

Then they plucked their robe off the floor and sped through the courtyard. Bodhi guided them between popcorn lines and book signings and through a crowded hallway, but Eli stopped in place when a particular booth caught their eye. The violet signage and bold title were too familiar to miss: BEYOND—MAKEUP ARTISTRY—REGISTER TODAY!

"We'll come back," Bodhi said, and tugged their hand, speeding through the corridor on the other side of the Exhibitor Hall until they hit the panel queue. Signs listed room numbers and schedule changes outside each designated panel area.

The printed sheet taped to Room 105C read FEARS, QUEERS, AND OTHER MONSTER MAKERS. A handwritten line above it spelled out: FULL.

Eli heaved an irritated sigh. Of all the panels and the days and the cosplays, they had to choose Saturday—convention prime time, when they were literally wearing Castor makeup—to miss a discussion with the creative team behind *Chaos Reign*.

"Yep," Bodhi said with a pop of her lips. "Sorry, honey. Maybe you'll catch 'em at the next show."

"Yeah, maybe," Eli replied, deflated. They wrinkled their nose in disappointment and pointed to an empty space against a wall. Bodhi nodded, following their lead, and then slid down to sit on the floor.

They'd only been there half an hour, but they were already in need of a break. At least Hall C was relatively calm, unlike anywhere close to the Exhibitor Hall, where vendors, booksellers, and artists set up shop for the weekend—bound to be slammed. They could usually go a couple hours without resting, but sometimes the crowds made it hard for Eli to catch their breath. Especially when they were cosplaying someone as popular as Castor. Missing the panel royally sucked, but sitting against the wall, scrolling through their phone, and enjoying a bit of quiet was a balm to their disappointment.

A part of them loved it: the cameras, the smiles, the compliments. But the rest of them wanted to do what they did best: hide in their tiny apartment with their circle light and their makeup tutorials, listening to role-playing podcasts and playing video games in their underwear. When they hid for long enough to need rescuing, Bodhi, bless her, never failed to drag them out for Taco Tuesday or brunch at Hamburger Mary's. Being an introvert wasn't *terrible*, but being an introverted influencer? Yeah, that definitely complicated things.

"You okay?" Bodhi asked, handing them a water bottle.

They took a sip. "Yeah. Should we attempt Artist Alley?"

"*Attempt* is the key word. I'm down if you are."

The moment Eli stood up, Room 105C opened and people started pouring out. A cosplayer in a Weasel fur suit, the seven-foot-tall marsupial from *Chaos Reign* who was also the party's rogue, lumbered into the hallway. Some attendees chatted with one another or flipped through the FaeCon guidebook, but most hovered outside the door, probably hoping to snag a picture with *Chaos Reign*'s star creators, Lee Gates or Theresa Jenkins.

Bodhi tapped their arm, pulling their attention to three clicking cameras pointed at them. Eli quickly shifted into character, holding their chin high and pointing their staff at a lens, then flashing a toothy grin and winking at another. Suddenly, they heard Bodhi say, "Yeah, that's them," and watched as she jutted her thumb over her shoulder, "but I don't know if they're doing interviews."

A Black woman with short, springy curls, wearing a Star Wars shirt with a "she/her" button pinned to the collar, leaned around Bodhi. She fixed her eyes on Eli and tipped her microphone toward them, silently asking for permission.

Eli blinked, taken aback. "Oh, me? As in, like, *me*, me? I'm just—"

"Eli Peterson, one of the youngest up-and-coming self-made special effects makeup artists in the game," she said, matter-of-factly. "Correct?"

"You make me sound *extremely* cool."

"It's my job to make things sound cool, including people." She extended her hand. "Pam Wippler, NerdsOut.com. The homegrown magazine devoted to the intersection of the queer community with creative industries and fandom spaces. I've got some questions if you're up for it?"

"Sure. Shoot."

"What's it like being openly nonbinary in the cosmetics industry?"

"Oh, I wouldn't say I'm *in* the industry. I literally just moved out of my parents' house, and I mainly focus on tutorials."

"Got your own place, huh? How's that feel?"

"Good, but kinda weird?" Eli said as they fiddled nervously with their badge. "Hopefully my family will see this whole makeup thing as a real job sometime soon. Right now, it's not that serious, though."

"You want it to be?" Pam asked. "Serious, I mean."

"Of course, yeah. I'd love to make monsters for a living."

"I bet." The cute gap between Pam's teeth showed when she grinned. "And what about your origin story? What, or who, got you into special effects?"

Eli's chest tightened. They should've expected that question. It was a standard checkpoint they constantly had to cross. "I started in eighth grade, actually," they said, and swallowed around the itch in their throat. *With Zach.* "With an old friend of mine. We used to practice after my parents went to bed." They could still hear his laugh, a little raspy, a little low. "Watched all the old horror movies, bought the 1965 Dick Smith do-it-yourself book." They remembered how his mouth felt against their pulse on their eighteenth birthday, sitting in the sand on Venice Beach, air still smoky and acrid from the New Year's fireworks. "Experimenting with latex and costumes and fake blood . . . It started something, you know. *We* started something." How Zach held his breath when Eli whispered *I'm not going with you* two days before graduation. "And it got me here, I guess."

"So what's next? Think you'll be fighting for the grand prize at the Cosplay Runway show in Seattle?"

They shoved memories away, narrowing their focus to *runway show.* "I'm not sure, actually. I haven't heard anything about it yet."

"Theresa is offering a twelve-month scholarship beginning this fall at Beyond in Hollywood to the winner. They'll be formally announcing the gig at the Cosplay Competition tonight. We'll see you there, right?"

"You sure will. Yeah, of course." Eli forced themself to smile normally, but every bone in their body hummed with excitement.

"Thanks for the interview," Pam said with a wave, then joined the Weasel cosplayer in the fur suit.

A scholarship to Beyond.

Suddenly Bodhi was there gripping their wrist and pulling them from their thoughts. "I'm starving, like, star-*ving*. Can we hit a food truck before we head to Artist Alley?"

Eli nodded absently.

Beyond was the best special effects makeup school in Southern California. And this was a shot at getting their foot in the door—at being more than an influencer by night and a server by day. This was the opportunity they'd wished for on every falling star and 11:11 and prepackaged fortune cookie throughout high school.

Their heart hammered in their chest, beating in time with two syllables.

Beyond.

CHAPTER TWO

Los Angeles-FaeCon

THE COSPLAY COMPETITION WAS HELD IN THE BALLROOM on the third floor. Fortunately, Eli and Bodhi arrived early enough to get seats. They weren't *great* seats, but that didn't matter. They could see the stage and the table where the judges, including Theresa Jenkins, would sit, and that was all that mattered. There were massive screens on either side of the stage, and the spotlights angled toward the makeshift runway that stretched from one wing to the other.

Ever since the missed panel and impromptu interview, Eli had scoured the Internet looking for more leads on the Beyond scholarship. The booth had been no help, so they had to rely on someone having leaked whatever information Theresa had let slip during the panel, and after clicking through twelve different Twitter profiles, they'd found it.

"So this Makeup Wars thing," Bodhi said, munching on some peanut M&Ms. "First there's glorified auditions, then there's the traveling battle of the baddest bitch, *then* the judges vote, those votes get combined with social media votes, and *that* determines the winner at the end? Did I get everything?"

"Yeah, you got it. I mean, it'll be fun, but I doubt I'll make it through auditions or win or whatever. I want to, I *hope* I do, but—"

"But?"

Eli sighed. "But it's probably best not to get wrapped up in this." If they were being honest, it was too late for that. Eli stared at their lap, thumbs rushing over keys as they typed, deleted, and then retyped the same post for Instagram over and over again.

What if gnawed at them. What if they didn't make it? What if they *did* make it? What if this was vindication for every twelve-hour shift they'd crawled through, every penny they'd dropped into their top surgery jar? Eli took a deep breath and tried not to be afraid. If they didn't win, they didn't win. But they had to try. *They had to.*

The entrance into the competition started on social media, and Eli was required to share a picture with #MakeupWars tagged at the bottom. Problem was, they couldn't decide between a selfie they'd taken earlier or a full-body photo Bodhi had gotten during the *Chaos Reign* meetup. One featured a half smile with their hand curled under their chin, showcasing their silver claws and the godforsaken foam run they'd perfected for their elvish ears. But the other showed their entire outfit, including their hooves and the slightly curved tail sprouting from the slit in their robe.

"All right, I'm doin' it," Eli blurted and tapped the selfie. "Ready?"

"Do it, bitch," Bodhi said, one cheek stuffed full of chocolate.

> Can't wait to compete with some amazing SFX artists for a chance to attend BEYOND! It's always been a big dream of mine to take classes from the best of the best and I can't wait to get latexy/ bloody/artsy with everyone during MAKEUP WAAARRSSS!! Thanks for the chance @theresa_chaos and @FaeCon. #MakeupWars

Eli hit "share."

Nervousness sloshed around in Eli's stomach. Cosplay competitions were one thing—a trophy or a medal, a check that might cover the cost of their materials, bragging rights at the next con—but a scholarship had the potential to fast-track their education. This could help them land a stable job instead of an unpaid internship. Beyond could change the trajectory of Eli's life.

"Kinda cool to finally see a makeup-centric cosplay contest. I mean, no doubt, I'm a costume fanatic, I *know* this shit is awesome," Bodhi said, and nudged them with her elbow. "But having something new and niche to add to the con lineup sure is a breath of fresh air."

The lights dimmed and applause rang out as a princess swathed in vibrant purple skipped to the center of the stage. Flowers were threaded through her thick braid, trailing behind her as she went, and a chameleon doll peeked from the basket looped around her arm.

"Damn," Bodhi said in awe, "look at that Rapunzel. I bet she'll place."

Eli sat higher in their seat and grinned as more cosplayers came and went. The packed ballroom clapped and cheered for every contestant, from first-timers to seasoned designers. Old-school characters in outfits from retired comics strutted across the stage, and new creatures from indie-developed games spread animatronic wings, inciting gasps from the audience.

Once all the contestants had taken the stage, the judges left to discuss who would place. Eli glanced around the ballroom, relieved to see clearly now that their contacts were out. Sometimes sclera lenses shadowed their peripheral vision, making it difficult to focus. Earlier, they'd almost dumped an entire In-N-Out double-double on themselves because they hadn't noticed the Robin Hood cosplayer standing beside them at the counter. Fortunately, Robin Hood hadn't spilled their Neapolitan shake either and had shyly asked where Eli had bought their fancy enamel pronoun pin. Conversation ensued, laughter followed. And in that moment, Eli remembered just how homey conventions could be.

Sometimes on bad dysphoria days or painfully long overnight shifts, they'd organize the pins on their lanyards and reminisce about how many artists they'd met and friends they'd made during weekends spent wandering Artist Alleys. Cons felt like home, even when Eli was almost spilling burgers and milkshakes on fellow enbies.

"Isn't there a *Chaos Reign* afterparty tonight?" Eli asked as they waited for the winner to be announced.

Bodhi nodded, bundling her big curls into a ponytail. "Yeah, but there's also a NerdsOut mixer and a lightning-round tabletop session. We could hit all three if we stick to a schedule."

"Us? *Schedule?*" Eli said through a laugh. "Yeah, no. Pick two."

"Oh, c'mon! Let's go to the mixer, do a lightning round, and then close out the night at the party. Makes sense, yeah?"

"Fine, fine, we'll give it a shot."

The lights dimmed again, and cheers rang through the room as the judges took their seats. Brett Howler, a famous cosplayer, took the microphone first, asking for a round of applause for all the contestants. He called the finalists to the stage and announced Rapunzel in third place and a Star Wars cosplayer in second. He awarded the first-place trophy to a massive full-body Dracon Warrior suit equipped with LED wings, 3D printed armor, and two giant reptilian heads.

Bodhi brought her mouth close to Eli's neck and whispered, "It's always someone on stilts."

Eli snorted a laugh. "True, but that face piece had to take days. Can you imagine the molds? The *glue*?"

"Oh, it's everywhere. Glue in the front, glue in the back, glue in the—"

"Nether regions," Eli said, and they both tripped into laughter. Then Eli gasped and almost toppled out of their seat as the words *Makeup Wars* floated across the screens hung above the stage. "Holy shit, okay, it's happening."

Bodhi took their hand and squeezed. "Here we go, sweets. Get ready."

Theresa Jenkins took center stage, wearing a sequined cape decorated in astrological constellations. Her short blond hair was slicked back, revealing silver elvish ear toppers and a dainty foliage choker. She was incredible, a powerhouse in the SFX industry, and Eli thought their heart might rupture if it beat any faster. Because if they won—*if they won*—they'd be one of her students. Their head spun at the thought.

"Thank you all so much for coming out tonight. How's everyone feelin'?" Theresa asked as she held her arms out, welcoming loud cheers, whoops, and whistles. "Good, good. Now, I have some exciting news to share with you. We talked about it during Fears, Queers, and Other Monster Makers, and I've seen the hashtag explode on social media, so . . ." A few people clapped or raised their hands, waving their phones in the air. "I'm unleashing *chaos* onto the special effects world! Are you ready?"

There were more cheers and even more hollers. Eli squeezed Bodhi's hand tighter.

"We're expanding the West Coast convention circuit to debut a summer showdown. This year, in tandem with the classic competitions we all know and love, I'll be turning our new Cosplay Runway into a battleground."

Theresa pointed to the crowd. "Over the next ten days, you'll be voting for your favorite artists during the virtual stage of Makeup Wars, an interactive social media competition to find the top five best makeup artists and cosplay designers in the country. I'll be sponsoring those creators at San Diego Comic Palooza, Anime Bay San Francisco, Oakland Heroes Expo, Portland's FanEx, and the final match during the Cosplay Competition at the infamous Sea City Comic Con in Seattle.

"With your help, I'll be choosing one artist to join me and my colleagues at Beyond for a full year of special effects and costume design education. Are you ready to help me find the next best special effects makeup artist?!"

Eli cupped their hands around their mouth and cheered.

Theresa swept her palm toward the big screens. "Let's take a look at some of our competitors!"

The screens shifted; animated blood dripped from the corners and cartoon cosplayers winked, framing a countdown next to the words *Entry Ends at Midnight*. The first face to appear was a well-known Indian American cosplayer stage-named Beverly Belle.

"Hell, yeah, Bev!" Bodhi shouted, pumping her fist in the air. "Show 'em what we can do!"

Eli vibrated in their seat as countless faces appeared with social media handles below them. There was Beverly Belle, the famous anime cosplayer. The ghoulish TikTok makeup artist Franklin Stein. Gary Harken. Cassie Anne Montgomery, the beauty specialist. Joe Morgan.

Eli had seen all their work float through their Instagram feed and pop into the "recommended" list on their Weblog channel. The nerves fluttering in their stomach turned heavy as they watched each new artist blink onto the screen. *So much fucking talent.* Eli swallowed, fiddling with a button on their robe. Maybe they should've thought this through more.

"Holy shit—holy *shit*, Eli!" Bodhi smacked their hand, pointing frantically at the screen.

Eli's selfie manifested, and the audience cheered. Something electric bloomed inside them, burning away their anxiety. Listening to the crowd shout and holler, watching their face, seeing their name beside creators they adored and envied—they couldn't help but grin. This was *it*. They were shooting their shot.

"I can't believe I—" Eli's voice faltered, snared on the jagged rock lodged in their throat. They stared at the screen. At that face. *His face.* Then everything inside them went careening toward their rib cage. They felt light-headed, seized by dizzy, panicked disbelief.

Right there, after Eli's selfie, was future Haunt Master Zachary Miller.

Zachary Miller, the boy who'd given them a promise ring junior year and practiced makeup with them late at night and kissed them on the mouth at prom and said *I love you* first.

Zachary Miller, the makeup artist who represented high-end brands like Hecate and HeartStopper, who'd attended the exclusive SFX workshop at Shockwave Studios in New York and had half a *million* followers on Instagram.

Zachary fucking Miller. The guy who owned the heart Eli had thoroughly broken.

Bodhi gasped. "Zach's back?" She whipped toward Eli, fangs poking over her bottom lip, eyes wide and unblinking. "I thought he was in New York, like, *permanently*?"

"Me, too," Eli croaked. Heat rushed into their face. They needed to move. To go. *Just go.*

"Hey, whoa, wait!" Bodhi said, flailing and grabbing their staff before it hit the ground. "Wait, wait, hold on, Eli!"

But Eli was already gone. They tripped over their own feet, and one hoof ripped, flopping against the floor as they made for the hallway. They clipped their horn on the doorframe, followed by their shoulder. There was a devastating sound, like a zipper coming undone, as the foam tore. They were going too fast, but instinct told them to *run*. To get away from the ballroom. To go somewhere safe and small where they could be alone with their heaving breaths and shaking hands. They pressed the down button on the elevator again and again and *again*.

Finally, the bell dinged, and Eli slipped inside.

They should've known. They should've anticipated this. But even if they had, nothing—not a damn thing—would've prepared them to see Zach's face on that screen.

"Okay," Eli whispered, pacing back and forth inside the elevator. "Okay, it's fine. You're fine. This is fine."

Memories rushed behind their eyes. A year ago, fidgeting with their purse in the passenger seat of Zach's truck. Trying and failing to find a way to say it. *I'm not going with you.* Weeks before that, dancing at winter formal. Fumbling under each other's clothes in the back row of a movie theater. Kissing Zach's jaw on the Venice Beach Boardwalk. Holding his hand as they queued for a panel at Anthrocon. Making plans together. Stitching their dreams together.

It felt like Eli had shot backward through time and jumped into their body two minutes before they'd shattered their own heart.

The elevator rocked to a stop, the bell dinged, and the doors opened.

Eli halted midstep. Their breath wobbled, stuck halfway to a gasp.

Zach's eyes were as green as they'd ever been. "Eliza—"

"Eli," they blurted and swallowed hard. "It's Eli."

"Eli . . ." he said, testing. Their name was a warm rasp in his mouth. "Been a minute."

"Yeah, yes. It . . . it sure has. I'm just . . . I'm gonna—" Another rip sounded. Their antelope horn fell, whacking them across their cheek and nose.

Zach winced. Jesus Christ, *he winced.*

"Go." *Run in traffic. Dive into the ocean. Walk into the desert and never return.* They held their limp horn in one hand

and gathered their robe in the other, stumbling over their limp hoof as the elevator door began to close.

Zach blocked the metal door before it bumped into them. "Got it?"

"Yep, sure do."

They tried not to give in. Tried to keep walking, defeated and trembling, but they couldn't stop themself. They had to look over their shoulder, to get a glimpse of the light stubble on Zach's cheeks and his dark bronze hair, to peek at the new ink snaking along his throat, to count the three—no, four—hoops punched through his earlobes. To memorize how his black button-down shirt clung tightly to his shoulders, and how his cold expression had hardly shifted, and how his lips hadn't formed a smile. Not even when he'd said their name.

Eli paused. Twisted their robe between their fingers, rallied their bravery, and looked.

Their heart ruptured.

The elevator doors had shut, and Zach was gone.

Again.

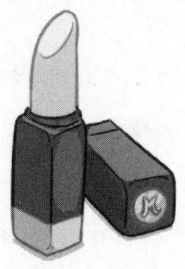

CHAPTER THREE

Los Angeles–FaeCon

ELI TORE OPEN KETCHUP PACKETS WITH THEIR TEETH AND squeezed the contents onto their plate next to a pile of thick-cut fries. They hadn't gone to the NerdsOut mixer or the lightning-round tabletop session *or* the *Chaos Reign* afterparty. In fact, they hadn't gone anywhere until Bodhi had found them standing awkwardly in the middle of the lobby, holding their broken antelope horn in a shaky grip. Bodhi had flown from the elevator, plucking her fangs off as she crossed the lobby to them as a few convention-goers and cosplayers had loitered outside the Exhibitor Hall and volunteers had floated around them, checking lights, arranging chairs, emptying trash cans.

Bodhi had waited until they were in the shuttle to say, "I ran into Zach."

And Eli had waited until they were safely inside their hotel room to say, "Yeah, I did, too."

Bodhi had only nodded.

She'd sat on the edge of the bed while Eli had swayed on their feet, staring at the floor as the minutes stretched. Eli had swallowed around the lump in their throat and gestured to the bathroom, and Bodhi had mirrored them, waving nonchalantly at the laminated room-service menu on the nightstand.

A full-face makeup removal was always satisfying. The way their skin flexed as silicone peeled away, how prostheses lifted, bubbling under their fingers like gelatin. Eli stayed in the bathroom, flashing playful smiles at their phone as they recorded the removal process for their Instagram story, steeped in fumes from alcohol-soaked cotton and the waxy crayon smell of the paint and glue. But once Castor was gone, Eli and their heartbreak were the only things left. Their smile faded, and their confident facade crumbled. When they got out of the bathroom, Bodhi was waiting for them with a feast.

"Okay, we have salt, we have sweet, we have beer," she said, pointing out each plate on the hotel-room desk. "Showers? Taken. Skin care? Done. Let's rip the Band-Aid off and jump in." She sat on the bed across from Eli, jamming her fork into a brownie sundae that sat next to a mountain of fries. "So, Zach's back."

"Yep, he . . . he sure is," Eli mumbled as they snatched a can of whatever craft beer Bodhi's girlfriend had bought them and took a sip. "So I think I'm gonna drop out of Makeup Wars."

"Absolutely not," Bodhi snapped. She swiped a flyaway off her forehead, brown cheeks dewy from her fancy rose-hip serum, and pinned them with a hard look. "That's *not* happening, Liz. You're doing this."

Eli popped a fry into their mouth, chewed, and swallowed. They remembered Zach's lips forming a name they no longer used. "He almost called me . . ." they mumbled, ignoring the discomfort squirming beneath their skin. They'd changed their name after Zach had flown to New York, slicing at syllables as if they were on an autopsy table. Snapped Eli away like a bone. Liz, too. And left the whole of it empty like an exoskeleton. "Not like he could've known or anything, but he just . . . He looked like he'd seen a ghost."

"Well, no offense, but you did the whole *I'm trans, hear me roar* and chopped, like, *all* your hair off, so I bet he was surprised," Bodhi said with a shrug. She grimaced. "But still, he knows you're nonbinary—he's known since forever. New hair can't be *that* shocking."

"He's known for as long as *I've* known, so yeah, like freshman year," Eli said as they grabbed a fork and dug into the brownie. "If he makes it through Makeup Wars, and he's going to, and I make it, then . . . then I'll have to compete against him, and I can't. I'm not—" It felt like the words

31

were rushing out faster and faster, along with all the air in their lungs.

"Oh, my God, do you hear yourself?" Bodhi asked, placing her hand firmly on their face and forcing them to look at her. "It's been a whole fucking year, Eli. You broke up! Breakups happen. Don't let old shit ruin this for you."

"I wouldn't call it *old* anything," they said under their breath. They pushed globs of melted ice cream around on the plate.

Bodhi signed. "C'mon, I mean, it's *Zach*. It's not like he'll be an asshole about it."

"Have you forgotten what went down?" Eli said, pinning her with a cold glare. "One, I told him I wasn't going to New York forty-eight hours before we were supposed to drive to the airport and get on a plane together. Two, we had plans, like actual, real-life plans: rent an apartment, intern at Shockwave after the workshop, get jobs, get married, and I—"

"First of all, I would've crossed the whole-ass country, hog-tied you, and brought you back to LA before I ever let you get married before your twenty-first birthday. And second, you did what was best for *you*, okay? You made a tough choice at the last minute, and it . . ." She sighed, smoothing her hand over their knee. "It sucked. It *hurt*. Trust me, I know it did, because it hurt me, too. These things just do, and sometimes they hurt for a while, but you can't *not* chase this huge, gigantic, monumentally important opportunity because your ex blew into town."

"He's a Haunt Master," Eli said dumbly, shielding themself from the passive-aggressive blade Bodhi had fit between the fluff. *Because it hurt me, too.* They wanted to bite her. Wanted to say, *I didn't ask you to choose me. You could've stayed friends with him.* But they didn't. "He's the next big name in horror, Bodhi!"

"Okay, he did two Haunt seasons—*two!*—and no one, not a single person, is impressed with two three-week Halloween theme-park gigs, especially when he was an assistant for one. That *Haunt Master* title is cute and all, but you can't bullshit a bullshitter. He was my best friend, too."

"Okay, whatever, he *will* be a Haunt Master. He's probably already on Universal's production team because he was everyone's favorite high school intern and he's got, like, nine hundred sponsors and a fancy Shockwave certificate to wave around and . . . and a *tattoo*? Did you see that? He got a fucking tattoo, Bodhi."

"Focus!" Bodhi said as she clapped an inch from their nose. "Repeat after me: I'm not dropping out of Makeup Wars."

Eli huffed.

"Say it!"

"I'm not dropping out of Makeup Wars."

"I'm going to *win* Makeup Wars."

"Bodhi—"

"Say it!"

"I'm going to win Makeup Wars."

Bodhi made a face and lifted an eyebrow. "I'm a badass makeup artist."

Eli's lips twitched as they fought a smile. They sighed, stuffing more brownie into their mouth. "I'm a badass makeup artist," they mumbled.

Bodhi grinned, snatching her beer off the nightstand. "Bodhi's always right."

They jabbed her playfully in the leg with their fork.

After that, laughter rang through the hotel room and Bodhi made a point of steering the subject away from Zach, talking about Eli's follower count and their first look for Makeup Wars instead. Eli smiled and pulled up inspiration on their phone. They let her believe they weren't dwelling and made an effort to ignore the thought of Zach, of what they'd been together, of who they were apart.

Once the lukewarm fries and the soggy brownie were gone, Bodhi and Eli drained the last of the six-pack, set the dirty plates on the floor, and brushed their teeth together in the bathroom. Half an hour later, Bodhi fell asleep while a Lifetime movie played in the background, curled toward the nightstand with her back to Eli.

Light from the TV bounced around the room, illuminating piles of clothes and Eli's tail draped over the dresser. They opened Instagram and tapped on the search bar, typed *Zachary Miller*, and hovered over his profile. They tapped again and flicked their thumb across the screen, scrolling through snapshots of Zach's life post-Eli.

He'd changed just enough to feel unfamiliar. Let his stubble grow out until it peppered his cheeks. Pushed hoops through his ears and wore his hair shorter than he used to. Eli opened a picture of Zach sprawled across a table at a tattoo parlor, the tattoo gun against his neck, carving a fine line that attached to a floral piece on his chest and shoulder. The caption read *Kicking off New York with my first tat!* That was two days after he'd left LA and four days after Eli had kicked his heart in the ass.

Eli mindlessly scrolled through their past. They paused over a picture of the two of them, Eli pressing a messy corn-syrup kiss to Zach's jaw and Zach laughing boldly, as he always did, cheeks dimpled, his crooked bottom tooth in full view. Eli's hair was still wheat-gold, pooling over their shoulder and thick as a horse's mane. Their eyes were clouded by white contact lenses, and their hand was perched gently on Zach's shoulder. They skimmed the caption, something about *love*, something about *future*, something about *always*. They shoved their phone under their pillow.

Sometimes Eli could go an entire day without Zach climbing into their thoughts. They'd film a tutorial, make themself lunch, work through an overnight shift, and then, after all that, as they sat on the Metro in the early mornings, they'd accidentally wonder what Zach was eating for breakfast. Where he was. If he was waking up next to somebody else.

Then there were times like right then, in that hotel room, clutching the crisp white sheets, when Eli thought about the harder things. About leaving and being left.

They had done their best to move on, to live their life, to scrub him out like an old stain, but no matter how hard Eli tried, thinking about Zach was inevitable.

CHAPTER FOUR

Los Angeles

ELI SHIFTED ON THEIR FEET, STANDING IN FRONT OF A TWO-top table, drumming a pen on their notepad. "No, sir, we can't put hash browns in a milkshake," they said, exasperated.

Not only did they work the late-night shift, they worked the late-night shift at a Denny's connected to the shittiest motel in West Hollywood, the Walk of Fame Roadside Inn. Police cars routinely patrolled the parking lot, and there was always someone pacing on the second floor. Sometimes they would see a cigarette ignite, glowing orange through the dark, or shadows would cross closed curtains, coming and going. Typically, Eli served the quiet inn patrons, taking orders from folks with flighty eyes and lonesome faces or couples who were strangers on every night but that one. Other times, Eli gritted their teeth and dealt with men who were six cocktails deep and wanted to *drink* breakfast foods at three in the morning.

"We literally can't put anything except ice cream, syrup, milk, and whipped cream in the milkshakes. I know, totally unfair," they said, in a high, overly friendly tone. "Anyway, how do you want your eggs?" Eli was finally able to scribble something on their notepad and then hurried away so they could punch the order into the POS system next to the kitchen window.

Max, the overnight cook, flipped pancakes on a steaming griddle. He scratched under his beard net and tightened the grease-stained apron tied around his bulky middle. "You almost out of here, kid?"

"Yeah, I was supposed to be gone a few minutes ago, but Linda asked me to put in an order for her while she cashed someone out. Watch table four, all right? Dude's about two drinks away from passing out."

"Course he is." Max flipped the hotcakes onto a plate. "Let Linda know on your way out. I can't do much from back here."

Eli rapped their knuckles on the steel counter. "Will do. See you on Sunday."

"Get home safe!"

They hung their apron on the kitchen door and clocked out at the front register, nodding to Linda, a silver-haired insomniac with a wide nose, shadowy crow's feet, and a smoker's cough. "Your table's got a sleepwalker," Eli said, cringing. "Could probably use some coffee. I can put a fresh pot on if—"

"*Again?* I swear, we don't never get a break, do we?" Linda rolled her eyes and blew out an irritated breath, waving them off with a dismissive flick of her wrist. "Go on, get. I'll take care of it."

They flashed two fingers over their shoulder as they headed for the door. "Bye, Linda."

"Good luck with your makeup stuff," she called.

They pushed through the front door, sinking into the lukewarm humidity of LA. Even in the early hours, when darkness still touched every corner of the city, summer stuck to their skin. Eli huffed, searching for autumn in the dead heat. Instead, they heard heels clicking on the concrete. Somewhere in the distance, a bottle shattered, and closer, dogs yipped, tearing through lots and alleys with joyful abandon. Eli put their knock-off AirPods in their ears and tapped the phone's music app. After a short ride on the rail and a two-block walk, they made their way through an overgrown courtyard and climbed the stairs to their apartment.

Air conditioning brought goose bumps across their skin, too cold and just right, as exhaustion settled deep, a weighty, familiar thing, pulling them closer to the king-size comforter draped over their mattress. Their keys clattered on the coffee table, and they kicked off their shoes, letting their clothes fall into small puddles on the floor as they pulled them off. They yanked off their binder last, inhaling a full, achy breath, and then crawled into bed, flopped on their stomach, and stayed like that, half covered by the comforter with their cheek two inches from the pillow.

They did calculations in their head, adding three hours of overtime to forty-five dollars in tips. "Ninety," they whispered. It wasn't a lot by any means, not with rent and bills and food and everything else. But they could put some away. Keep saving until they had enough to move forward with Dr. Tamura.

Make more tutorials, clock more overtime.

Win Makeup Wars, get the scholarship.

Beyond could change everything.

Eli peeled their eyes open and watched the sky turn navy through slots in the blinds. Their thoughts were slow and soupy, lingering like yesterday on the horizon. When they thought of Makeup Wars, they thought of FaeCon and then of Zach's eyes fixed on them in the elevator.

They rolled over and glanced around their apartment. Zach would've made a comment about the unpacked boxes pushed against the wall. *Put your stuff away, babe. Make it homey.* He would've stopped by on his way to the Pantages Theater for his opening shift, bagels in one hand, smoothies in the other, and Eli would've fucked him on the floor while morning traffic clogged the streets. They hated imagining what life could've looked like with Zach and couldn't stand dwelling on memories reshaped by regret. But Makeup Wars was their future and Zach was their past, and they couldn't think about one without thinking about the other.

They inhaled sharply and squeezed their eyes shut again, burrowing under the blankets only to toss them away a second later. They hunted for a semiclean shirt and found a sports bra next to their laundry basket, pulling them both on. They tugged the blinds open, flipped the switch on the freestanding lamp, and walked into the bathroom, pushing lotion bottles and a curled toothpaste tube off to the side.

Eli propped their phone against the mirror, turned on their circle light, and opened a pastel eyeshadow palette. They swiped lazily at their cheeks with a cleansing cloth. Next they pressed foundation into their skin and concealer under their eyes, then powdered. They added another layer of concealer, trapping dark circles beneath silky makeup, and powdered again. Los Angeles was barely awake outside their apartment, but Eli found the quiet comforting.

They worked diligently. Dabbed balm on their lips and primer on their eyelids, then sculpted their eyebrows and applied pale pink eyeshadow with a damp brush. Their thoughts narrowed to the point of their eyeliner, the shimmer dusted on their cheeks. They twitched, smudging black beneath their eyebrow, and immediately went to work cleaning, concealing, reapplying. Once they finished, Eli stared at their reflection, brightly lit in blushing tones. Eyes like rose petals, lips sticky with gloss, brows arched, and lashes fanned by black mascara.

Like this, they looked soft and wild and ready to bloom. They snapped a few selfies, tilting their jaw up and down, chin pointed left, then right, and grinned, tongue stuck between their teeth. They posted the last one to Instagram, smile blazing, the neon white from their circle light reflected in their eyes, and typed out the caption:

> Anyone here heard of Area X? Get ready to see the finished product!!! I'm coming for you #MakeupWars!

A notification flagged the top of the screen. They stared at it, unblinking.

HauntedByZach liked your photo 15s.

West Hollywood was never boring. Bikini straps peeked under crop tops, and button-down shirts billowed open. On the weekends, mimosas were poured from glass decanters on open-air porches at popular brunch spots, and chic fusion food trucks lined the sidewalks in front of thundering nightclubs. The city never failed to come alive, igniting like a torch on the Southern California coast.

Eli sidestepped a skateboarder, tossed pocket change into an open guitar case, and crossed the street on Santa Monica Boulevard. Colorful banners fluttered behind a sushi restaurant, pinned from a ratty fence to the roof of Los Primos, a lime-green taqueria on wheels. Picnic tables were scattered between parking spaces, and a makeshift salsa bar filled a foldout table.

Bodhi sat with her heeled boot propped on the seat, grinning at Stella, a beautiful Filipino woman with pin-straight black hair and an Atlas moth tattooed on her throat. She was older, better, and prettier than anyone Bodhi and Eli had ever hung out with before. She had an alligator smile, marketed for raves at night, and freelanced for MAC Cosmetics during the day.

"Hey, I already ordered everything. Two chicken, two barbacoa, right?" Bodhi asked, patting the space beside her.

"Yeah, perfect. I'll Venmo you." Eli slid onto the bench and smiled. "How's it goin', Stella?"

Stella dragged her perfectly manicured nails through her hair. "Keeping busy. Bodhi sent over a few clips from your Instagram. Anything else you think I'll need before I put this video together?"

"Just the final look," Eli said. "Thanks again, by the way. I would've done it myself, but I know jack shit about compilations."

"No worries, I do this stuff all the time. Videos get more people in the door than flyers do, so." She smiled and shrugged. "What's on the agenda? Tacos, makeup, ice cream?"

"Tacos, ice cream, makeup," Bodhi corrected.

A Los Primos cook hollered, "Siete!"

"I got it. Salsa, yeah?" Bodhi slid off the bench seat and walked over to grab their order.

"Yeah," Eli and Stella said in unison.

Stella waited for Bodhi to hover over the salsa bar before she flashed a grin, leaned in, and pinned Eli with a mischievous look. "What's this I hear about somebody's ex coming back around?"

Eli heaved a sigh. *Of course.* "She told you? *Seriously?*"

"She tells me everything."

"Yeah, he's ..." *Back, and I don't know what to do.* "It's really not a big deal."

"Bodhi thinks it's a big deal." Stella's grin stretched.

"I think *what's* a big deal?" Bodhi asked as she returned with a tray full of tacos, salsa cups, and pickled jalapeños.

"The ex."

"Oh, Zach? Yeah, he's a big fucking deal," Bodhi said, and pushed Eli's tacos toward them. "Have you texted him yet?"

"*What?* No, obviously not." Of course, Eli had drafted six different texts to Zach, but they hadn't sent a single one. Too many variations of *How are you* and *It's been a minute* and *I hope you're doing well* haunted their message app. They'd tried again—*I'm sorry for everything* and *I miss you* and *Can we talk?*—but they'd deleted those, too. Bodhi certainly didn't need to know that, though. "He liked my post this morning. Like, right after it went live."

"Which means he follows you," Stella said.

Eli shook their head. "He doesn't. I checked."

"'I checked,'" Bodhi parroted under her breath and bit into a taco.

"Yes, I checked," they said forcefully.

Stella nodded, wiping her mouth. "And this is the high school sweetie, right? The one that got away?"

Bodhi grimaced. "*Got away* is a bit of a stretch—"

"Can we seriously not do this?" Eli said, staring at the table. Their cheeks flushed hot, and their fingers twitched and jerked in their lap. Talking about Zach was one thing. Talking about Zach like he wasn't a wound was something else entirely, especially when everything about him still hurt. "A year isn't *that* long, and I really, *really* don't want to talk about it."

Bodhi stopped chewing and exchanged a quick glance with Stella. Speakers under the ice cooler blasted hip-hop while people stood around, sipping Jarritos and eating tacos. Eli didn't move. They stayed still, waiting.

Finally, Stella cleared her throat. "But . . . he's doing this contest thing, too, isn't he? You'll probably run into him if—"

"If I make it through Makeup Wars, yes," Eli said, tempering the heat in their voice. "But I highly doubt I'll make the top ten, and I definitely won't make the top five. And . . ." They stopped to take a breath. "My main concern is money right now, since I have, like, *none*, and scouts for high-end brands will probably be scrolling through the hashtag looking for new ambassadors. So worrying about pulling off the best makeup I can is a lot more important than figuring out what I'll say to Zach if I run into him again."

Bodhi sighed through her nose. "You *want* that scholarship. I know you do. Beyond is all you've talked about for years, Eli."

"Yeah, and Zach is all you've talked about since FaeCon, so can we please stop?" Eli said, then snatched a chicken taco and stuffed it into their mouth.

Bodhi's lips thinned, and Stella looked away, picking through the basket of tortilla chips. Cigarette smoke wafted through the air from a group standing near the sidewalk. Eli inhaled deeply, sucking in dry heat and the sour smell of the city—stale beer bottles in a recycling bin, charred meat wafting from sizzling grills.

They wanted to forget about Zach, but sometimes, most of the time, when they caught themself trying to escape a memory, they imagined newness. What being with him now might've been like if Eli hadn't tossed his heart in the gutter. They hated it, *hated it*, but they couldn't stop. And seeing him again? Talking to him? *Competing* against him? Eli didn't know if they could do all that.

"You still looking for a doctor?" Stella asked innocently.

Eli breathed a little easier, thankful for the subject change. "I found someone in Newport Beach. She's trans, too. Great reviews, offers a payment plan, definitely *doesn't* take my insurance. But, I mean, I've got almost half saved, I think. Not including post-op stuff."

"These puppies were three G's each," Stella said. She squished her breasts between her arms and laughed, swatting Bodhi's hand away. "Nothin' like a hefty dose of gender-affirming debt, but it was worth it. For me, at least.

"Some trans folks don't need surgery, don't want surgery, don't wanna *deal* with surgery, you know how it is. But damn." She looked at herself again, lacy blue bra peeking from beneath her strapless dress. "You won't catch me complaining."

Eli laughed with Bodhi and Stella.

"If I get a few more brands on board," Eli said, "I should be able to book a consult sometime this fall. Maybe get on the schedule after the first of the year? I don't know, we'll see." They poured chunky green salsa over their last taco.

"Uh-huh, and if you do, somehow, maybe, possibly get that Beyond scholarship, you'll bring in way more of those high-quality work-from-home influencer dollars," Bodhi said, testing the waters. She arched her eyebrow. "And, you know, get in with the Hollywood big shots."

"Yeah, somehow." Eli sighed.

"Maybe," Stella reiterated, pitching her upper half over the table so that she was almost nose to nose with Eli.

"*Possibly*," Bodhi teased and leaned in closer, too, whispering playfully against their ear.

Eli tried not to laugh and failed miserably. "Listen, I hear you, okay? Beyond is the dream. It's been the dream since I *could* dream. But I'm not putting all my eggs in one basket."

"Okay, sure, but I know how skilled my best friend is," Bodhi said, matter-of-factly. "So I'll put a few eggs in there for you."

"Fine, fine, whatever. Ice cream? There's a McDonald's on the way to my place." Eli stacked their empty cardboard trays and tossed them into the trash. They smiled at Bodhi, an apology written in their tense mouth and tight shoulders, and she smiled back, looping her arm around their elbow.

Later, after Eli had smoked a joint and Stella had gone home, they would apologize for snapping at Bodhi, and she would apologize, too. But Zach's name would still burn between them like a hot coal, tossed back and forth, singeing skin. Eli and Bodhi would do what they always did: talk around useless, painful things, as if attaching anger to loss might make it feel different.

Better, not different.

Bodhi would say, "He left me, too. Didn't even say goodbye," and so much more would prickle under the surface, dying to be said.

Eli would say, "I know, I'm sorry," and hope with every fiber of their being that Bodhi would let the rest remain buried.

It would go on like that, a still sore bruise they both shared. Bodhi would be ready to talk about Zach, ready to stop the bleeding and start to heal, but Eli would be unable and unwilling to let him go for good.

CHAPTER FIVE

Los Angeles

"OKAY, WHAT CAN I DO TO HELP?" BODHI ASKED AS SHE held a gluey paintbrush in one hand and a metal palette in the other.

"Well . . ." Eli tipped their head from side to side. Two matching Pros-Aide transfers, glue-based prostheses that blended seamlessly with skin, accentuated their bone structure, carving their cheeks into sharp lines. They wanted to replicate the same subtlety from their Castor cosplay, two parts human, one part something else. "You can hold this branch-antler thing while I glue the edges down."

Outside the bathroom, Stella sat on an oversized pillow in front of their coffee table, typing on her rose-gold laptop. She leaned sideways until her face appeared in their mirror. "I've almost got this finished. How long 'til the money shot's ready?"

"Like, twenty minutes?" Eli said with a grimace. They took the paintbrush from Bodhi and dabbed tacky Pros-Aide over the pantyhose stretched across the bottom of the antler. The branches they'd constructed came from the floral section at the local craft store—the type of fake foliage middle-aged women stuffed into vases or bundled to look chic atop kitchen counters. The pantyhose worked like an extra foundation, cut into small squares and attached to Eli's forehead, helping to hold the antlers in place. "Okay, one . . . two . . ."

They let the antler go. It wobbled but stayed upright, decorated in pink and violet flowers. Eli exhaled with a smile.

"Bambi, but make it body horror," Bodhi said, leaning around their shoulder to study Eli's face.

"Bambi, but make it VanderMeer," they corrected.

They attached the other antler. Exhaled again when it stayed upright. Then they smoothed the edges at the base of their antlers with another layer of Pros-Aide, concealer, and body paint. Small acrylic eyeballs were added, following their jawline and painted to appear both deer and human. Fake flowers were bundled on their temples, climbing the antlers like vines. Twigs collected from the planters in the courtyard scaled their cheeks, ears, and throat.

"The headpiece is last," Eli said. They gave their reflection a once-over. "Can you make sure the curtain is good to go?"

Bodhi nodded and turned around to adjust the blackout curtain hung from the shower rod, creating a plain backdrop.

Eli swallowed hard. They were done. Audition look complete. Now they needed a few pictures—*good pictures*—and a short video for their Instagram story plus the compilation Stella was putting together for their Makeup Wars submission. They'd *entered* the competition with a cute selfie, but this was the real deal now. *Crunch time.* They needed their official submission to rake in votes and secure their place in the final five. With Stella's editing skills on their side, Eli's makeup might stand out from the crowd. Adding some strobe-light effects, music, and slow-motion close-ups could potentially give them a leg up, too, and given how many aspiring artists were banking on Makeup Wars, they needed all the help they could get.

Eli pressed a few more white spots onto the bridge of their nose and carefully smeared dark paint on their top lip. They reached for the handmade headpiece on the counter. Thin brown branches fanned away from a rigid headband with green and brown moss dripping between each pair of narrow arms, peppered with faux wisteria, hydrangea, and lavender spears. It fit snugly, as it was supposed to, and transformed their makeup into a fully formed character.

"Okay," Eli whispered, and nodded to themself. "Hit the lights."

"You look fuckin' wicked," Bodhi said, turning off the overhead bathroom light and angling the circle light to cast a golden glow over their face.

Stella appeared, leaning against the doorframe with her arms crossed over her chest. "Damn, kid. You've got skills, that's for sure."

I do this every day, Eli told themself. *Another shoot, another makeup, another paycheck.*

They tipped their head. Smiled. Snapped their teeth at the camera and batted their individually applied lashes. Eli had become horrible, beautiful, and mutated. Their nose was sculpted to look like a deer snout, face flecked with spots and flowers, skin glowing pastel pink and baby blue and sunset mauve. Pale contacts turned their eyes milky gray, and their ears were round and high, painted to match their exaggerated anthropomorphic features.

"Did we get the shot?" they asked, straightening their back for a face-forward picture. Simple, no smile, no playfulness. Once the shutter closed, Eli grinned, pitching their shoulder toward their ear and flashing a peace sign at the camera.

"Yeah, we got a few," Bodhi said. She jumped in front of the circle light with them, arms around their waist, grinning for another picture.

Stella was next, sticking her tongue out as she tipped into the frame, pointing at Eli's flowery antlers.

Now Eli had one thing left to do: post the video, use the competition hashtag, and wait for the results. They looked past their phone, attached to a dock on the circle light, and stared at their reflection. Bodhi and Stella followed their gaze. They wanted to laugh, to brush off their swelling anxiety, but no matter how hard Eli tried to downplay what this meant, what it *could* mean, their heart still reached for Beyond.

They blinked. Inhaled, exhaled, then snatched their phone.

"I'll add that last ten-second clip to the end of the compilation and AirDrop it to you. Cool?" Stella tossed the words over her shoulder as she plopped on the pillow in front of the coffee table.

"Yeah, cool, awesome," Eli said absently. They stared at themself for a long time, flipping through their photo album, enhancing brightness and deepening shadows, and finally chose the perfect shots. "Okay," they whispered, glancing nervously at Bodhi. "I'm doing this, I guess."

Bodhi shook her head. "You're winning this."

"Stella?" Eli called.

"Yeah, incoming!" Stella rocked to the side, waving her phone at the bathroom. "Should be there in, like, two seconds."

Eli's phone buzzed. "Got it."

They saved the video and drafted an Instagram post. Their thumbs hovered over the screen, typing, deleting, typing again.

What if this was all for nothing? What if I'm not good enough for any of this?

They chewed on the inside of their cheek, glancing at their reflection again—bones heightened to look stronger, deadlier, skin polished in beautiful shades, antlers knifing the air around their face—and nodded.

Whether they were good enough or not, they'd created something extraordinary, and they wanted the world to see it.

Eli typed the caption:

> Alright everyone!! Here's my official #MakeupWars submission. ♡ the showcase look was inspired by one of my fave books . . . Jeff VanderMeer's ANNIHILATION!! Can't wait to see the amazing submissions from the other #MakeupWars competitors! Fingers crossed!!! #VoteEli #MakeupWars #SFX #MakeupWarsAudition

Before another wave of hesitation stopped them, Eli hit "share."

They changed their profile icon to a picture of them in their competition makeup, added selfies to their story, and drafted a separate post highlighting their showcase look. They posted a four-square grid—a serious face-forward shot, the picture of them grinning and flashing a peace sign, one of them playfully poking an eyeball on their jaw, and a cute outtake with Bodhi and Stella—and captioned it *Here we gooooo!!*

Bodhi gripped their shoulders. "You did it," she squealed, craning to look at their phone.

Notifications flooded their feed, and comments appeared. Eli tapped on the official hashtag and scrolled, scanning through the different makeups: bloody horror, perfectly applied lash strips on glamorous beauty pieces, anime characters brought to life, dramatic video-game weaponry clutched in metal gauntlets. They flicked their thumb. More pictures filled the screen. Excitement buzzed as they browsed beautiful designs. The hashtag was full of seasoned artists, up-and-coming influencers, and experimental cosplayers. Somehow, Eli's makeup stood out, though, and hope sent their head spinning.

They paused, thumb hovering over the screen as their euphoria slowly fizzled out. *There you are.* They forced their smile to stay put, enduring the leap in their chest as Zach's profile filled the screen. He'd gone with horror-fantasy. *Of course he had.* A brow piece with clean, invisible edges shaped into jutting horns. Fangs clipped over his canines; mouth open in a snarling grin. Blood dripped from intricate latex sigils carved across his face and neck. Glossy black paint turned his horns razor-sharp, and his green eyes were whitened by a circle light. Dark and witchy, on brand and riskless. *Flawless.* Exactly what Eli had expected.

"Lucifer himself," Bodhi mumbled. "Should've known."

Eli "liked" Zach's picture. "He'll place," they said, and kept scrolling.

"Yeah, probably," Bodhi said, and nudged them with her elbow. "But you will, too."

They smothered a laugh. "We'll see, huh? Finalists get announced in three days."

"You should take a hiatus," Stella called from the other room. "Get off social media, do yoga, drink turmeric lattes, make hemp brownies, whatever, but don't obsess. Staring at your phone'll give you a seventy-two-hour panic attack." She slid her laptop into a padded black sleeve and slung her purse over her shoulder, crossing the room to kiss Bodhi on the mouth. She kissed Eli, too, right on their silicone cheek prosthesis. "You've got my vote."

"Thanks, Stella. Maybe I'll preplan some content and let Bodhi change my password."

"*Brave.*" Bodhi said, and laughed under her breath. She nodded as Stella opened the front door. "Pizza night for the new *Chaos Reign* episode, yeah?"

"Yeah, my place!" Stella flicked her hair over her shoulder, and the door floated closed.

Eli sighed. The pictures were taken, the submission was posted, and now they were alone with Bodhi in their apartment. They twisted their fingers together, glancing from the floor to Bodhi's face.

"I've got Pineapple Kush, Sour Diesel, and Honey Gold," they said, flashing a half smile.

Bodhi smiled, too. "Sounds like a plan, but I get to wear the big horns."

"Antlers," they corrected.

"Whatever, *antlers.*"

Eli took the headpiece off and handed it to her. "Careful, they're a little heavy."

The antlers looked cartoony paired with Bodhi's blue jeans and white crop top. She sat on the bed while Eli dug through the nightstand, unearthing a powder-blue joint and a lighter. They flopped next to her, balancing their uncertainty with being alone in their safe space with their best friend.

They lit the coiled paper at the tip of the joint and set their lips against the round butt, inhaling sour-sweet smoke. Their lungs were used to the burn, the immediate evacuate response, and relaxed as gray plumes billowed from their mouth. They handed the joint to Bodhi, and she took a drag, passing it back to them, they to her, again and again.

"I'm sorry about earlier," Eli said. They stared at the popcorn ceiling, shooing anxiety away with the smoke. "I should be over it by now. Over *him.* But I just . . . I'm not, I guess? It hurts—it still hurts a lot, like *a lot.*"

"No, you were right," Bodhi said. "I've been hounding you about it. That's my bad." She tapped loose ash into a dirty coffee mug on the nightstand.

"We should be able to talk about it."

"*Should*, yeah."

"I'm sorry."

"Stop apologizing. It's fine, we're fine."

Eli heaved a sigh. "Do you miss him?"

Bodhi blew a few smoke rings, and her bloodshot eyes flicked toward the window, tracking headlights between the blinds. Finally she said, "I don't know. Can you miss someone you're pissed at? Like, really, *really* pissed at?"

I hope so, they thought. "Maybe."

"Zach could've texted me," she said, weighty and snappish. "It's not like I took sides."

"I don't know if he sees it that way."

"Is that how you see it?"

Eli swallowed hard, nodding. "A little bit, yeah."

Bodhi's nose twitched. She handed over the squat joint, pinched and sallow where the smoke had poured through the paper. "I understand why you did what you did, but that doesn't mean *I* wouldn't have done it differently. Zach never gave me the chance to tell him that, so." She shrugged, scrolling through her phone. "That's his problem, I guess."

"What would you have done?"

"You don't want me to answer that."

"I do."

Bodhi heaved a sigh, then said, "I would've given my best friend a heads-up. I would've given my boyfriend, who'd planned an entire cross-country trip, a chance to prepare. I would've ..." She paused, clearing the anger from her voice. "I just ... I think I deserved *at least* a warning. And I think ... excuse me, I *know* you owed Zach more than a stereotypical beach breakup, Liz. You're better than what you did to him."

Ouch. Eli suckled at the joint. "I don't know about that."

"Shut up," Bodhi said dismissively.

"If I'm better than what I did to him, then why are you still pissed at Zach, huh?"

"Because he's better than what he did to me," she said, smooth as a blade. "I'm not the one who broke his heart. I get it—I was always your friend first—but he could've called. He could've *answered*. I texted. I DM'd. I tried. But, I don't know. Damage was done, I guess."

"I'm sorry. I didn't mean to hurt you. I tried to ..." Eli paused searching for the right words. *Cauterize it. A lot of hurt, not a lot of blood.* "I tried to do the right thing. You know that, don't you?"

Bodhi didn't answer, and Eli couldn't bring themself to ask again.

Yellow light striped the ceiling. Their limbs sank into the bed, and they pulled nervously at the bottom of their binder. Smoke cushioned every thought, softening the sharp edges where memories and worries jabbed at them. They hummed. Resisted the urge to check their Instagram and instead traced a lavender spear near Bodhi's temple. Slowly, Eli closed their eyes.

"So, yeah, I'm gonna let you change my password," they said, exhaling a long-held breath. "If that's okay."

Bodhi smirked. "Probably smart."

Eli nodded. "Probably."

"You did great. Really great, Eli."

"We'll see."

She huffed out a laugh. "Yeah, sure, okay, *we'll see*. I'm telling you right now, right here, that you did something awesome."

"I believe you," they said, and a part of them did. They opened Instagram and clicked settings, then handed her their phone. "Do it before I change my mind."

Bodhi snatched their phone. "Send me shit to post. Pictures, captions, tags, all of it. I don't wanna screw up your *brand*," she teased.

"Will do," Eli said.

They watched light scale the ceiling again, still painted like a deer, still thinking about Makeup Wars and Beyond and Zach. Again, always *Zach*. But a future, too. Finally, a future, a goalpost, something else to chase.

Something better to hope for.

CHAPTER SIX

Los Angeles

SUNLIGHT SENT A MIRAGE DANCING ABOVE THE VENICE Beach Boardwalk. Umbrellas slouched together, shading trinkets laid across towels and artwork propped on makeshift easels. Shops blasted music, tattoo machines buzzed, and street performers bounced through impressive gymnastics while vendors sold pink-skinned tourists overpriced Gold's Gym muscle tees. As always, Venice was uncomfortably awake, wide-eyed, and a little feral.

Eli narrowly missed running into someone in a sun hat as they skirted the crowd on a yellow longboard. They tipped their head back, soaking warmth into their tan cheeks. Neon kites speckled the sky, and briny air whipped under their tank as they careened past Small World Books. The last two days were a blur—opening Instagram, staring at the log-in screen, sighing, closing the app, then working a double, covering a midshift, and, of course, smoking themself stupid at one in the morning. They'd binged a new anime, ordered cheap sushi, and nudged Brand Managers about promised product they hadn't received. They'd only browsed the Beyond website once, scrolling through syllabi and graduate work and staring helplessly at the top of the home page: *Makeup Wars Scholarship Opportunity!*

It had been a long two and a half days.

"Yo, hey," Bodhi called, seated on the patio at the Sidewalk Café. She adjusted her sunglasses and pointed to the empty chair across from her. "Took you long enough. I almost ate all this shit by myself."

They kicked their skateboard upright and hopped over the gate separating the patio from the boardwalk. "Sorry, I slept through my alarm. Cajun fries?"

"Obviously. How was work?"

"Someone passed out in a urinal," they said, and dipped a peppery fry into ranch dressing. "Like, dick out, forehead against the wall."

Bodhi almost choked on her lemonade. "I bet Linda *loved* that."

"She threatened to pour hot coffee on 'em." Eli laughed, biting into their tuna melt. "Thanks for ordering," they slurred, one cheek stuffed full, and sucked mayo off their fingers. "What'd'ya get?"

"Chew your food, you animal." She chuckled, jabbing her fork into a colorful salad. "Cobb with extra egg."

Eli hummed in response.

"So how we doin'? Only a few hours left, yeah?"

They stuffed the sandwich into their mouth. Bit. Chewed as slowly as they could. Swallowed. Six hours, to be exact. Half a day for people to scroll through the hashtag and cast their votes.

They licked around their straw, sipping too-sweet strawberry lemonade. "I hotboxed my apartment last night."

"Is it even possible to hotbox an entire apartment?"

"Exactly," Eli said, flashing a sarcastic grin. "Anyway, great, awesome, I'm doin' amazing, clearly."

Bodhi rolled her eyes. "*Clearly.* Do you want your password back yet? Or should we wait 'til later?"

"Definitely later." They subconsciously touched their phone, itching for the flick, tap, flick, scroll, glance, scroll. "How's everything at the boutique? Shelly still being aggressively asshole-ish?"

Bodhi groaned, chomping on fries. "I swear, I just need to get through this internship and start building a clientele. Can't be a stylist unless I've got folks to style, you know?"

"The cosplay designing has gone well, though, right?"

"I mean, it's money, which is always nice, but it's not . . ." She shrugged and jabbed at her salad. "It's not steady. I could do both, but I need an actual *job* job to make that happen."

Eli wiped their mouth with the back of their hand. "Think Stella could get you in at Nordstrom?"

"She'd be a great referral, but I'd still have to pay my dues, and this internship at Aura might fast-track me anyway." She blew out a sigh. "Two more months to go."

Eli and Bodhi ate their lunch and drank two more lemonades each, scraping ranch cups with fries until they'd finished everything. After that, Venice welcomed them with hot sand and cool blue water. Eli curled their toes as white foam framed their feet, then sprawled on a towel while Bodhi joined an impromptu volleyball game. They waded through lucidity, napping on their stomach, then their back, then their stomach again. The day passed like that, between bouts of nervousness and drowsiness. At one point, Eli jolted awake, watching seagulls dive for fallen potato chips, and told their runaway heart to relax.

Be present, they thought. *Don't get lost in something that hasn't happened yet.* But everything was too close, too *right there* to ignore, and Eli didn't know what to do with the *what if.* They sighed, scrolling through the work-group chat to see if anyone needed coverage, clicking Instagram and flicking the app away, checking Twitter and closing it once *Makeup Wars* crossed their timeline, hovering over an unanswered text from their mom:

Mama 🌸: How are you, sweetie? How's the apartment coming along?

They dimmed their phone and squinted at the bright sky.

They hadn't told their parents. Hadn't uttered a single word about it because if they didn't make it through Makeup Wars, and Eli was ninety-eight percent sure they weren't going to, they'd have to deal with parental pseudoworry for months. The *See, honey, we told you* paired with hugs and forehead kisses. College brochures tucked subtly into their bag after a visit home. Prodding questions—*So what's next? You can't work at the diner forever, can you? You're so talented, you'd be a great realtor, huh?*—and reassuring their family that makeup *would* be their career, somehow, some way.

But right then, sitting on the beach listening to waves crash and laughter echo from the boardwalk, Eli wanted to unload and not hear a single combative word afterward. Just *Okay, Eli*, just *Is that better, Eli?* No reassurance. No critique. Just someone who would listen.

They hovered over their mom's contact for a long moment, then heaved a sigh, scrolled to a different contact, and put their phone to their ear.

Stella's voice came through the other end. "Hello?"

"Hey, hi, it's Eli. Got a minute?"

"Oh-ho-ho, today's the big day, huh?" Something rustled in the background. A zipper. A spray bottle.

"Yeah, I guess. So can I just . . . Can I just vent?"

"Is this a 'let me holler' call or a 'course-correct me' call?"

"The first one."

Rustling resumed. Another spray. Stella said, "All right, you're on speaker. Go for it."

"I know I'm probably not gonna make it through," they blurted, swallowing around the itch in their throat. "There's, like, a thousand submissions, and most of them are set-ready makeups, and I'm definitely not the best by any means, but I hope something happens. I *need* something to happen. Maybe . . . maybe not Beyond, but more sponsorships, more influencing gigs, something that'll tell me this isn't for nothing, you know? Because I get it, I do, this industry sucks, it fucking sucks, and it's so competitive and mean and hard, and I just . . . I want it more than I thought I would." They closed their eyes and breathed deeply. "The scholarship. A shot at this, a *real* shot. I didn't think it'd get in my head, but it did, and now I'm afraid of what'll happen if I don't make it."

"Nothing," Stella said, easy as a breeze. "You'll keep doing makeup. That's what'll happen."

Eli took another deep breath. "The rational part of me knows that."

"Not puttin' all your eggs in one basket, remember?"

"That's what I told myself, yeah."

"Hoping for something doesn't mean you're weak, Eli. Just means you're human. If you don't make the cut, you don't make the cut. If you do, you do."

"I know," they said, sighing.

Footsteps hit the sand, fast pitter-patters. Bodhi skidded onto the rumpled towel beside them.

"Look, you'll be fine . . ." Stella said, but her voice was muffled by Bodhi's big breaths.

"I know we're supposed to wait, but you need to see this. Now. Like, *right* now," Bodhi blurted.

Eli narrowed their eyes. "Sorry, Stella. Bodhi's having a meltdown—"

"Oh! Hi, Stella!" Bodhi said, snatching their phone. "Hi, yeah, it's me, no, Theresa released the live-voting results. Yeah, okay, yes—yes, we'll call. Okay, bye!"

Eli's lungs emptied. "We still have an hour."

"Yeah, we do, but . . ." Bodhi's fingers flew across their phone, typing, swiping, typing again, then she spun the device around. "I got a notification from your account. Look."

They focused on the screen, which was open to Theresa Jenkins's Instagram post. The words *Makeup Wars* were bolded at the top, followed by a timer ticking backward, counting down. 55:52 . . . 55:51 . . .

"Read the caption," Bodhi said.

> The countdown begins! Follow your
> favorite artists as they battle it
> out LIVE for the top five spots on
> the Makeup Wars website! Link in bio
> #MakeupWars

Eli swallowed hard. Sunlight stung their shoulders, and sweat dampened their ribs beneath their tight sports bra. The drone of the beach, the tourists, the locals, the vendors and eateries and bars dulled into an indistinguishable mess. Even Bodhi's voice barking at them, *Go, go, click the link, c'mon*, sounded faraway.

Hope was a hell of a drug, tipping their thoughts too far, leaning into a future reshaped by something they might not get. They stared at Theresa's post until the timer hit 55:49.

Anxiety opened like a pit in their stomach, and they said, "Maybe I should wait."

Bodhi heaved a frustrated sigh. "I already checked, just go, c'mon."

Eli opened the website. They stared past their phone at the waves rolling over the sand and a white sail cruising past the buoy, afraid of what they might find if they peeked at the results. Bodhi grabbed their wrist and steered until their phone was an inch from their nose.

She pointed at a circular avatar in the middle of the screen and hollered, "Earth to Liz! That's *you*!"

Their eyes darted to their Instagram avatar. Votes kept ticking, adding length to the bar next to their name. *Eli Peterson: 4th*. And the text above the five avatars—*Current Finalists*.

They inhaled shakily. "That's me ..."

"Yeah, dumbass. Of course that's you," Bodhi said.

They scrolled to the top of the page. Their lungs squeezed again.

Zachary Miller: 1st

Kept reading.

Beverly Belle: 2nd

Cassie Anne Montgomery: 3rd

Eli Peterson: 4th

Rhonda Riot: 5th

Suddenly, the avatars faded, disappearing and reappearing. Rhonda's avatar was gone, replaced by Eli. Self-taught gore specialist Madison Colley had climbed to fourth place.

Eli rolled their bottom lip between their teeth. "There's time. Someone can still knock me out."

"Okay, yeah, sure, but if I were you, I'd shout at my ridiculous follower count and remind them to vote," Bodhi said. "There's time for that, too."

Eli stared at the bar next to their name.

Bodhi clapped. "Eli, seriously!"

"Okay, okay, fine, you're right, I . . . What do I say? I'm not even . . ." Eli trailed off, gesturing wildly at their face and blinking away from their phone to stare at Bodhi over the top of their sunglasses. "I'm wearing sunscreen, that's it!"

"Yeah, and . . . ? People love a good nude. Do it."

Eli rolled their eyes. "*Ha ha.* Seriously, though, should I put on bronzer or—"

"You do *not* have time. Lip balm, sunglasses, smile, that's all you need."

"I don't know if you've forgotten, but this is a *makeup* competition."

"Oh, my God, just use a filter!"

They stood, pacing in front of their towel, staring at the countdown on their phone. "Fine, okay, I'll just . . ." They huffed and blew out a sharp breath, then opened Instagram and walked toward the water. "Make it work, I guess. What do I even *say*, Bodhi?" They shifted nervously. They never, like *never*, posted anything without wearing a full-face. Not unless they were showcasing skin care. The idea that people would see them without makeup, promoting themself for a *makeup competition*, made their anxiety spike. "I'll just wait," they said, firmly, like a commitment. "I should wait, it's not like—"

"I'm going to murder you," Bodhi snapped, laughing. "You literally do this for a living."

Eli whined, glancing at their phone, at Bodhi, at their phone again. Finally, they said, "Okay, but what if it backfires and—"

"Eli!"

"Okay, Jesus, fine . . ." They clicked the icon on the top left and held their thumb on the "record" button. "What's up, everyone, this is Eli," they said through a groan and shook their head, deleting the story video. "I can't do this, seriously, I can't. What if I jinx myself?"

"I'm this close to drowning you in the ocean," Bodhi said, pinching her fingers together. "I'm not fucking kidding. Just do it!" A family nearby paused mid-sandcastle assembly to glance at them.

Eli whined but hit the "record" button again. "What's up, everyone! I'm chillin' at the beach, waiting for the top five to drop. Have you voted in Makeup Wars yet? Check out my submission video and swipe to vote!" They flashed a wide grin, sunglasses settled on the top of their nose, waves crashing behind them, and added the video to their story.

Bodhi bundled her hair into a ponytail, palms reddened from hard swats to the volleyball, and said, "See? Easy."

They shot her a weak glare. "Not easy. Excruciating, actually."

"What can we do to distract you for the next forty-five minutes?"

Absolutely nothing. No matter what they did or didn't do, all Eli was going to think about was Makeup Wars and Beyond and seeing Zach's name in first place. They kicked salty water into the air and shrugged, enduring a constant wave of butterflies in their stomach.

"A street dog with extra mustard might help," Eli said, which wasn't the least bit true, but it'd give them a reason to get on their skateboard and go somewhere. Movement sounded like the best plan. Time passed when people moved. "I'd say let's smoke a blunt first, but I might have a panic attack."

"Yeah, no weed until after the voting's over. Does Lorenzo still have his grill down by Nighthawk?"

Eli nodded and brushed off their feet, slipping on their Vans, sand still crunchy between their toes. They stuffed the towel into their mini-backpack and stepped onto their board. Bodhi stayed beside them, riding a shorter, decorative skateboard covered in stickers. Small wheels scratched the concrete, an unmistakable, comforting sound. Wind hit their cheeks and late-afternoon sun cooked their upper half, but even right then, zigzagging through the crowd, all Eli could think about was what happened next. With Makeup Wars. With Beyond. With their stupid, awful diner job and their career-not-career dangling just out of reach.

Lorenzo sat in a lawn chair behind a rolling grill, occupying his usual spot across from the hair salon. His belly slouched over striped board shorts, bald head covered by a floppy hat. He jutted his chin at the pair as they kicked their skateboards upright.

"Lookin' good, Lorenzo. Still got peppers and sausages?" Eli asked and bumped their knuckles against Lorenzo's fist.

"Sure do. You two want everything on 'em?" he asked and stood, tossing two fat hot dogs onto the grill.

"Yeah, everything. Extra mustard for me, extra mayo for Bodhi."

"Cool, it'll be eight," Lorenzo said.

"How's business? Still upcharging tourists?" Bodhi asked, handing him a ten and stuffing the extra bills into the tip jar.

"Yeah, three-dollar traffic fee for anyone in fuckin' Mickey ears," he said.

Eli snorted out a laugh, desperately trying to focus on the popping grill, Lorenzo's mustache-topped grin, and Bodhi's loud cackling. Their phone burned in their pocket.

"Kids still good?" Bodhi asked.

"Ah, yeah, you know the drill. Soccer practice on Tuesday, cookout on Sunday, hip-hop class on Wednesday. It's a shit show, but it's worth it." Lorenzo handed them each a hot dog topped with onions and peppers.

"Thanks, man. See you around," Eli said.

They ate as they walked, making their way to one of the hills separating the boardwalk from the beach. Bodhi flopped on the grass. Eli felt her eyes on them, staring from behind her pink-tinted sunglasses. They munched quietly, smearing sauce on their mouth, watching the sun skip across the water, wondering if it was over, if they should even check, if they should give it another hour or another day or another week before they opened the Makeup Wars website and looked at the finalists.

Bodhi crumpled her napkin and cleared her throat. "Eli, it's six."

"Is it?"

She waited, watching them, and then gently said, "You want me to check or—"

"No, no," they blurted. Their stomach knotted, but they still swallowed the last of their street dog. Everything paused. They stared at the sun hovering over the sea and dug their fingers into the grass, waiting for an epiphany, something that might put them at ease. Nothing came. They were stuck in the middle, smack-dab between *I made it* and *Of course I didn't make it.*

"Eli . . ." Bodhi smoothed her hand over their knee. "Hey, it's okay. It's just a contest."

"You know that isn't true," they mumbled and tried to smile. "But thanks."

Their phone buzzed in their pocket.

They held their breath, pulled out their phone, and inhaled a tiny breath. *You again.* Their heart pressed hard against their ribs. A hundred notifications hovered over the Instagram icon, but only one text lit the screen.

> **Zachary Miller** ♡: Congrats. See you in San Diego.

Eli's throat cinched. "I'm in," they whispered. "I did it—I made it."

Bodhi shrieked. Her arms were around them before they could open Instagram, before they could see where they'd placed, before they could process a single goddamn thing. *I forgot to delete the heart emoji next to Zach's name*, they thought, and laughed, because they had to, because it was all they could do.

This is the beginning. This is my chance.

They burst into ecstatic laughter, and their heart ignited.

CHAPTER SEVEN

San Diego~Comic Palooza

ELI STOOD IN AN EMPTY BATHROOM—THE BIG, SOLITARY one with the picture of the block-shaped family on the sign— adjusting their binder and dabbing balm on their lips. Their reflection blinked back at them, face sculpted by contour and shimmery highlight, lashes coated in light-brown mascara, eyebrows plucked and filled. They gripped the edge of the sink, scanning their button-down black shirt and frayed high-waist denim shorts. Last week, they'd received a welcome email with warm congratulations, the address to the convention center where Comic Palooza would take place, and directions to the green room, but the publicity team hadn't sent a dress code. They checked their email again, reading and rereading the message from the Makeup Wars team, and grabbed their train case off the changing table.

Everything had happened in a blur, so fast, *too fast*. One minute they were on the grass, laughing and hollering next to Bodhi, and the next they were in San Diego, hiding inside a Taco Bell. They bought a Baja Blast as payment for occupying the bathroom for *at least* twenty minutes and inhaled briny air as they stepped onto the sidewalk. They chewed on the plastic straw, staring at the blue-windowed convention center on the other side of the street. Someone cosplaying Cloud Strife walked by with a foam sword resting on his shoulder and a few Sailor Scouts waited at the intersection, sipping blended coffees and fiddling with their lanyards.

Bodhi was stuck in traffic, because of course she was stuck in fucking traffic, and Eli couldn't wait any longer. They'd have to walk into the convention center alone, and find the green room alone, and meet the other competitors alone. Which they probably, maybe, *possibly* could've avoided if they'd texted Zach back a week ago. But instead, they'd liked his follow-up celebratory post—a picture of him grinning, one eye closed in a wink—and spent five days reading his text, typing out responses, and hitting "delete."

Here we go, I guess.

Eli rallied courage, or desperation shaped like courage, and followed Usagi, Rei, and Michiru through the intersection. They dipped around Animal Crossing cosplayers, a family posing for pictures with Elsa and Anna, and made their way to badge pickup inside the air-conditioned lobby.

A girl with fiery hair waved them to her portion of the six-sectioned ticket booth and asked, "Picking up?"

"Yeah, yes, I'm actually here for Makeup Wars . . . ? I don't know if I get a badge or something else, but I'm Eli—Eli Peterson," they said, smiling nervously, fingers slick from the condensation around their soda.

"Oh!" She beamed and pawed through manila envelopes stacked behind the counter. "I'll just need to see some ID, please."

"Sure, it shows a different name, though. Is that okay?" Eli asked, swallowing hard.

"Totally fine. It looks like you're . . ." She trailed off and narrowed her eyes at an envelope, plucking it open, reaching inside, and glancing at the badge. "Yeah, okay, cool. It looks like they registered you under one name and used another for your badge. Is this correct?" She flashed the badge: ELI—@EliSFX.

"Yeah, they probably used my legal name. Badge name is correct, though," Eli said. They handed her their ID and subconsciously touched the pronoun pin clipped to their collar.

"No worries, I'll update your file. You might wanna let the Makeup Wars team know since most convention centers don't share the same system."

"Will do."

"You're good to go. There's a green room sticker on your badge, and your badge'll get you a free large specialty coffee at the Grind. Good luck!"

"Thanks," Eli said, and hooked the Comic Palooza badge to their lanyard.

The green room was behind the Exhibitor Hall near the main stage in Hall H. Eli pinned their soda cup in the crook of their elbow and typed a quick text.

> **Eli Peterson:** go to badge pickup to get your guide and lanyard and stuff
> **Bodhi Babe:** Okay will do
> **Bodhi Babe:** You good?
> **Eli Peterson:** i don't kno if good is the right word

Good? Yeah, no. Eli was terrified.

They followed the online map past a pretzel cart, two coffee stands, and a pop-up cosplay repair booth before finally finding Hall H. Next to the hall entrance, a printed sign on a plain door read GREEN ROOM—VIP ACCESS ONLY. Eli glanced at their badge and twisted the knob, peeking inside.

A bulky man wearing a black baseball cap sat in a folding chair, gaze pinned to the flatscreen on the far wall. Eli cleared their throat. The man turned, eyes flicking from the TV, where *Infinity War* played, to Eli and then back to the screen again.

"Panelist, moderator, or makeup person?" he asked.

Eli closed the door behind them. "Makeup person."

"Cool. Snacks and drinks are in the back."

Eli pinched the edge of their badge, waiting for him to check the sticker, but his attention was glued to Tony Stark. They scanned the room for familiar faces, one in particular, but Zach wasn't there. Someone read a book on the sofa, and two other people sat at a high-top table. Eli recognized them: Beverly Belle and Cassie Anne Montgomery.

For years, they'd watched Beverly and Cassie Anne rise through the influencer ranks. Beverly, a Bengali cosplayer and makeup artist with an affinity for perfectly executed character portrayals from popular anime, had been mutuals with them on Instagram for a while, but they'd never had the courage to talk to her. And Cassie Anne—peak Florence Pugh, boss babe, beauty makeup master—always seemed like a hornet. Bright from afar but would definitely sting.

They clutched the handles on their train case. *Do I just walk over?* That was probably the right idea, but Eli beelined for the snack table instead. They stared at salami slices and soft cheeses, squishy sourdough and purple tortilla chips, and mentally practiced their introduction.

I'm Eli, I've heard so much about you—

Ugh, no.

Hi, I'm Eli, I loved your Princess of Heart cosplay.

I'm Eli Peterson, I can't wait to work alongside—

"Eli?" They recognized Beverly's windy voice from her Instagram live tutorials. "Eli Peterson, right? You did the Area X makeup?"

Shit.

Eli turned around, nodding. "Oh, hi, yeah, that was me. That *is* me. I'm—yeah, I'm Eli. I really love you—your work! I love your work," they said, scrunching their nose. "Sorry, I'm a mess."

"No, no, don't be sorry!" Her glossy bubblegum-pink lips split into a grin, and her dark eyes were framed in white liner and dramatic lash strips. She grabbed their upper arm and squeezed. "I totally love your work, too. You should kick it with me and Cassie while we wait for everyone else."

"Is that okay?"

"Yes, yes, yes," Beverly said, and tugged on their arm, sliding her warm hand to their wrist. "Here, let me take this." She took their train case and set it against the wall next to her giant rolling trunk and Cassie's four-tiered wheeled train case. "Cassie, this is Eli Peterson, special effects master. Eli, this is Cassie Anne Montgomery, beauty expert."

Cassie ran her coffin-shaped fingernails through cropped brown hair. She gave them a once-over and offered a barely-there smile. "Ah, right, the baby."

"Be nice, Cassie," Beverly said, stifling a giggle.

Eli thumbed at the edge of the lid on their Taco Bell cup and quietly said, "The baby?"

"Nineteen, right? That makes you the youngest," Cassie said, and stuck out her hand. "You're really fucking talented, by the way. It's a pleasure."

Oh. They shook her hand and nodded. *Of course.* "Zach's not much older than me, but he's, like, a special effects god, so." They shrugged. "Guess I'll just change my bio and roll with it. *Eli Peterson, I'm baby.*"

Beverly laughed, flicking a crunchy pink curl over her shoulder. Her wig was high quality, big and thick and perfectly styled. "You'll have to fight me for it. If anyone's baby, it's *obviously* me," she said, and batted her lashes.

The door opened and closed. Eli was too busy laughing to look over their shoulder, but as soon as they heard Zach's warm, soft chuckle, they froze.

"Who's baby?" Zach asked. He rolled his oversized matte-black kit around the table and propped it against the wall. The sleeves on his gray shirt were rolled to his elbows, and his jeans were ripped at the knees, as always. Eli tore their eyes away from him, catching the bend at his waist as Zach leaned down and accepted a kiss on the cheek from Cassie. "When'd you get here?"

"Bev's fighting Eli for the honorary title of *baby*," Cassie said. She rested her hand on Zach's arm—*Why, exactly, was she touching him?*—and smiled, the familiar kind that sent all the blood in Eli's body rushing toward their toes. "I took a red-eye last night. Figured I'd get here early and check out the con."

"Should've texted me, I would've tagged along," Zach said.

Cassie smirked and said, "Next time."

Eli wanted to sink into the floor. They fiddled with their cup, standing awkwardly between Beverly and Cassie as Zach shook Beverly's hand. He looked at them last, and his smile thinned.

A chin nod was all Eli got, followed by a lackluster "Hey."

"Hi," Eli said. They opened their mouth to ask a question. Something. *One* thing. But an obnoxiously loud voice boomed through the room before they could.

They rolled their eyes. *Here she comes.*

"What's up, guys?" Rhonda shouted. She whistled, slinging her arm around Cassie's shoulders and swatting Eli with the back of her tattooed knuckles. A guy wearing an embarrassing RHONDA RIOT—ARTIST TEAM shirt placed two, no, *three* train cases on the table instead of the floor with the rest of their stuff.

Beverly met Eli's eyes and lifted her brows.

Cassie ducked away from Rhonda and, worse, leaned against Zach. Their arms pressed and elbows touched. Eli didn't know where to look, so they nodded slowly, studying

Rhonda's platform boots and her tightly laced corset. Her navy hair was roped into a French braid, and a spiked collar ringed her fair throat. Eli had been nontalkative mutuals with her on social media since sophomore year, but she'd become insufferable ever since she'd landed one—yeah, *one*—music-video gig last year.

"Who's ready to come in second?" Rhonda said, laughing louder. "I'm kidding, come on. How's it goin', Beverly? Still doin' the cosplay stuff?"

Beverly's smile tightened. "Sure am."

"Oh, hey, you're the newbie, huh?" Rhonda asked, gaze flicking around Eli's face. "Drugstore brand fanatic?"

Eli inhaled sharply, tempering the urge to snap. "Cheap makeup gets the job done," they said, and dragged their eyes from Rhonda's feet to her nose. *Wannabe rock star.* "Your lashes popped, by the way. I've got glue if you need it."

Rhonda rolled her lips together and laughed in her throat. She didn't say anything, just whipped toward Zach and Cassie and said, "Glad to see you two stayed close after Shockwave. Did you ever get that referral, Zach?"

Stayed close.

Zach's eyes flitted to Eli. He wrung his hands, a nervous movement.

Jealousy wasn't anything new. Eli had been jealous of flat-chested GQ models, and Insta-celebrity makeup artists, and

Orange County trust fund babies for, well, *forever*. But they'd never experienced prickly, awful *relationship* jealousy before. It stuck in them like a sea urchin, spines pointed outward, piercing delicate places.

"Yeah, I did," Zach said, exhaling.

Eli grabbed their soda and their train case.

"Pretty sure we're getting called to the makeup trailer, like, any minute," Cassie said, tracking Eli toward the door.

"I'll be back in a minute," Eli said, smiling at Beverly on their way out, mindful of their quick steps. They kept their eyes away from Zach. Away from Cassie. Away from their friendly touches and whatever had happened between them in New York.

Eli put their back against a wall once they'd turned the corner. They stood there, eyes closed, and let everything they hadn't wanted to think about stampede over them.

Cassie was probably a fantastic kisser. She was probably super fucking flexible, and made all the right noises, and did all the right things in bed. She probably liked rough, gross, awesome sex, and looked perfect when she woke up, and paid three hundred dollars for a Brazilian wax once a month. She probably thought Eli was Zach's bratty little ex-whatever who couldn't bear to see him standing close to someone else.

She was probably sweet. She was probably good to him.

Eli shut their eyes and heaved a sigh. They couldn't shake the thought of Zach kissing Cassie. Couldn't stop picturing it. They wondered if she'd been there when he'd gotten his tattoo.

Get it together.

They stared at the ceiling until the world tipped into place again. Their heart still raced and their eyes still burned, but Eli breathed through the nervous, unearned anger until it settled like a rock in their throat. Hard and unyielding but manageable.

Zach could kiss whomever he wanted, he just couldn't have Beyond.

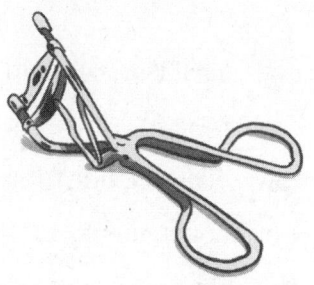

CHAPTER EIGHT

San Diego-Comic Palooza

THE RECTANGULAR MAKEUP TRAILER IN THE COURTYARD outside Hall H was plastered with a vinyl banner that read MAKEUP WARS! SPONSORED BY BEYOND SPECIAL EFFECTS AND COSTUMING. The trailer was fit for a movie set, big and spacious with laminate flooring and individual stations. Eli had ditched their soda for the complimentary con coffee and set the cup and their train case on the station labeled with their Instagram handle. Zach unpacked beside them, sighing as Cassie pointed at the paper taped to her station's mirror.

"So the theme's *Eternal*, huh?" Cassie arched her brows, glancing at each contestant.

An identical paper with the bolded word *Eternal* was taped to Eli's mirror, too. They took it down and set it on the counter next to their palettes and paints. "They included that in the email, right?" they asked.

"Oh, yeah, probably. I wanted to wing it, though. At least for the first challenge," she said, catching their gaze in the mirror with a wink. "See if I've got what it takes flyin' by the seat of my pants."

Eli nodded slowly. They couldn't imagine walking a day in her shoes. Having enough money to fly across the country for an elite workshop like Shockwave? Please. Not breaking a sweat over opportunities like Makeup Wars? Eli could *never*. But they'd seen her brightly colored Instagram, browsed her minimalist website, and no one, not a single person, pulled off the looks she did without a few trial runs.

If she wanted to peacock, she could. Eli had other things to worry about, like making sure their makeup didn't look like a cheap Halloween mask.

Focus.

They lined sponges on a clean napkin, clipped their brush belt—a mini-apron with slots for makeup brushes—around their waist, and carefully laid out their foam facial prostheses. As soon as Eli had seen the theme at the bottom of the email, they'd thought *vampire*, but *vampire* was predictable; *vampire* would be everyone's immediate go-to. So Eli had brainstormed, poking through their unpacked manga collection until they'd come across a dingy green plushie.

Shenron the Eternal, the wish-granting, godlike serpent from *Dragon Ball Z*, fit the theme perfectly.

Eli tapped their phone and looked over the Makeup Wars guidelines.

Everyone must start with a clean face.

No prepackaged prostheses.

Two-hour application time limit.

Assistants are welcome, but they may not help with application, painting or assembly, only setup, cleanup, and organization.

All artists will be given ten minutes for final looks before stage queue.

*Judges will score in individual categories, including but not limited to Set Ready, Creative Development, and Clean Application. Livestream viewers will vote in one category: Look Delivery. Those scores will be combined to determine 1st, 2nd, 3rd, and 4th place. The higher your scores, the higher your placement. While social media scoring is public, we encourage contestants to avoid self-rejecting and remember that the in-house judging panel uses a private scoring system. **Both** scores accumulated throughout the competition will help determine the final winner in the last runway.

They scrubbed a makeup remover cloth over their face, wiping until the sheet was varying shades of beige and brown. Beverly stripped away her wig and raked her hands through long black locks. Rhonda peeled off her lashes. Cassie did, too. Eli tried not to watch Zach remove the silver hoops from his ears.

A Makeup Wars volunteer stood just inside the doorway, smiling at everyone. She checked her phone, waited with one finger raised, and said, "Welcome to Makeup Wars. You have two hours. Your time starts . . . now!"

Rhonda whooped. Hard-rock music erupted from a Bluetooth speaker on her station.

Eli steeled their expression and kept their anxiety from showing while they sipped their coffee. Their hands trembled—*Stop shaking*—and adrenaline made their head spin—*Don't freak out*—but they had to get it together, had to *keep* it together. They'd practiced this makeup at home twice, once alone, once with Bodhi. They knew which paints to blend, where to glue, and how to speckle their skin to look scaly and inhuman, but standing next to Zach at Comic Palooza made everything much, *much* harder.

Beverly whistled and asked, "Is *everyone* doing bloodsuckers?"

"The theme *is* Eternal," Cassie said.

"Pretty sure that means we're all doing vampires," Zach said through a laugh.

"Undead makeup is my thing, so I've got this in the bag," Rhonda said, leaning closer to the mirror as she dabbed liquid latex on her forehead.

Eli rolled their eyes but stayed quiet, ignoring Zach's quick glance at their station. They smoothed down their coarse brows with a glue stick, powdered, and applied the flexible foam forehead piece. The loud *whir* of their travel-sized blow dryer drowned Rhonda's music, and Eli got lost in familiarity. They knew makeup. They knew color theory and foam and application. They just needed to breathe.

Once their forehead piece was glued and dried, Eli placed a wide prosthesis over the bridge of their nose and two thin, scaly pieces on each side of their face, elongating their cheekbones and sharpening their chin. Beverly sang along to whatever terrible music Rhonda played, and Cassie snorted, glancing at Zach's scrappy old brush belt.

"I can't believe you're still using that thing," Cassie said.

Zach shrugged. "Yeah, it's seen better days."

Eli glanced at his brush belt, and their throat closed. Cheap liquid latex still clung to the pleather loops from nights spent practicing zombie makeups on each other. Purple paint from a cosplay practice run stained the strap. "I'm surprised Shockwave didn't give you a new one," they said, and wished they could snatch the words and swallow them.

One year. Twelve *entire* months. And that was the first thing they'd thought to say to him.

Zach tipped his head to the side, carefully stretching a silicone appliance in the hollow of his cheek. "They did. I packed both, but my brushes were in this one, so," he said, and shrugged, catching Eli's gaze in the mirror, "figured I'd use the one I'd already committed to."

Their vocal cords were clenched in an iron grip, and their stomach bunched and knotted. *Committed*. What a choice word. "Makes sense."

"Does it?"

"You upgraded," they blurted. "Don't know why you wouldn't take advantage of better options."

Zach laughed under his breath, licked his bottom lip, and stared at his reflection, tearing at dry latex to make a fake wound. His movements were brisk and hard, fingertips moving too quickly, ripping at the edges until he cursed and glued them back down. "You know, I get why you of all people wouldn't understand this, but some of us actually go through with our decisions. I'd decided to use this brush belt, so I'm using it."

"Oh, yeah, weren't you supposed to be there?" Cassie asked. She leaned around Zach's shoulder and flashed a curious smile at Eli. "You were on the Shockwave roster for the first two days and then disappeared."

Eli's pulse quickened. They needed their hands to stop shaking. They needed to paint and speckle and powder. They needed to find an escape hatch. "It's . . . it's complicated, I—"

"It's not that complicated. They bailed at the last minute," Zach bit out, flexing his jaw. "Which, I mean, it's fine, right? It's not like they care about how anyone else feels," he said, following his lashes with a gray pencil, "or think about who they're hurting. Or give a shit about amazing opportunities or plans they'd made or promises they'd broken. It was probably just a fluke, right?" He glared at them, palms flat on his station, forcing a pained smile. "You just weren't feelin' it? *Right?*"

Rhonda lowered her music on the other side of the trailer.

Cassie made an awkward *O* with her mouth and turned back toward the mirror.

Eli's chest hurt. They fought back the heat in their face and shook their head. Anger boiled under their skin, lashing like a viper. "Looks like you were *feelin' it*, though," they said, hushed, like a mean secret, and jutted their chin at Cassie. "Already made new *friends*, huh? You guys seem close." They didn't—couldn't—look at Zach, but they felt his gaze on them. Their eyes stung, vision blurred, and they knuckled at their lash line before anyone noticed the wetness gathering there.

They wanted to rewind and take everything back, all of it, every word they'd said. They should've stayed silent, should've let Cassie and Zach talk about his stupid goddamn brush belt and kept their stupid goddamn mouth shut. But now the trailer was dead silent, and the only thing Eli could hear was their own rabbit-fast heartbeat. They swirled a fine-tipped paintbrush in a water cup and steadied their hand while staring themself down in the mirror. Carefully, they applied a layer of ivy-green base paint.

The trailer door opened. "One hour left," the volunteer said, and slipped away again.

Rhonda cleared her throat. "Well, then," she rasped, masking laughter, "this just got a lot more fun."

"C'mon, what's up with the music?" Beverly said, like a loud, cheery distraction. She flicked through her phone, and the theme song of *Blood Reign*, a popular anime, filled the room.

Do not cry. Eli kept painting, then sponged another, darker shade around their hairline. *Do not fucking cry.*

They bent thick brush quills and speckled their face, splattering varying shades of yellow and green to add depth and texture to the makeup. Zach's harsh tone echoed behind every thought.

It's not like they care about how anyone else feels.

Eli held their breath. They'd rehearsed what they'd said to Zach that night. Perfected the breakup until it was just a script, until they could say the words without choking. Did Zach think they hadn't fallen apart after he'd driven away? Did he think Eli hadn't sat on the beach, staring at the ocean until Bodhi had finally found them? *Or think about who they're hurting.* Did he seriously think Eli hadn't been *hurt*? That losing him hadn't broken their heart, too? They swallowed around the lump in their throat and glued branch-like horns to their temples.

Their face was finally gone, masked by scales and reptilian features. They tipped their head one way, then the other, checking for anywhere the paint might've thinned, and glued patches of fluff over their ears, using hairspray to splay the fur outward.

"Ten minutes until final looks," the volunteer said, leaning into the trailer.

Eli bit back a curse. They still had to paint their hands, glue talons to their fingernails, put their contact lenses in, *and* get dressed. Everyone worked furiously. Zach finished powdering his face, adorned with structure-enhancing prostheses and ghoulish paint, Cassie carefully glued down her spindly lashes, Beverly pulled a crimson wig into place, and Rhonda splattered fake blood on her face, shirt, and pants.

Time sped by, and just as Eli finished drying the paint on their hands, the trailer door flew open again.

"All right, contestants! Please grab anything you'll need for last looks and follow me," the volunteer said, propping the door open with her foot.

Get dressed. Do touch-ups. Take the stage.

They snatched their tote stuffed with last-look materials and stumbled along behind everyone else, stealing a moment to open Instagram and check their notifications.

Beverly slowed her quick steps and fell into stride beside them. "That was rough," she whispered, grimacing. "I know not *everyone* knows about you two . . . but a lot of us do. You good?"

"Yeah, yes, of course. I'm totally fine!" Eli stammered, clearing the thickness from their throat. They really, seriously didn't need to worry about what other influencers thought of them. They hadn't made their breakup public, and they thought Zach had kept it quiet, too, and knowing their private life had wound up on the makeup world radar made their cheeks burn. They forced a smile, glancing over Beverly's extravagant gothic cosplay. A sturdy collar ringed in lace circled her throat, and knee-high pleather platform boots were buckled around her calves. They gestured to her hoop skirt and high-collared, bell-sleeved top. "You look amazing! You're Selena Luna from *Blood Reign*, right?"

She pointed to her cheek, painted with the signature cracked-porcelain look her doll-turned-vampire character was known for. "Sure am. I can't believe you busted out a full-face Shenron, though. Seriously, you look incredible."

"Thanks, yeah . . . The foam run for this was ridiculous. I hope the judges don't think it's too dated."

"Dragon Ball? Dated? Please, it's one of the greats. And I mean..." she trailed off, dragging her gaze to Rhonda, whose assistant stumbled at her heels. "At least you didn't go with an *original character* for a freakin' Cosplay Competition," she whispered and rolled her eyes.

Eli wrinkled their nose. "Yeah, that's ballsy."

The volunteer ushered them into Hall H and through the stage door. Each contestant had a small station stocked with a mirror and vanity to store their bags and finish last looks. Around them, cosplayers fixed wigs, changed batteries for light-up weapons, and laced boot covers over their shoes. The Sailor Scouts Eli had seen outside the convention center earlier straightened bows and flat-ironed pleats in their skirts. Giant mecha cosplay suits were assembled with the help of friends or assistants.

Eli ducked behind a circular curtain serving as a dressing room. They peeled away their clothes and put on their costume—plain black pants, a high-necked black top, and a forest-green hooded cloak—careful not to damage the strategically placed zipper on the side of their shirt that allowed for quick solo assembly. Next, they tied their scaly boot covers around their shins, smoothing them down until the rubber treads on their knock-off Doc Martens were nearly invisible under curved claws.

Someone shouted, "Five minutes, Makeup Wars!"

Shit. They were running out of time. *Okay, where's my tail?* They dug around in their tote for a skinny foam tail curled neatly and secured with a zip tie. *Just breathe.* They glanced at their reflection in the mirror, and their heart dropped into their stomach. *Contact lenses!* Everything was happening too fast.

As Eli almost crashed into an Optimus Prime, Rhonda picked at her nails, already standing in a puddle of neon light at the front of the staging queue. She chatted with one of the stage techs, saying, "I'm not sure if I'm going first or not, but I have the largest social media presence of anyone here, so it'll probably be smart to save me for last. *Wow* factor, right?"

"I'll give you a hundred bucks, cold, hard cash, if you glue her mouth shut," Cassie whispered, mock-gagging in front of the middle vanity. She glanced at Eli as they hovered close to the mirror, sliding their contact lenses over their eyes with a trembling index finger. They almost didn't hear her gasp, but they definitely heard what came next. "Oh, honey, your edges," she said, wincing. "Your cheek prostheses are totally lifted."

Eli almost ignored her. Almost pretended they hadn't heard. But their red eyes betrayed them, darting around their reflection and snagging on the one, two, *three* edges popping away from their skin. They wanted to crawl under the vanity, tear the makeup off, leave the convention center, and hide in their apartment for a solid week.

"Just do a quick fix-it with Spirit Gum," Cassie said, dusting translucent powder over her nose. She looked perfect, hair tucked under a cropped black wig, body wrapped in a shiny catsuit. "It'll look totally fine. You've got this, don't worry!"

"Thanks, yeah, I'll just . . . I'll figure something out," Eli said. They dug through their tote, looking for Spirit Gum or Pros-Aide or fucking *tape*. Anything that could keep their prostheses in place.

Panic speared them, and it felt like their bones had been upended inside them, knees wobbling, eyes stinging. *Don't you dare cry, it will ruin everything.* Their quivering hands wouldn't cooperate.

"Fuck, okay," they whispered, glancing at their reflection, the tote bag, then their reflection again. They crouched to look under the vanity. Nothing. Dug through their tote again. *Nothing.* It was over. They wouldn't come back from a mess like this. Theresa Jenkins would take one look at their amateur makeup and cut them from the competition. "God dammit, I know it's—"

"Eli, stop," Zach said, appearing beside them. His floor-length black coat was buttoned to his collarbones, and a bloody bite mark reddened his throat. He was a vampire from Doomsday, a popular video game, and the subtle blue veins on his paled skin, and the gorgeous gore makeup down the left side of his neck, and his accentuated bone structure, and, fuck, *everything* about him looked stupidly perfect.

All they could think to do was turn and snap at him, but as soon as they opened their mouth, Zach took their chin between his fingers. Eli instantly froze.

"It's not that bad," Zach said.

They exhaled through their nose. "It's pretty bad."

Zach smeared translucent Spirit Gum over the lifted edges with a flat silver spatula. His thumb feathered across Eli's jaw, and he hovered there, cradling their face in a bright, familiar way. They stared, because looking at him was all they'd wanted to do for months, and looking at him right then, backstage before their first runway, convinced Eli's shoulders to relax and their heart to slow.

"You'll win with this," Zach said, and pressed the spatula to the corner of their mouth, smoothing sticky glue over a lifted edge.

They shook their head, but their voice refused to budge. *Not with you here.* Zach's fingers buckled around their chin, keeping them still.

Across the stage, a member of the tech crew called out, "Makeup Wars! Thirty seconds!"

Zach tipped his head, glancing around Eli's face, then he met their eyes and dropped his hand. He gave them a quick once-over, but his lips became a thin, steady line, and he was unreadable behind black, saucerlike contact lenses. Eli waited for something else, another word, anything.

Talk to him.

Eli opened their mouth, but nothing surfaced. Not *Thank you.* Not *Why are you helping me?* Nothing. Zach didn't wait for them to speak. He walked away, taking his place in the queue.

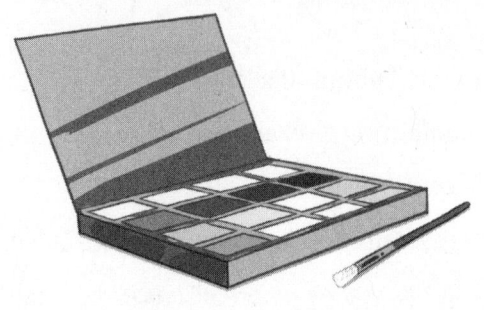

CHAPTER NINE

San Diego-Comic Palooza

THIS IS IT.

Neon lights beamed, and the audience roared. Theresa Jenkins filled a massive screen hanging above the far side of the stage. She held a microphone in front of her mouth, grinning at the crowd.

"Welcome to round one of Makeup Wars! The theme for Comic Palooza is *Eternal*. Our artists have been hard at work creating amazing cosplays and makeups to unveil at tonight's runway. Are you ready, San Diego?"

The audience clapped and whooped again, and a spotlight beamed toward the empty space in front of the stage wing where Eli stood, shifting their weight from foot to foot. They chanted to themself, *Get dressed, do touch-ups, take the stage.*

"Everybody smile," Beverly said, holding her phone out to snap a selfie of the lineup.

Eli grinned, showing off dainty fangs clipped to their canines, and held a hand-painted orange Dragon Ball under their arm.

Music boomed. The volunteer stood at the entrance to the stage, one finger perched against her earpiece, and motioned with her other hand, counting down. *Three. Two. One.* "And ... go!"

Theresa's voice careened through the ballroom. "Zachary Miller!"

Zach walked onstage, and cheers filled the air. Eli craned to watch him, tracking his long strides from one end of the stage to the other. His cosplay was vampiric, and grotesque, and perfect. The veins and burst blood vessels he'd painted on his skin were subtle enough to look natural under the stage lights and eerily *real* enough to cause a double-take. He turned toward a camera, smiled to show his fangs, waved, and playfully snarled as any good vampire should. Then he was back, slapping Cassie's palm as he slipped past the lineup and disappeared backstage.

That quick. Ten seconds, maybe.

Get dressed, do touch-ups, take the stage, walk, turn, walk, smile, walk.

"Beverly Belle!"

Beverly skipped onstage and twirled, blowing a kiss to the audience. Her makeup was perfectly executed, beautiful and haunting, and there wasn't a stitch out of place on her cosplay. When she walked backstage, Eli nodded to her and said, "Good job, you killed it."

She blew out a big breath and nudged their shoulder. "It's packed out there, like, standing room only."

Eli nodded and kept breathing, kept watching, studying the way Cassie lifted her chin and pushed out her chest, following Rhonda's tightly set shoulders and cocky grin. The lights dimmed as Eli waited, listening for their name.

Walk, turn, walk, smile, walk.

They still felt the ghost of Zach's fingertips on their jaw and knew every place on their face where the glue was barely holding. But when Theresa called out, "Eli Peterson," they forced their legs to carry them forward and walked into the spotlight.

Cosplay competitions had always been a must-see for Eli. Almost every convention had one, and nothing ever sounded better than plopping into a chair and relaxing after a busy Saturday. But standing on the stage looking at a sea of faces was an entirely different experience. They took calculated steps and skimmed the crowd, baring their fangs in a wide smile. The audience cheered, clapping and hollering and whistling. *Keep going.* They looked for Bodhi, but the lights were too bright, and the ballroom was too big, and Eli could barely breathe. Having thousands of people stare at their Instagram on a daily basis never felt *awesome*, but standing in front of hundreds of people, asking to be judged . . . ? Yeah, Eli hadn't been ready for that.

They whipped their tail and balanced the Dragon Ball in their palm. A camera crew member swooped by for a close-up, blasting Eli's face on both screens above the stage. *Smile. Wave.* They lifted their hand and curled their claws, and the audience erupted again. Off to the side, the judges jotted notes, seated behind a white table. Theresa Jenkins floated her pencil up and down, gesturing to Eli as they walked off the stage. They finally, *finally* exhaled.

Cassie clapped lazily. "Nicely done, makeup baby."

Eli noticed the place where Cassie's shoulder pressed against Zach's arm. They nodded curtly and tried to smile. "Thanks. It's nerve-racking out there, though."

"It's not *that* bad," Rhonda said, primping her navy ringlets with hairspray.

Everyone, including Eli, rolled their eyes.

The tension wilted for a moment. Eli tipped their chin toward their chest to hide in their phone. They flicked through Instagram, tapped the Makeup Wars hashtag, and then immediately closed the app, too overwhelmed by shots of the stage in Hall H to keep scrolling. Theresa Jenkins and

her cojudges, Scott Brant, another professional makeup artist, and a local video-game designer Daisy Li, were counting
Instagram votes, tallying their scores, and debating who
would stay and who would go home. Their phone buzzed,
startling them.

> **Bodhi Babe:** YOU DID AMAZING!!
> **Eli Peterson:** i'm super glad i didn't puke
> **Bodhi Babe:** Seriously you looked awesome
> **Bodhi Babe:** Are the judges looking at you
> guys up close or no?
> **Eli Peterson:** pre-judging happens for the last
> round of the competition. so not this time.
> **Bodhi Babe:** You get an assistant for the final
> runway right?
> **Eli Peterson:** yes yes which sure woulda been
> nice tonight
> **Bodhi Babe:** Don't worry I'll have your back in
> the boss fight

If I make it that far, Eli thought. They sighed at their phone,
watching three dots bounce in Bodhi's text bubble.

> **Bodhi Babe:** Stella wants to grab snacks and
> bubble tea after. You down?
> **Eli Peterson:** uhhh yeah, unless they send
> me home in which case i'll be ugly crying the
> whole time
> **Bodhi Babe:** Pppfffttt babe you are NOT
> going home.

"All right, Makeup Wars. Let's get you back onstage," a volunteer said. She pointed to the stage queue. "Same order as before—yep, Zach's first, then Beverly, uh-huh . . . All right, and . . . One, two, three . . ." The lights dimmed, and excited cheers filled the ballroom. "Go!"

Eli almost tripped over their boot covers as they followed Rhonda onto the brightly lit stage. Lasers shot from left to right. Applause and cheers filled the air. Hope needled their heart. *I want this.* They remembered their lifted edges, and Zach saying *You'll win with this,* and how the ballroom had roared at the sight of their makeup. *I want this. I want this. I want this.* The contestants stood center stage, Zach at one end, Eli at the other.

Theresa Jenkins sighed into the mic. Her lips were painted black, and she wore a shimmery silver top over pearl-white pants. "I'm absolutely blown away by the talent standing in front of us tonight. Every single artist on this stage brought their A game," she said, steering her attention to the contestants. "Seriously, guys. You made it tough for us."

The audience clapped again.

Daisy Li leaned forward, tucking a strand of rosy hair behind her ear. "The hardest part of being a judge is deciding who goes home and who moves forward in this competition. Four of you will join Theresa, Scott, and the incredible Margaret Madness in San Francisco next week-end, and one of you will pack up your kit and end your time in Makeup Wars."

"Scott, would you do the honors?" Theresa asked.

Scott nodded, wearing a piece-for-piece T'Challa cosplay. "In fourth place, Cassie Anne Montgomery, who beauti-fully captured Queen Crymah!" Everyone cheered as Cassie stepped forward. "In third place, we have Beverly Belle's ren-dition of Selena Luna!" The crowd hollered, and Beverly let out a relieved sigh, curtsying to the audience. "And in sec-ond place . . ." The music paused. "Zachary Miller! With his Doomsday Biter cosplay!"

Eli swallowed, staring at the double doors at the very back of the ballroom. *I'm going home.* Their eyes burned. Not even two weeks into the competition, and it was already over. They were about to be the first person eliminated. They tried to straighten their shoulders, tried to smile, tried not to look devastated as they stood next to Rhonda.

"One of you is the winner tonight, and one of you is going home," Scott said. "Theresa?"

Theresa Jenkins took the microphone. "Thank you both for sharing your impeccable skills with us tonight. San Diego, are you ready to meet your winner?"

The lights dimmed again. Hard-hitting electronica filled the air and then died, leaving silence behind. Eli inhaled a slow, steady breath. *Smile, wave, get backstage before you fall apart.* They thought about their influx of followers, how the publicity would help them get more work. *You'll be okay.* Thought about top surgery and using next year's tax return to start a savings account for Beyond. *You'll make it happen.* Thought about their parents and the inevitable *I told you so.* Thought about making it on their own, not giving up, never, ever giving up. Thought about—

"And first place goes to . . . Eli Peterson!" Theresa hollered. "Eli, your Shenron the Eternal cosplay blew us away. Innovative, classic, and creative. Congratulations!"

Applause filled the ballroom. They gasped, exhaling through a short, surprised laugh. *First fucking place.* Adrenaline whipped inside them like a riptide.

"Rhonda Riot, I'm so sorry, but your Makeup Wars journey ends tonight," Theresa said.

Eli stepped back into the lineup. Beverly squeezed their arm. Cassie bumped her shoulder against theirs. They reveled in thrill, relief, and shock. Someone touched their elbow, fingers gently scratching. When Eli turned, they found Zach leaning around Cassie's back, watching them.

"Told you," he whispered, and for the first time since they'd seen each other again, Zach smiled.

Eli smiled, too. Somehow, they'd made it through the first Cosplay Runway, and Zach had helped them win.

♡   ♡   ♡

Stella tipped the lip of a silver flask against Eli's bubble-tea straw and poured vodka into their drink. She narrowed her eyes, concentrating, while Bodhi scanned the café, overly paranoid about the nonexistent security guard who might catch them.

"How's it feel?" Stella asked, sipping from the flask before she tightened the lid and stashed it in her purse.

Eli didn't know how to explain the feelings slithering through them. They were happy—of course they were happy—but they couldn't stop thinking about Zach's spatula pressed to their skin, smoothing down the edges of their foam face pieces. They wouldn't have won if he hadn't helped them. They would've placed second, maybe. Or third or fourth. With an amateur mistake like that, they might've gone home. They probably *should've* gone home.

Bodhi poked their shin with her heeled boot and said, "Yeah, how're you liking that first-place title, huh?"

"I didn't expect it at all, like, not even a little bit," they confessed, sipping their spiked taro-milk tea.

They chewed on a tapioca pearl and shifted on the mustard-yellow sofa. The night café, fondly called Tea Light, was filled with postcon cosplayers and attendees. Candles glowed in glass jars on round tables, and booths lined the wall across from the barista station. Jazzy hip-hop played over the speakers, overrun by lively chatter. Around the room, ferns hung from macramé baskets looped over hooks in the ceiling. Eli watched someone dressed as Daenerys pop a pink straw through the top of a cup, dragged their gaze across a *Chaos Reign* group crowded around a table, and noticed a familiar set of shoulders on the far side of the room.

"Well, you should've," Bodhi said.

Stella drummed her teal fingernails on her cup. "Yeah, you looked amazing. Shenron was a great idea."

"I guess it was," Eli said, looking away, staring at their lap, then the bar, then Bodhi's glittery pink lanyard, but their eyes kept flitting back to Zach.

"What—oh . . ." Bodhi heaved a sigh, following their line of sight. "We can leave, Eli. We don't have to stay."

Before Eli could stop themself, they said, "I'll be right back."

"No, do *not*," Bodhi hissed under her breath, scrabbling for their hand. "Liz, I swear to God. You're kicking your own heart in the ass at this point. Don't go over there."

Eli watched Zach wring his hands, face turned toward the floor, foot bouncing incessantly. He was nervous and alone, and something about seeing him like that, dressed in his old leather jacket, barefaced and anxious, pulled Eli back into his orbit.

Stella laughed. "Let them go, they've gotta deal with this at some point."

They didn't bother responding, just grabbed their tea and crossed the room. Maybe they were still high on adrenaline, still reeling from being onstage, or maybe they couldn't stand to see Zach look so . . . *lonesome*. He glanced at them once, then again, and his jaw shifted back and forth.

Eli traded their cup from one hand to the other. "Thank you," they blurted, and sighed. "For helping me earlier. I'd probably be packing my shit and going home if it weren't for you."

Zach stayed perfectly still. His deep green eyes flicked from Eli's ratty Vans to their face, blotchy from glue removal. "Don't worry about it," he said.

"I don't . . ." They trailed off and shut their mouth, locking the rest away. *I don't know what happened in the trailer, but I'm sorry about that, too. I'm sorry for everything. It hurt me too. It still hurts.* "I don't know," they said, and swallowed hard. "I think I should probably worry a little bit."

"Why's that?" Zach asked, lifting a brow. His mouth was set, but a smile teased at his lips.

"Because you're my biggest competition," Eli said.

Zach met their eyes. They stayed like that, staring at each other, until a hand met Eli's wrist and someone craned to look around them.

Cassie grinned, bouncing in place. "Hey! Zach, Eli, this is Brandon, my husband," she said, and turned, gesturing to a tall, stocky guy with a scruffy beard and stretched earlobes. "Babe, this is Zach, my friend from Shockwave, and Eli, the total fucking dark horse who just swept the first runway. Up top, baby makeup artist!" She lifted her hand, and Eli high-fived her.

"It's good to finally meet you, man," Zach said.

Brandon nodded and said, "Yeah, seriously. We'll get dinner in San Fran?"

"For sure."

"Eli, you're welcome to join us. We'll make it a Makeup Wars outing," Cassie said. She grabbed Brandon's hand and shrugged toward the exit. "See you next weekend."

"Yeah, see you later." Eli lifted two fingers in an awkward wave.

Cassie had a husband. Of course she had a husband. Why *wouldn't* she have a husband? Still, Eli's stomach crawled into their throat. For years, they'd never been jealous when it came to Zach, and all it had taken was a pretty, talented girl getting a kiss on the cheek to throw them into a spiral. Cassie was brilliant, and beautiful, and competitive, but none of those things made her a threat, and Eli felt a little gross for not giving her a fair chance when they'd met hours ago.

In the end, they'd weighed their options: top surgery, a healthy savings account, enough money to live on, or going to New York with Zach and nothing else. No money, no job, just pockets full of hope and some graduation gift cards. Eli didn't have Zach's last name. They hadn't lived in a big house, hadn't picked out a brand-new car on their fifteenth birthday, hadn't come from a powerful family. They'd lived *fine*, sure. But they hadn't lived like Zachary Miller, and they definitely didn't have the cushion he did. But none of that was Cassie's fault.

Eli's lips parted. They sighed, smiling painfully.

"Me and Cassie were partners during the workshop. We did all our projects together and used each other as canvases," Zach said. He smiled, too. Lips curved knowingly, eyebrows lifted. "She's a little cold at first, but she's got a big heart."

"Yeah, no, she's really nice," Eli said, toeing the floor. "I'm sorry about what happened in the trailer. I came over here to thank you for helping me, and Bodhi's waiting, so I should go."

"You can't sit for a minute?" he asked, louder, uncertain.

Eli chewed on the inside of their cheek.

Zach scooted over. "What've you been up to? How's the new place?"

They knew the moment Zach had asked them to stay, they would stay, despite Bodhi's eyes searing holes into their back.

They sat, elbows resting on their thighs, and nodded slowly. "I've picked up more hours at the diner. Tourists are everywhere, but you know how it is." They sipped their tea. Vodka bit their throat. "New place is cool. It's small, but it's on the west side. No roaches. The air conditioning works, so," they shrugged, "it's got everything I need, I guess."

"No roommate?"

"Bodhi's dad got a job in Culver, so she's staying with them to save money. Kind of freaky to find people on Craigslist, right? You know, with my transition stuff, and my weird routine, and me being an anxious mess—"

"You're not a mess," Zach said, too gently.

Been a mess since you left. Eli swallowed hard. "How was New York?"

"Like LA but tall," Zach said. An accidental smile ghosted across his mouth. "The workshop was great. I made connections, got some referrals, learned a hell of a lot."

They studied the stubble peeking through his skin, hunting for familiar places on his handsome face—ridiculous jungle eyes, and long eyelashes, and the tiny scar on his forehead. Eli remembered putting their thumb there, feeling the pocket of missing flesh. *Fell off a horse*, Zach had said, eyes closed, resting his cheek on Eli's thigh, *fifth-grade Jesus camp*. They blinked. Zach met their eyes, staring back at them.

"That's great." They steered their gaze to their lap. They should *not* have done this. They should've walked away, they should've texted him, but they never, ever should've let themself get this close—

"She's pissed at me, huh?" Zach whispered. He grimaced and shifted his eyes to the other side of the café. A fleeting, frightened glance.

"What? Oh, Bodhi. Yeah, you," Eli stopped to take a sip, "you might wanna call her."

"Or I could talk to her now."

"Probably not the best idea. She's been drinking," they said, and shook their half-gone tea.

"Seriously? You spiked your bubble tea?" Zach didn't wait for an answer. He snatched Eli's cup, took a sip, wrinkled his nose. "You *really* spiked your tea. *Wow.*"

Eli's knee touched Zach's thigh. They scoffed and grabbed their drink back. Zach's fingers were warm, his knuckles bony and hard. They tripped into laughter, and everything inside them wanted to get closer, to put their shoulder against Zach's, to scoop their hand around his thigh. But they didn't, because they couldn't. Because if they leaned toward him, everything would spill from them. All the avoided truth. All the explanations. And it was too late for that. Too late for the two of them.

"I'll see you in San Francisco," Eli said. They stood before they changed their mind. "I promise you won't have to rescue me."

Zach's smile softened before it disappeared completely. "We'll see about that."

CHAPTER TEN

Los Angeles

Zachary Miller: You bringing any cosplays for the actual cons?

Eli Peterson: nah, i'm just bringing my runway cosplays and regular clothes

Eli Peterson: you?

Zachary Miller: Same, I think

Zachary Miller: You excited?

Eli Peterson: obviously??

Zachary Miller: To get your ass kicked?

Eli Peterson: hahahahaha suuurrreeee

Eli Peterson: I WON the last runway soOooOOOoo

Zachary Miller: I took it easy on you

Eli Peterson: i know i know

Zachary Miller: What time's your flight?

Eli Peterson: ass early in the morning

Zachary Miller: Mine too. Maybe we can swing some shitty airport coffee?

Eli stood in the middle of their apartment with a joint pinched between their lips, staring at the bouncing cursor on the screen. They sucked smoke into their lungs and exhaled gray plumes. Brakes squealed outside their window, and they heaved a sigh. It wasn't like they'd *planned* this. They might've *thought* about texting Zach, but they hadn't gone through with it. Not until Zach had toed the forbidden no-exes-allowed door open and stepped into Eli's life again. Now Eli didn't know how they were supposed to *stop* texting him. Every time their phone buzzed, they hoped it was him. Every time they checked their Instagram they scanned the likes and comments for his username.

They could be friends, right? Exes could be friends. Eli could absolutely, one hundred percent be friends with Zach.

They took another long pull off the joint and tapped ash into an old cereal bowl.

> **Eli Peterson:** yeah, maybe
> **Eli Peterson:** text me when you get through security?
> **Zachary Miller:** Will do 😊

Smiley face. Eli squinted. Was it a flirty smiley face or a platonic smiley face? They squinted more. Could smiley faces *be* flirty?

"Oh, my God, no. *No!*" They tossed their phone on the bed. "No, self. We're not doing this. Nuh-uh. Nope." They finished the joint and flicked the butt into the cereal bowl, narrowly missing the spoon. "We're packing, we're going to the barbecue, we're not flirting with Zach. The end. No more texting. Done. Nada. That's it."

They unzipped their duffel bag and shoved clothes inside—jeans, shorts, two skirts, a few shirts, and a crop top—then stomped into the bathroom and packed their skin care. It was over. Zach and Eli were done. They wouldn't come back from a breakup like that. They *couldn't.* And Eli certainly didn't need their heart to claw at Zach from afar, hoping for . . . what? Something new? Another chance? Not with Beyond on the line. Not when Zach had the power to snatch their dreams away. Eli sighed again, zipped their toiletries case, and pawed through the top drawer, hunting for eye drops.

Makeup kit, packed. Outfits, folded in their duffel. Skin care and toiletries, ready to go. They packed the hooded wool coat Bodhi had altered in their hard-shell rolling case with the rest of their runway gear. *There.* They plopped their duffel on top of the case next to the front door. *Done.*

Eli exhaled, flapping their lips, and grabbed their buzzing phone.

Zachary Miller: Any chance I can bait you into telling me what you're cosplaying?

Eli smirked, thumbs hovering over the keyboard.

Eli Peterson: i'll give you 3 guesses
Zachary Miller: Hmmm okay.
Little Mermaid?
Eli Peterson: nope
Zachary Miller: Damn
Eli Peterson: 2 more
Zachary Miller: Okay, okay
Zachary Miller: Maleficent?
Eli Peterson: nooooppppeee
Zachary Miller: SERIOUSLY?!
Eli Peterson: 1 more. better make it good
Zachary Miller: Okay, fine. Let me think.

Eli grinned at the screen. Three dots bounced. Stopped bouncing. Bounced again.

Zachary Miller: The Cheshire Cat?
Eli Peterson: N O P E
Zachary Miller: Fuck. C'mon, really?!
Eli Peterson: bet i can guess your fairytale makeup
Zachary Miller: Bet you can't
Eli Peterson: you're gonna be Beast obvi

A second passed, then another. Eli didn't know why, but their pulse quickened, anxiety sitting low in their throat. They smiled, laughing softly as another text appeared.

Zachary Miller: You know me too well

♡   ♡   ♡

Eli hadn't been back to Laguna Niguel, their hometown, in two months. They'd texted their dad and called their mom, but this was the first time they'd booked a train ticket and gone back to Orange County. They didn't *hate* being down south, but OC was ridiculously conservative, overly white, disgustingly rich, and mildly unfriendly to anyone outside those first three categories. Sometimes they didn't understand how their parents did it. Staying, working, living, making ends meet. Their dated one-story house, bought with cash in the '70s by Eli's grandparents, was the kind of fixer-upper that was never actually *fixed*. But it was paid off, same with the family car, and once Grandma and Grandpa retired to Nevada, Eli's parents put down roots. Truthfully, the Petersons were expert pretenders, sliding through social circles wearing thrift-store clothes, ordering takeout from restaurants with coupons from the *OC Shopper*, and, for Eli, collecting free breakfast and lunch at school every day.

Becoming an influencer had changed everything, but it hadn't changed *enough*.

"Liz!" Their mom, Claire, waved from the open passenger window of a black Corolla idling at the pickup curb in front of the train station. "Good trip, honey?"

Eli slid into the backseat. "Yeah, it was fine. Can we stop by the store on the way? I forgot to grab ginger ale."

"Your father forgot hot-dog buns, so that's already part of the plan," Claire said, casting a narrow glance at Eli's father, Gary, who heaved a sigh.

"Looks like we ruined the barbecue, kid," Gary teased, catching Eli's gaze in the rearview mirror. They shared the same heart-shaped face and dark blue eyes. "How's LA? New apartment lookin' good?"

Eli nodded. Anxiety brewed low in their belly. They knew what was coming—talking about the competition—and they really, seriously hoped their parents wouldn't fly off the handle about it. "Still unpacking, but yeah. Everything's good."

"Everything went okay with the work transfer, too?" Claire asked, staring at the visor mirror and plucking at her short blond bob.

Now or never. They picked at their cuticles, watching cookie-cutter houses and perfectly trimmed hedges rush by the window. They'd mentioned Makeup Wars to their parents, but they hadn't included the *first-place* part or the *traveling* part or the *taking time off work* part. "Yeah, totally fine. Hey, so, speaking of work, I, uh, I kinda did something spontaneous," Eli said, and dug their thumbnail into their palm. "I entered that Makeup Wars contest I told you about, and I got in."

"Oh, that's wonderful," Gary said, grinning as he turned into the grocery store parking lot. "Congratulations!"

Eli nodded. "But—"

"But?" Claire unclicked her seatbelt and craned to look at them.

"But there's traveling involved, so I'm taking some time off work to make it happen. Everything's fine!" they blurted, catching themself on the seat when the car lurched to a stop. *Don't freak out.* "I have plenty of vacation and sick time, and the team at Denny's is cool with me going. I've already talked to my manager, she promised I'd have a job when I got back, it's totally fine."

Gary adjusted the silver glasses perched on his nose. "How long are we talking here, Eli? You can't just up and leave your job."

Claire heaved a short, frustrated sigh, the kind Eli couldn't stand.

Eli said, "Four weeks, four conventions, but it's fine—"

"Four weeks?" Claire parroted, shaking her head. "You can't be serious."

"I'm home for a few days in between shows. I'm still working every Tuesday and Wednesday, but I need Thursdays to do test runs for my runway looks, and we usually fly out Thursday or Friday, so my weekends are being covered while I'm gone. It's fine, I promise! Linda's on board with the schedule change until Makeup Wars is over." They paused to catch their breath, surprised they'd made it that far without being interrupted. Their throat tightened, but they inhaled and kept going. "The winner gets a scholarship to Beyond. It's a really, *really* good makeup school, and I . . . I have an actual shot at this."

Gary pulled the keys from the ignition and slid out of the car. "And this school is accredited? It's a *school*?"

"A trade school, yeah," Eli said. They fell into step between their parents, shivering as the automatic doors opened, sending a chilly gust across their face, and walked into the grocery store. "Like, the best school for special effects."

Gary and Claire exchanged suspicious glances. Someone thrust a cart toward self-checkout, and Eli leaped to the side, hurrying to keep up with their parents. *Sell it. Make them believe in you.* Gary stuffed a pack of hot-dog buns under his arm and pointed to the soda aisle. "Go grab the ginger ale," he said.

"Dad, c'mon," Eli whined.

"We'll talk in the car; we can't be late. Go on."

Eli huffed and did as they were told. Once they were in the backseat, holding two liters of ginger ale, they waited, chewing on the inside of their cheek while the silence thickened. Claire's nails clicked together, a nervous habit, and Gary kept his eyes forward, staring at the road. They'd expected a shitty reaction, but they'd hoped that maybe this time their parents would take their future seriously. For once.

They pulled out their phone and reread messages from Zach. *Do not.* They swiped his text bubble away and Texted Bodhi instead.

> **Eli Peterson:** so this is a nightmare
> **Bodhi Babe:** What's up?
> **Eli Peterson:** in OC with my parents. just told them about makeup wars
> **Bodhi Babe:** Oof yeah I bet they're THRILLED. Want me to come get you?
> **Eli Peterson:** nah i'll be okay for a while
> **Bodhi Babe:** I'm making food with my grandma later. Come by if you want.
> **Eli Peterson:** will do ♡

"I really think you should consider the fact that you just moved into a new apartment. You've got bills now," Gary said.

"When have I *not* had bills, Dad? I started paying rent when I was sixteen." Eli rolled their eyes, thumbing through the popular makeup hashtags on Instagram.

Claire made an indignant noise. "We never charged you *rent*! You had all that free money coming in, so we asked if you could help with groceries and . . . and . . ."

"Mom, it's fine. I offered, I get it. But that wasn't *free* anything. I worked for that money, and I'm working even harder now. I've got savings, I'm expecting at least three sponsorship payments in the next few weeks, *and* I'm using some vacation time. I did the math. I've got it covered."

"You're almost twenty, Eli. Your gap year is pretty much gone, you're *still* pulling overnights at a diner, and now you've got your own place and your own responsibilities. You can't blame us for being a little skeptical of your social media job, okay? It's not reliable, and it's definitely not sustainable," Gary said, clearly attempting to keep his voice level and calm. "We can all agree on that, can't we?"

"Yes, we can," Claire mumbled.

Eli tipped their nose closer to their phone, ignoring their mom's held breath and their dad's eyes in the rearview mirror. The car stopped along the curb in their aunt's neighborhood. Laughter and splashing echoed from the backyard. Before they could change their mind, they unfastened their seatbelt and shoved their phone over the center console, hitting play on a video.

"That's me," they said matter-of-factly. Neon lights flashed across the stage at Comic Palooza. The audience applauded as they were announced the winner. "This isn't some little online contest, and this isn't an *unsustainable* social media gig. This is big, and I don't want you guys to think I'm being a dumbass about it."

Their mom clucked her tongue, smiling softly at the video. Gary shot her a glance and smiled, too.

"We know how much you *enjoy* makeup, sweetheart . . ." Claire said, sighing. She looked at Eli over her shoulder. "We just worry, you know that. Wouldn't it be a little safer to take a few online classes? Or enroll down here at Saddleback and transfer to a university later? You know you can stay with us while you get on your feet. Our house is your house."

"I *am* on my feet," Eli said, even though they were maybe, possibly on *one* foot. But they were standing. Wobbly, yeah, but upright. "I'm doing this, okay? If I don't win, I don't win, but I have to try."

Gary offered a tight-lipped smile. "That's very good," he said, gesturing to the video. "People with imaginations like yours make incredible architects. Bring home big paychecks, too. The detail and color, you could take skill like that and run with it. Become a designer or—"

"Or a makeup artist," Eli snapped. They shoved the car door open and got out, carrying the ginger ale toward Aunt Ashley's two-story white house.

They flexed their free hand. They'd braced for this, for the boring, repetitive advice their parents always gave. Worrisome *what ifs* and excuses. They'd been raised in a world where money played the hero and villain, and that made them understand why their parents wanted them to have something secure. Claire and Gary would've been overjoyed if they were miserable at a bank, or completely unfulfilled as a realtor, or bored out of their mind as an architect. But the American Dream their parents thought everyone still wanted sounded like a prison sentence, and Eli refused to subscribe to it. Still, they'd hoped for something different, something that prioritized their happiness and not their income. For their parents to finally say *That's great, honey* and not a single thing after that.

Just *Good job.* Just *Congratulations.* Just *We'll cross our fingers for you.*

Eli opened the front door. "Ash? We're here!"

"Liz? Oh, hi, baby. Yeah, we're in the back," Ashley hollered.

Like most houses in the suburbs, Ashley's décor was varying shades of gray and beige. Feel-good accessories from high-end boutiques were hung on the walls, and framed family portraits lined the staircase. Eli pushed their sunglasses to the top of their head and set the sodas on the kitchen island, already packed with chips, dips, and cut fruit. Their cousins were in the pool, hugging inflatable animals and swatting a beach ball over a detachable net.

Uncle David lounged under the shady gazebo, sipping a light beer. "Hey, hey, family, there's ribs on the grill. Burgers and dogs are up next!"

Gary and Claire walked behind Eli. Their dad squeezed their shoulder as he made his way to the backyard, and their mom sighed as she met Ashley in front of the barbecue. Another weekend in Orange County. Another day of polite niceties, the smell of chlorine, and watching their parents pretend to relate to the more successful branches on the family tree.

No one ever said it, but Eli knew they were the oddity. The one Peterson who refused to comply, who wouldn't beg for attention from rich assholes or pretend to be someone they weren't. Not that Ashley and David were *assholes*, but . . . c'mon, they had a fucking pool.

Eli stripped off their tank, poured a glass of lemonade, and laid a towel next to the gazebo, basking like a lizard in the sun.

"How's the big-city life, Eli?" David asked.

Here we go again. "Goin' great, actually," they said, sighing.

"Still doing the cosmetics stuff?"

"Yep," they said, popping their lips.

Ashley walked over with a platter of ribs and sat next to Gary on the loveseat. Claire stood, resting her hip against a wooden gazebo leg. "Your mom said you've been taking a gap year," Ashley said, feigning delight. "That's exciting!"

"If that's what we're calling it now, sure." Eli fingered sticky ribs onto a paper plate and gnawed on one, retreating back to their towel. "Technically, it's been an I-have-a-real-job year, but gap year works, too." They licked barbecue sauce off their fingers and flashed a smile.

Their aunt nodded slowly, shooting Claire a quizzical glance. Eli was thankful that Gary started talking about the stock market, leaving them to their food and the sunshine. They kept to themself for the next few hours, trading sun for shade, ribs for potato salad, and napped on and off as the afternoon sizzled.

They'd almost made it out unscathed—gone for a swim with their cousins, listened to music, read a sample of a book on their phone—but, of course, as the family gathered for dessert, their uncle sighed and said, "So no college, huh?"

Eli jabbed their fork into a gooey brownie and huffed out a laugh. "Trade school," they said.

"Right . . ."

"We're still talking things over," their dad assured David. "Nothing's set in stone."

Ashley sighed. She had a blond bob and a small, straight nose like Eli's mom's. She'd been the one to gasp at Eli's shaved head the first time she'd seen it, casting pitying glances at Claire after Eli had walked at graduation. She didn't understand the makeup stuff or the nonbinary stuff, but she'd never said anything outright *horrible*. Her judgment was held in passing glances. Always tucked away in hidden apologies.

"I think makeup is a great interim." Ashley extended her palm to them as she would a feral cat.

"And a great career," Eli said.

"Well, yeah, sure, but you're still considering a degree, right? I mean, a bachelor's doesn't open every door, but it doesn't hurt." She laughed, nodding as if she'd told an ultimate truth. "Not that makeup isn't super fun! I bet it is, huh?"

"It's fun, yeah," Eli said, resisting the urge to start a fight. *And stressful and hard and demanding.* "Speaking of which, I have a thing I need to get to."

"What? I thought we were dropping you off at the station tonight?" Claire spoke through her teeth. "Liz, please. Just stay."

Eli's cheeks burned. They stood, towel in one hand, purse in the other, and forced another painful smile. "Wish me luck at Makeup Wars. I'll call before I get on the plane."

"Now, hold on a minute," their dad said.

"It was nice seeing you, Ashley. Bye, David," they said, and walked away before they changed their mind or snapped at everyone. Their cousins hollered from the pool—*Bye, Eli! Have fun in San Francisco!*—and Eli turned, laughing, "Thanks, guys! See you later!"

They heard Ashley say, "San Francisco . . . ?" just before the front door closed behind them.

Eli Peterson: how long are you at grandmas?

Bodhi Babe: Uhhhh a while. You coming?

Eli Peterson: getting a Lyft to the train station, so yeah. i'll be there in a couple hours

Bodhi Babe: You okay? Need me to drive down there?

Eli Peterson: i'm okay, just gotta get outta here.

Bodhi Babe: Grandma says she'll make extra vada pav anndd doughnuts

Eli Peterson: are those the curry potato burgers?

Bodhi Babe: Yes dumbass

Eli Peterson: tell grandma she's my favorite human

Bodhi Babe: I'M YOUR FAVORITE HUMAN

Eli Peterson: okay tell her she's my second fave

Bodhi Babe: Fine

♡   ♡   ♡

The Burman household was always delightfully chaotic.

Bodhi's parents, Bhavita and Steven, bustled around the house, Bhavita hollering about oil spitting from a bubbling pot, Steven crowing, *Honey, it's fine*, as his wife stormed into the kitchen. Olivia, Bodhi's grandmother, batted Bhavita away and dropped a glob of dough into the gurgling oil.

"Coconut doughnuts," Olivia said. She jutted her thumb over her shoulder, gesturing to the marble island where Bodhi and Eli munched fried dough balls. "Don't you feed these kids? Look at your daughter—starving, skinny." She made a mock-disapproving noise.

"*Skinny?*" Bodhi barked through laughter. Powdered sugar flecked her chin. "Hardly, Nani. But I'll let you keep feedin' me."

"Thank you for cooking, Olivia," Eli said.

"*Mess*," Bhavita hissed, scrubbing the counter with a rag. She looked like Bodhi. Strong nose, russet skin, long face. Beautiful and ever scowling. "I swear, Mama. *I swear.*"

Olivia dropped more dough into the oil and pulled her apron tighter around her thick middle. "You're welcome, Liz. You can take those." She waved half-heartedly at the remaining pile of doughnuts. "Next time, I'll make mango-filled."

"Can you two, like . . ." Bhavita shooed Bodhi and Eli, flapping her hands toward the staircase. "Go, please? I need to get this—*Mama, stop*—place clean."

Bodhi shrugged and took the plate, bumping Eli with her elbow. The pair climbed the stairs and walked into Bodhi's bedroom. She hip-checked the door, sucked sugar from her fingertips, and kicked dirty clothes toward the overflowing hamper in the corner.

"So your parents suck," she slurred. She sat cross-legged on her bed, cheeks bulging with fried dough. "We knew that, didn't we?"

"They don't *suck*. I mean, okay, maybe a little, *sort of*, but they're just . . . dense. I thought they'd get it by now." Eli tapped their phone and opened another text message from their mom. Guilt panged in their chest.

> **Mama 🏵:** We love you so much and just want the best for you
>
> **Mama 🏵:** Send us pictures from your makeup contest! MUAH! ♡

"They're afraid I'm wasting my life," they added quietly. "Can't blame 'em."

"Oh, c'mon. You're not *wasting* anything," Bodhi said, and shoved a doughnut in Eli's mouth. "I think it's hardwired into parental brain matter to associate anything artistic with immediate failure. Even Zach's parents still give him grief about it."

They stopped chewing. *Still*. As in *now*. As in Bodhi had *talked* to him. Their heart jumped. "What . . . ?"

Bodhi stopped chewing, too. Her eyes widened, and she hastily swallowed. "Oh, right, yeah. He . . . he called. Twice, actually. I forwarded the first one, and then—"

"What'd he say?"

"I . . . I mean—"

They couldn't control the hot flare inside them. "What did he *say*, Bodhi?"

"A lot, Eli. He said a lot."

"Okay, and ...?"

"And I don't know, I'm still processing."

"Processing?"

"Yes, processing. It was hard, like, really, really hard. I've never heard him sound—"

"Like *what*?" Eli asked eagerly, rudely.

"*Sad!* Jesus, Liz, you broke his heart," she bit out, snappish and too loud. "You totally fucking wrecked him, okay? He thought he'd done everything wrong. And he . . . he thought I was leaving him, too, and he didn't want to take *me* from *you*, so he blocked my number while he was in New York because he didn't trust himself not to ask about you. I mean, seriously, you emotionally curb-stomped him, and he still put you first." She spoke with vigor. Righteously. Like all the anger she'd smothered had rushed to the surface. "Yeah, I want to punch him in the dick, yeah, I'm pissed at him, yeah, I hate that he disappeared, but I've missed him, too, okay? I *miss* him, and now I've heard his side, and I'm mad because I love you both. This sucks. The whole thing. You, him." She paused to stuff another doughnut in her mouth. "So," she flashed her middle finger, "to you both."

Eli stared at her. Their heart lurched, and they swallowed the urge to shout, blinking away the sting in their eyes until they were certain they wouldn't cry. "I know I wrecked him," they spat. Their nose burned. Despite their attempt at steadiness, their voice still wobbled. "But I didn't ask him to stay away from you, and I didn't ask you to pick Team Eli, okay? You think I don't know how shitty this is? You think I don't get it—"

Bodhi sighed. "No, I know. I'm sorry."

"Don't be. He called me out in front of everyone at Comic Palooza, but he's been . . ." They knocked their hand against their phone, lying next to the plate of doughnuts. "Texting me, too. I don't know what's going on, but I'll take a step back if you think I should."

"Called you out?" She raised an eyebrow.

"Yeah, called me out about our breakup. Like, not directly, but enough to make sure everyone knew what he was talking about."

"That's . . . yeah, that's not cool."

"Emotionally curb-stomping him isn't cool, either."

"Okay, maybe my word choice was a little harsh—"

"*A little?*" Eli felt their chin dimple and clenched their jaw. They met her softened gaze. "You have no idea what it's like to realize you're not good enough for the person you love, okay? I know I hurt him, I know I screwed up, *I know.* And I know you got hurt in the crossfire, so if you have anything else you've been *dying* to say, go ahead."

Bodhi chewed her bottom lip. A strained moment passed, then another, disrupted by Bhavita's shrill voice, plates clattering, and Olivia's belly laughter. Carefully, Bodhi grabbed Eli's palm and squeezed, blowing out a tired sigh. She didn't ramble or ask for answers. Just held their hand and endured the awkward silence. They stared at the rumpled polka-dot comforter, trapped in a vicious cycle—the night of the breakup, the weeks that followed, Comic Palooza, sitting with Zach at the café—and tried not to tense when their phone illuminated.

Zachary Miller: Something Greek? Hades or Cerberus?

"Do you think that's smart?" Bodhi asked. She let their hand go and pointed at their phone.

"What?"

"Talking to him again. Is that smart?"

"I can't *not* talk to him, Bodhi. He's literally my competition. There's no avoiding him."

Bodhi gave a curt nod. "I just don't want you to get hurt, that's all," she said, and it felt like a conclusion. Like the eruption they'd started had come to an end and the ash had finally settled. For Eli and Bodhi, at least. "What's that about, anyway?"

Damage is already done, Eli thought. In the end, they'd broken themself by breaking him, and there was no taking that back. Being near him in San Diego had felt terrible and hopeful and *good*, and they didn't know how to stay away. Didn't know if they *could* stay away. They popped another doughnut into their mouth and chewed, swallowed, then tried to smile. "He's trying to guess my cosplay."

Bodhi flashed a playful grin, and things felt normal again. "So the dreaded Haunt Master is already afraid of you, huh?"

"I don't know if *afraid* is the right word," they said, and typed out a response.

Eli Peterson: wrong again, beastie

CHAPTER ELEVEN

San Francisco–Anime Bay

"CHECKING IN?"

"Yes, the reservation should be under Eli Peterson," Eli said. They glanced at the off-white floor as they stood in the lobby of the sponsored hotel for the San Francisco Anime Bay convention. Backpack straps dug into their shoulders, and they ran their finger across their black-painted thumbnail.

"Okay, perfect. You're in room 2024. Pool access is on the twelfth floor, and complimentary breakfast is served every morning from six to ten on the second floor. If you have any questions, please let us know. Enjoy your stay." The host smiled, gesturing with a flat palm to the elevators at the far end of the lobby. "And have fun at the convention!"

Eli nodded, clutching their room key in one hand and the handle on their rolling case with the other. "Thanks," they said, walked to the elevator, and tapped 20. Two other people stood in the elevator with them, chatting about panels, movie showings, and con-sponsored bars near the convention center.

Usually, Eli would've been doing the same thing, talking over panels and cosplay with Bodhi. But for the first time ever, Eli was alone for an entire weekend. They gripped the handle on their suitcase tighter and tried to avoid the obvious solution to being stranded—hanging out with Zach. The elevator dinged, and the doors slid open. Eli's train case, situated on top of their suitcase, almost toppled to the floor as they trudged down the hall and shouldered open room 2024.

The curtains were cinched, but Eli could still make out the fluffy white comforter and the blank television. To the left, the small closet sat adjacent to a vanity, and the bathroom housed an oversized bathtub and a glass-walled shower. They dropped their backpack and propped their cases next to each other in front of the closet. Light slipped beneath the bottom of the curtains, and the air conditioner whirred softly.

Eli put their back against the wall and stared at the ceiling, running their index finger along the top half of their phone, jutting from their front pocket.

After they'd left the barbecue, their parents had sent more long-winded texts—*It's our job to worry, don't be mad at us for having your best interest at heart, you're a great makeup artist but everyone needs a backup plan, we can't wait to see pictures from the convention, it's okay to enjoy your summer but don't forget to apply for financial aid before the window closes at Saddleback, career motivation is important*—and Eli had responded with two thumbs-up emojis and a smiley face. They swallowed hard. Footsteps padded along the hallway, and muffled laughter came from the room next door. Loneliness was an awkward thing, especially when they were surrounded by like-minded people, in proximity to someone who knew them better than anyone ever had, and unable to do a damn thing about it. Eli flapped their lips and banged the back of their head against the wall.

Focus.

They could be lonely *and* productive, at least. They unpacked their suitcase first, swatting wrinkles out of their cloak and combing the brown fur on their chest piece, then went to work arranging their skin care in the bathroom. Once everything was done, and they had nothing left to put in a drawer or hang in the closet, they positioned their circle light in front of the mirror and opened Instagram.

"Hey, everyone, Eli here . . ." They groaned and started over. "Hi, guys, it's Eli—" Another groan, another hard tap to the screen. "I'm here at Anime Bay, getting ready for another shot at . . . God dammit . . ." They flicked the app away and gripped the edge of the counter, staring at their reflection. *Another shot at Beyond.* Another two hours spent assembling a makeup in the same room as Beverly and Cassie and Zach. Another day wondering if they were cut out for something like this, for an opportunity like Beyond, for the life they'd always wanted.

No matter how often they reminded themself that special effects were their passion, their *thing*, their dream, their parents' worried voices still fit under every thought. Because what if Gary and Claire were right? What if Eli was squandering precious time chasing something unattainable? What if they couldn't live in the city they loved, pay for the surgery they needed, make enough money to survive, *and* have the job they wanted? What if pretending to have their shit together was the only real way to get through life? Like their parents had, like most people did.

They heaved a sigh and dug through their makeup kit, pressing concealer over the bags under their eyes. They shielded themself with dark eyeshadow and sharp liner, heavy contour, and bold eyebrows and snapped a selfie in front of the giant window. Typing out a caption was easier than recording a video. They could fake their way through text, but they couldn't mask the tremble in their voice or the uncertainty in their eyes if they updated their story. They hit "share."

> Just checked in at my hotel for
> ANIME BAY!!! Can't wait to take the

stage again. This week's theme is
Fairytales & Folklore and I've got
something pretty cool to show you
all. Still can't believe I get to be
here with so many talented artists.
The runway is tomorrow . . . keep
your claws crossed for me! Tag any
cool trans/queer comic artists who
are at Anime Bay in the comments
and I'll try to stop by their booth
♡ #MakeupWars #VoteEli #BenNye
#StageCrewBodyPaint

A few red hearts floated across Eli's screen, and a message dinged their inbox.

> **BeverlyBelle_BB:** Heyy!! you're here?
> **EliSFX:** yeah, i just checked in and unpacked
> **BeverlyBelle_BB:** awesome! wanna hit the con? I still need to get my badge and stuff
> **EliSFX:** sure 😊 give me 5

Eli changed out of their airplane clothes and slipped into a pair of high-waisted dark-washed jeans and an old anime T-shirt they'd cut into a crop. They grabbed their lanyard and slung their black purse over their shoulder, checking for wallet, yes, room key, yes, phone *and* battery block, yes and yes. Before the door had shut behind them, Beverly's voice careened through the air.

"Of course they put us on the same floor," she said. Her cute noir maid outfit, all bows and lace and hoop skirt, was paired with fluffy cat ears and exaggerated eye makeup. "I figured they would, but sometimes things get wonky with hotel bookings. How're you? How was your flight?"

"I'm okay, I think. Just nervous. Flight was really short, so not too bad. How 'bout you?"

Beverly bounced in place as the elevator dropped. "I got really, *really* cool news," she blurted. "Like, big news. I can't even tell you about it because it's still under wraps and I don't even know if I'm in yet, but I'm still freaking out."

"Oh, shit, really? Big news, huh? How big?" Eli flashed a toothy grin.

"Like, I had to sign a nondisclosure *big*," she whispered. Her smile widened and she sneaked her arm around their elbow, staying close while they walked through the revolving door and onto the sidewalk. "Just keep your fingers crossed for me, okay? I need all the luck I can get. Also, smile!" Beverly held out her phone. Eli smiled, winking for a selfie.

Like most con-sponsored hotels, the Marriott was only two blocks away from the convention center. Since it was Thursday, day one, the entrance into the building wasn't packed. The crowded days were Saturday and Sunday, sometimes Friday, too, and Eli was relieved to see open space between groups of cosplayers and short lines at snack stands.

"So . . ." Beverly aimed a curious glance at them. "You and Zach talked after the runway last week?"

Eli sighed. *Of course.* "Cassie told you?"

"Zach told Cassie, who told me, yeah."

"Yeah, we talked. But I mean, it's not like we *talked*, you know? We're cool. We're doing this competition together. We have to find a way to make it work," they said and shook their head, following Beverly to the badge pickup line in front of the Exhibitor Hall. "Is everyone talking about us or—"

"No! No, no, I swear. You know how it is. You two were the endgame SFX couple, you stopped tagging each other in posts, Zach went to Shockwave without you . . . People were whispering for a while, the drama died out, and then you guys went feral in the makeup trailer, so." Her smile thinned, and her brows knitted. Eli hated that look, like they were a kitten in the rain. "It can't be easy doing this whole thing with him, but I'm glad you two are cool now."

"I hope we are," Eli said. They cleared their throat, thumbing through Instagram, past the selfie Beverly had tagged them in and updates from other influencers. When they glanced up, Beverly was still peering at them sadly, curiously. "It's fine, seriously," they blurted.

She sighed. "Can I say something? I know we're not close, but we're friends, I hope."

"Yeah, we're friends. Go for it."

"I think he still . . ." Her smile faltered. "You know, I think he *still*—"

"I *can't* go there, okay? I really, really can't." Eli's heart floundered.

"All right, I hear you, I get it. As long as you know. Anyway, badges, Exhibitor Hall, Artist Alley?"

They wanted to walk back to the hotel, crawl under the crisp comforter, and burrow in the dark like an armadillo. Entertaining the idea that Zachary Miller might have feelings for them was off-limits. *Danger zone. Caution: rip currents—watch out!* And after being catastrophically bombarded by how Bodhi felt about everything? Yeah, *no*, Eli seriously couldn't deal. But they forced a smile and nodded, pointing to the open space in front of the pickup desk.

"Sure, yeah. Sounds good," they said.

Once Eli and Beverly had their badges, Eli adjusted the pronoun pin clipped to their lanyard, and Beverly fastened her badge to the heart-shaped fanny pack around her waist. Eli's chest still ached, weighed down by the gross revelation that other makeup artists *had* gossiped about them. *Endgame SFX couple.* Damn, people were probably *still* gossiping about them. They wrung their hands, scanning plushie booths and manga spines.

Artist Alley was located next to the panel rooms. Aisles lined with comic creators, fan artists, and independent shop owners filled the space. Eli glanced at their phone, meandering between booths until they came across a few artists mentioned in the comments section on their Instagram post. Beverly cooed over *Haikyu!!* key chains and *Beastars* zines. Eli skimmed a table stocked with *Yuri on Ice* buttons and reached for a comic called *Shadow Deliverance.* A handwritten sign read SUPER QUEER! BLOODSUCKERS! TRANS VAMP! SEXY! LAST COPY! Their fingers knocked against someone's knuckles.

"I'm so sorry, go ahead," Eli said, glancing from the table to the person beside them.

Zach's throat worked around a swallow. He looked as good as he always did, short auburn hair pushed away from his face, wearing an old-school *Wolf's Rain* T-shirt and fitted black jeans. "Guess we were too busy looking down, huh?"

"Yeah, guess so." They handed him the comic. "Heard this was good. You should give it a shot."

He considered them for a moment, eyes flicking from Eli's shoes to their nose. "I'm pretty sure you went for it first; you should take it."

"I'll get a copy online or something. No big deal."

"Better idea—I'll read it tonight and you can borrow it in the morning."

Eli's lips betrayed them, curving into a smile. "Sure, yeah. We can do that." They short-circuited. Once Eli started smiling, they couldn't stop. *Oh, my fucking God.* They turned their gaze to the ground, nodding. "I'm sorry we couldn't get coffee at the airport. I overslept, and the Metro was packed."

"Yeah, I'm used to you bailing on me." Zach flashed a sarcastic grin and narrowed his eyes. "Kidding. But I wish you would've said something. I could've given you a ride."

Ouch. "I . . . yeah, I didn't think about that. Maybe we can get coffee tomorrow morning?"

"That'd be cool."

"Hey, what's up?" Cassie said, popping her head around Zach's arm. Her bubblegum lips quirked. She gave Eli a one-armed hug and held her phone up, shimmying it side to side. "Did you get Theresa's email? They want us for a video shoot. Something about event promotion, I guess?"

"I got a notification," Beverly said, pinning a new button to her fanny pack. "What time?"

Eli pursed their lips. "Email?"

"She just sent it out a few minutes ago," Cassie said. "Six, I think?

They opened their email app and tapped the bolded message in their inbox, sidestepping out of the aisle while Zach paid for the comic. "Promotional material for social media, highlighting Anime Bay," they mumbled. "Full-beauty makeup looks, one to two hours maximum."

Beverly nudged their arm with her elbow. "Easy enough."

Eli nodded. That was one way to put it.

♡   ♡   ♡

Unsurprisingly, Theresa Jenkins wasn't actually in the room for the shoot. She'd provided four Makeup Wars assistants and a video tech who hung a makeshift green screen in front of a tripod ring light. Beverly and Cassie fixed their makeup in the bathroom, whispering to one another behind the closed door. Zach put his back against the wall, arms folded, and Eli stood next to the closet, awkwardly scrolling on their phone, attempting to keep their nervousness masked and their attention fixed on something, *anything* else.

Their mind did cartwheels, though, flipping through imaginary situations. They wanted to understand how Zach could go from snarling at them in the makeup trailer to helping them win the runway, laughing with them at the café, texting them throughout the week, asking them to meet him for coffee, and landing . . . where? What were the two of them supposed to become? *Friends?* Eli's throat tightened. They wanted that; they'd always wanted that. But they'd had something different with Zach for a long, long time, and they didn't know if they had what it took to unlove him romantically in order to love him platonically.

Love wasn't fair. It was a learned thing, familiar and indomitable, and they couldn't picture a world where their heart stopped reaching for Zachary fucking Miller.

"You okay?" Zach asked.

Eli nodded. "Yeah, why?"

"You've been flicking your home screen back and forth for two minutes."

"Right, yeah. Just, you know . . ." Their cheeks heated, and they shoved their phone in their pocket, taking a deep breath. "Nervous, maybe? Thinking too much, I guess."

He arched an eyebrow. "Dwelling isn't thinking."

"Okay, well, I can't really help it, so," they said, huffing.

Zach laughed in his throat. "You still haven't told me about your runway look."

"And I'm still not going to."

"I get it, you're scared. I'd be scared of me, too," he teased.

"Please." They scoffed, raking their eyes from his scuffed boots to his black-rimmed lashes. "Me? Scared of *you*? Yeah, no. Sorry, Haunt Master, but you're not that intimidating." Eli forced the flutter in their chest to fade. They weren't scared of Zach's skill; they were scared of everything else he had power over. All the memories suspended between them and how they wanted to kiss away his smug smile.

"It's okay, you can say it."

"Not happening."

"No judgment, seriously."

Eli hummed. "Uh-huh, sure."

He laughed again, harder and louder, and Eli laughed, too. They missed the sound of Zach's breathy laughter, how his shoulders shook and his nose scrunched.

What the hell are you doing?

They straightened their back and muted another giggle. Quiet thickened between them again, a reminder that nothing was normal, that they'd gone from being everything to each other to being . . . *this*, whatever it was.

"I'm sorry about San Diego," Zach said suddenly, in a rush. "I didn't mean to be a dick. I shouldn't have said that shit to you, I just—"

"It's fine," Eli said just as suddenly. "You don't need to be sorry for that. You don't . . ." they trailed off, trying to find the right words. They could *not* do this. "You don't owe me anything, okay? Not a big deal."

"It *was* a big deal to you. I know it, I saw it on your face, Eli."

Eli didn't know what to do or say or how to feel. They were trapped, expected to be professional while their heart tore itself up. "That was last week," they said, and met his eyes. "I'm fine, it's fine, we're fine."

Zach sighed through his nose. His jaw tensed, his brow furrowed, and his lips parted again, to say something, to give another apology, to make Eli feel worse, but the video tech cut him off.

"We're ready to go," the tech said, adjusting the tripod.

"Great," Eli blurted. They shot Zach an apologetic look and cleared their throat. "Cassie! Beverly! C'mon, they're ready for us."

Cassie and Beverly swept into the small space, makeup flawless, hair styled, outfits smoothed, and accessories perfectly placed. Eli almost regretted keeping it casual in their Strawberry Panic T-shirt and tight jeans. At least Zach was dressed down, too, still wearing his outfit from Artist Alley.

"Let's get third and fourth place from last week first, then we'll do the top two, and then we'll get a group shot," a volunteer said, gesturing to the green screen next to the bed.

Cassie and Beverly hung off each other, linking elbows, throwing arms over shoulders, pressing cheeks together, and spouting one-line quips for the camera.

Beverly said, "This isn't just a battle," while Cassie blew a kiss at the camera and added, "You better armor up."

The video tech replayed their portion of the video on his laptop and nodded approvingly. "Good job, girls. That was great. Eli, Zach, you two are up."

Eli stood in front of the green screen. Zach's arm touched their shoulder. They didn't shift away, but they tensed, blinking at the floor.

"Okay, so, let's get you two a little closer. Zach, can we get you to say, 'This is a bloodbath,' and Eli, you placed first last week, so your line is the main tag. Just look directly at the camera and say, 'This is Makeup Wars.' Yep, Eli, shift to the side. Yes, like that, and Zach, a little, right there, awesome."

Zach and Eli were almost flush together. They stood chest to chest. Zach's chin touched their ear, and Eli's knuckles brushed his thigh. They hoped the ring light washed out their blush. Hoped Zach couldn't hear their heartbeat or feel the tremble on their breath.

"And . . . go!"

"This is a bloodbath," Zach rasped, lips lifting into a dangerous smile. He looked incredibly sexy, and he was *way* too close, and Eli wanted to, literally, jump off a building.

They lifted their chin, rallying courage, and winked at the camera. "This is Makeup Wars."

"Yes! Loved that, guys. Beverly, Cassie, let's get you two in here, and if you all could just clown around. Hug, kinda tease each other, make the viewers think you're all friends. Cool?"

"We *are* friends!" Beverly said, barking out laughter. "Do people seriously think we're not friends or something . . . ?"

"It *is* a competition." Cassie threw her arm around Eli's shoulders, hauling them close.

They knocked into each other, laughing hard, harder, until they were barely able to stand, bouncing off each other, grabbing shoulders, tangling fingers. At one point, Eli rested their forehead on Beverly's shoulder and Cassie kissed them on the cheek, and when they tried to balance on one foot, they almost toppled over. Zach caught them. He perched his hands on their waist as Beverly hugged him from behind.

"You good?" Zach asked, still laughing.

Eli was hyperaware of the camera, their rising pulse, Zach's steady gaze. They nodded, leaning back to rest against Cassie, who kicked her foot out like a dancer. "Yeah, you?"

The video tech clapped. "That's a wrap! Thanks, everyone!"

Zach met their eyes but didn't answer. His fingers slipped away, leaving an echo on Eli's hip bones.

♡   ♡   ♡

The Castro—San Francisco's gay district—came alive after dark. Cassie had insisted on a group dinner before the competition, and despite being broke as hell, Eli had agreed to tag along. They didn't have much money, but they had enough for an appetizer. Probably, *hopefully*. They walked next to Beverly, listening and nodding as she rattled on about a new manga series, and tried not to stare at Zach's broad shoulders as he strode beside Cassie and her husband on the sidewalk in front of them.

Queer flags whipped above shopfronts, and the group followed a crosswalk painted like a rainbow.

"C'mon, it's this way," Cassie said, pointing down the street.

Eli grinned. They'd kept to themself in San Diego, but with Beverly's arm looped around their elbow and Cassie's laughter ringing through the air, they felt utterly *seen*. Friendship had never been easy. Anxiety? Too hard for most people to deal with. Being an introvert? No fun at parties. But they'd become a part of something memorable, and somehow, their little makeup group felt like the real deal. Like something that might outlive the competition. That big, bright feeling glimmered inside them, and they instantly wished they could teleport Bodhi and Stella to San Francisco.

A Batman patch spanned the back of Zach's denim jacket, stealing Eli's attention while nightclubs boomed and people laughed on dinner patios. They nodded along as Beverly talked about the epic fight scene she'd read on the plane and tried not to panic when Cassie steered the group toward a packed restaurant. Usually, they would've looked up the menu beforehand and scanned the prices, but the evening had unraveled quickly after the video shoot. One minute they were standing in the hallway, laughing about their cheesy promo script, and the next they were saying *Sure* when Cassie pitched the idea for dinner.

"Oh, an Arabic place! Hell, yeah, I haven't had shakshuka in forever, let's do it," Beverly said.

"This place looks pretty small. Think they've got a big enough table?" Zach asked.

Cassie waved dismissively. "We'll push two together. Is everyone good with getting a bunch of stuff and splitting the bill? Figure it'll be easier that way."

Ice shot into Eli's stomach. They swallowed hard and pulled out their phone, trying to sneak a glance at the menu.

"Of course!" Beverly clapped excitedly. "I definitely want to try a little bit of everything."

Fuck. They couldn't afford an equal split of four fancy entrees and a *just-not-that-hungry* excuse for an appetizer.

Zach cleared his throat. "Why don't we all order whatever looks best and get share plates?" he asked.

"That works, too," Cassie said pleasantly.

Saved for the second time. Eli chewed their bottom lip and painted on a smile, nodding excitedly. "Sounds good."

Maybe Zach's idea was a coincidence, or maybe he'd remembered Eli's strained relationship with money, how they'd always insisted on matinee movie tickets and preferred date nights at cheap diners instead of chic cafés. They'd never said the word *poor*, never given their situation a name, but they'd never shopped at Zach's favorite stores, either. Never had the newest gaming console, or name-brand *anything*. Never went to theme parks or bragged about extravagant vacations.

They glanced around, watching Cassie dig a sleek black credit card out of her bag, and Zach prep the Apple Pay on his iPhone, and Beverly fish a few twenties out of her bra.

"So, what's everyone thinking?" Eli asked, rallying faux confidence. They'd used drugstore makeup for high-end looks, sewed together discount fabric for immaculate cosplays, and slipped clipped coupons into billfolds at pricy eateries . . . If there was anything they knew well, it was how to fake it 'til they made it. Before anyone could answer, they blurted, "I'll get the lebna and pita."

Nine dollars. Cheapest thing on the menu. Easy; done.

"Perf," Cassie purred, eyeing the menu. "I'm leaning toward the baked cheese, I can't lie."

Once everyone settled on their plate of choice, they ordered at the counter and scooched two outdoor tables together. Eli sat with their back to the restaurant's window, looking out over Church Street, and Zach took the chair beside them.

"So, tomorrow," Beverly said, squealing excitedly. She flapped her hands and scrunched her nose. "Are we ready for another runway, gang?"

"Well, my wife—who used to sleep like a bear, by the way—has somehow evolved into an actual fuckin' owl, so she better be ready," Brandon teased, earning a hard swat from Cassie. "Because I'm super over being woken up by midnight foam runs."

"Keep complaining and I'll start making you be my model again," Cassie quipped.

Everyone laughed, and Eli tried to dismiss the weight of Zach's boot against their ankle beneath the table.

"I didn't think this whole thing would be a big deal, honestly," Zach said, shrugging off his jacket. "I mean, I knew it was a competition, but I didn't know it'd get so much hype."

"People love cosplay," Beverly said. She set her bony elbow on the table and cradled her chin on the heel of her palm, glancing between everyone. She grinned, catlike and coy. "But if we're talkin' about big deals, I have to admit . . . I was really, really nervous to meet all of you."

Unanimously, Zach, Eli, and Cassie said, "*What?*"

"I'm serious!" Beverly crowed. She pushed out her bottom lip and mock-pouted. "Look, I have a lot of followers—*whatever*—but I've been stalking you for years," she said, pointing at Zach. She shifted, jutting her finger at Cassie. "And you, ma'am, are totally intimidating online, okay? I mean, I stitched you on TikTok and had a panic attack because I was *sure* you thought I was some dumb weeabu girl." Before Cassie could respond, Beverly whipped toward Eli. "And you! I never, ever had the courage to talk to you, but I always hoped we'd run into each other at a convention. I, like, prepared for it. Like, I have a script."

Eli blinked, dumbfounded. "You . . . *what*? I know we're mutuals, but I assumed you never saw my stuff. I just—"

"I saw it," Beverly assured them, wide-eyed.

"Yeah, no, everyone saw it. You've got a huge cult following. Might not be mainstream, but it's there," Cassie said. She gave Eli a smile and flicked her gaze to Beverly. "Bev, what're you even talking about, though? You're influencer royalty. When you stitched my TikTok, I gained a thousand followers. We never talked because I was always super fucking afraid of you," she said so seriously that it silenced the table.

Beverly's jovial expression fractured. She knitted her brows and tilted her head, blinking at Cassie. "But you're not afraid of anything," she said confusedly.

Cassie snorted and sipped her drink. "If only that were true."

Zach stayed quiet. His small, knowing smile spoke volumes, and Eli knew—they *knew*—he'd been aware of Cassie's insecurities from day one. That's just who Zach was. Someone who paid attention, filed away information, and course corrected to make everyone around him a little more comfortable. No wonder Cassie had latched onto Zach. Eli had fallen in love with that same gentleness a long time ago.

"I was terrified of every single one of you," Eli said, yanking the spotlight off Beverly. Brandon nodded, commiserating, and Beverly gestured to them with an open palm as if to say *Why, though?* "All of you have more followers than me, more sponsorships than me, more connections . . . You think I wasn't scared? Cassie, I thought you'd eat me alive." They laughed in their throat, trying to lighten the mood. "Bev, if you'd walked up to me at literally *any* convention, I would've trembled like a chihuahua."

"Oh, shut up," Beverly said, cackling.

Eli shook their head and grinned. "Dead serious."

Something inside their chest unlatched. Something tiny, secret, and afraid of . . . *this*—connection, friendship, future—broke like a rusty lock, and Eli felt it all. The delirious happiness, the safety, the hopefulness. They shrugged and glanced around the table, avoiding Zach's attentive gaze.

"Well, here's to being fuckin' terrified of each other," Cassie said, and lifted her glass. "But what're we *really* toasting to, gang?"

"Makeup Wars, obviously," Beverly said.

Eli lifted their lemonade. "Friendship."

"Winning," Zach joked, and immediately laughed. "Oh, c'mon, I'm kidding! To the chance of a lifetime."

They swallowed hard and clanked their glass against his.

The table rang with laughter, but Eli still felt Zach's boot against their ankle and still recognized his steady gaze.

"Scared of me, too?" Zach asked under his breath.

Chills scaled Eli's arms. Their heart thundered. They remembered kissing Zachary Miller for the first time and being scared, and thrilled, and nervous. Now, all they could imagine was being *his* again. It was fear, yeah. It was something else, too.

"Course not," they said.

Zach scared the hell out of Eli. He made them reckless. He made them *brave*.

CHAPTER TWELVE
San Francisco-Anime Bay

ELI WAS SPRAWLED ACROSS THE BED IN THEIR HOTEL ROOM, phone perched on their chest, staring at the ceiling while a muted Lifetime movie played on TV. They thought about yesterday, the promo video, Zach's apology, that long, late dinner, Beverly saying *I'm glad you two are cool now*, and wondered what, exactly, *cool* meant. Their phone buzzed once, then again a few seconds later.

Bodhi Babe: Excuse me but 👀

A link appeared beneath her first message. Eli tapped it and was redirected to the official Makeup Wars Instagram. Comments and likes stacked under the video they'd recorded last night. The green screen had become a brightly colored background filled with blinking stars and face charts. They increased the volume.

Oh.

Eli thought they'd understood how close they'd been to Zach last night, but watching the video made them realize how ridiculously narrow the space between them had actually been. Zach's eyes left the camera and drifted to Eli, his smile ticking upward as Eli spoke. Their chests were barely an inch apart, faces tipped toward each other, and when the video flashed to the next scene, a slow-motion recap of the group hugging and laughing, Eli had to remind themself to breathe. Zach's index finger had snuck through their belt loop. Eli's smile had softened when they were pulled upright, tugged gently, laughing as Cassie balanced against their back and Beverly wrapped around Zach's middle from behind. Eli and Zach had looked at each other the whole time, face to face, trading barely-there touches.

Oh, shit.

They scrolled through the comments.

> **MakeupIsLife13:** ommmgggg eli and zach!! are they back together? can someone confirm??
>
> **Trend_Set:** holy shit everyone looks AMAZING
>
> **Hearteyes:** ELI & ZACH! LOOK! AT! THEM! #goals
>
> **SFXnerd_09:** Beverly and Cassie have stolen my heart but Eli and Zach ♡ we stan perfection

sunandstars: I want someone to look at me the way Zach looks at Eli
BeautyBaby: Are they still together? Holy shit!
LipstickValerie: are you kidding me?! eli is looking at him like he hung the entire fucking sun
daniellemua: omfg kiss already
janellemakeovers: CASSIE ANNE IS A BABE
MakeMeUp: I'm here for the Zach and Eli content thank you very much

Eli scrambled to sit up and almost fell off the bed. They flicked the app away, ignoring the absurd number of followers they'd gotten overnight, and called Bodhi. They held their phone in their lap, listening to the ring tone.

Finally, Bodhi's face lit the screen. "So, that's quite a video," she said, toothbrush jammed in her mouth.

"Did you see the comments? Do these people not understand how real life works? We don't ship actual human beings, right? That's still a thing? That's still, like, fandom standard?"

"I mean, yeah, obviously. But you and Zach were public for, like, *ever.* I think people are just excited to see a queer couple in the spotlight."

"Okay, except we're not a couple."

"Uh-huh, but you *look* like a couple." She paused to spit, then looked at her phone with a raised brow. "Did something happen?"

"Bodhi, seriously. *Really?*"

"Hey, don't get pissy. You're the one with puppy-dog eyes in that video, not me."

Eli groaned, propping their phone against the lamp on the nightstand.

Bodhi leaned closer to the screen. "Not to be a bitch about it, but you do remember that *you* broke up with *him*, right? Remember just, oh, two days ago, when you said he's *literally* your competition?"

"Yes, obviously," they snapped.

"Because I remember that, too. I also remember you not being stoked about it. You've actually been pretty torn up—"

"Point, Bodhi. Get to the point."

"Maybe he's not over you, either," she said, and shrugged. "Maybe you guys aren't done."

"What happened to *not* wanting me to get hurt?"

"Yeah, of course I don't want you to get hurt. I don't want him to get hurt again, either. But I know *you* and I know *him*, and there's obviously some shit you two need to work out," she paused, angling her foamy lips at the camera, "... *together.*"

I don't want him to get hurt again, either.

Again. The word landed like a hornet on their cheek.

Eli's phone buzzed. A message flashed at the top of the screen.

Zachary Miller: Hey, still down for coffee?

They bit their lip.

"What? What's wrong? I mean, besides the obvious," Bodhi said.

"We're supposed to get coffee."

"Who?"

"Me and Zach."

"Oh, right, yeah. That's normal. Coffee dates are *totally* normal."

"It's not a date!"

Bodhi hummed suggestively. "Okay, well, have fun at your coffee-not-date with your ex-boyfriend."

Eli whined, rolling their forehead against the bedframe. "I hate you."

Bodhi snorted out a laugh. "Stop acting like this wasn't bound to happen. I knew it, he knew it, you *definitely* knew it."

"What? Nothing happened. Nothing's happening."

"Yep, right, sure. Well, text me after you get totally platonic coffee."

Eli whined again.

"Love you, bye," Bodhi said.

"*Fiiiinnnnee.* Love you, too. Bye."

They sighed, fiddling with the hem of their shirt, and grabbed their phone again.

Eli Peterson: yeah, meet downstairs in 20?
Zachary Miller: See you then

♡　♡　♡

Zach chose a café two blocks away from the hotel with a Travelocity sticker on the door and a ten percent discount for anyone with an Anime Bay badge. Eli sat on one side of a square table next to the window, palms wrapped around a dewy glass. They licked the peak off their whipped coffee and tried not to look too nervous as Zach sat across from them.

"That video shoot was fun last night." Zach cleared his throat, thumbing the handle on his steaming mug.

Eli nodded. They needed to test the waters, to know where Zach stood when it came to who they'd been together and what they might become now. Exes. Rivals. Friends, maybe. "It was, yeah. Bodhi sent me the link this morning," they said.

He laughed under his breath. "She sent it to me, too. I'm guessing you saw the comments?"

They sipped their coffee, nodding. "Yep." They popped their lips and offered a mock cringe. "We're pretty popular."

"That's one way to put it." Zach tugged at the frayed edge of his long-sleeved shirt. The braided chain around his neck had been a gift from Eli two Christmases ago. "I know you said everything's fine between us, and I probably picked the worst time to try to apologize to you, and I meant to bring it up last night, but we ended up at dinner with everyone . . . I just need you to know that I *am* sorry about San Diego, Liz." He paused, blinking away from the table to meet their eyes. "Is that still okay?"

"Is what okay?"

"Calling you Liz."

"Oh." They nodded curtly. "For you, yeah."

"For me?"

"You, Bodhi, my family. But just . . . just use Eli if we're, like, you know, out, I guess? In a group?"

Zach's smile softened.

"And stop apologizing to me. I should be apologizing to you, not the other way around," Eli said.

"For what?"

Those two words rang like an alarm in Eli's skull. "Everything," they blurted, laughing through it, breathy and sad. *I didn't mean any of it.* "I fucked up, I know I did." *I should've told you the truth.* "I got scared, and I made . . ." *A mistake.* They sipped their coffee to buy time, to clear the thickness from their throat. "A choice. I waited until the last minute because I thought I'd change my mind about New York. I'm sorry for making everything harder than it needed to be."

"It would've been hard either way," Zach said, still fiddling with his sleeve. "Good thing Instagram doesn't know the whole truth. I don't think we'd be that shippable if they knew how big of a mess we were."

"We weren't a mess. And it's not past tense, it's me. I'm the mess," Eli said. They glanced at Zach and found him looking back, smile soft as ever. "And they shouldn't be shipping people in real life anyway. It's creepy."

Laughter sputtered from Zach. Eli laughed, too. At least they still had this. Laughter and coffee. Being close, inching toward the truth, making the conscious decision to be gentle with whatever this was. Whatever they were. Eli could be thankful for that. As quiet settled between them again, Eli watched him, content to stare at his eyes and his jaw and his pierced ears. Zach did the same, gaze scaling Eli's face, catching on their eyelashes, staying there for too long, then flicking to their mouth, and throat, and freckled temples.

Zach set his elbow on the table and propped his chin on his palm. His smile split into a delighted grin. "Big Bad Wolf," he purred, and lifted a brow.

Eli didn't register the comment at first, but the moment they did, their eyes narrowed. "Bodhi told you," they deadpanned, and huffed. "Fuckin' traitor."

Zach's grin sharpened. "Oh, Grandmother, what big eyes you have."

"Shut up, it's gonna be awesome."

He hummed, scooping whipped foam out of Eli's cup. He sucked his finger clean. "I don't doubt that."

Heat rushed into their cheeks. They turned toward the window, watching cars roll across hot concrete and people hurry down the sidewalk. "I'm glad you're here," they said absently, accidentally.

They caught the edge of Zach's smile in the reflection on the glass. "Me, too."

♡　♡　♡

The staging for last looks at Anime Bay was cramped and hot.

Eli could barely breathe through their foam prostheses—wolf snout glued securely over their nose, brow piece curving around their eyebrows, accentuated cheekbones jutting from their face. They leaned toward one of the standing vanities backstage and slid an amber contact lens into each eye.

Cassie stood beside them. She sprayed her red wig, fixed with seashells and fishing net, and cursed under her breath. "I'm out," she said softly, sighing as she looked at her reflection. "I definitely didn't do enough."

"You look great." Eli squeezed her arm.

Across from them, Beverly stood in front of a full-body mirror, tugging her black robes into place. Giant foam horns curved away from her head, and delicate silicone prostheses changed her bone structure, turning her into the perfect Maleficent. Zach folded furry boot covers over the tops of his hoof-shaped shoes, pupils shaped into squares by yellow, goatlike contact lenses. Eli's stomach clenched into knots. Last week felt so, *so* distant compared to being backstage, flicking brown paint on their throat and straightening the wolfish ears attached to a beige headband.

Zach and Beverly looked incredible. Cassie was right to worry. Eli was, too.

They rushed through final touches, dusting powder over transparent edges, feathering paint to look like fur on their jawline, tugging clawed gloves onto each hand. *Okay.* They exhaled sharply and stepped back to look at themself. *Okay, it's totally fine.*

"Oh, what big teeth you have," Zach cooed, propping his hip against the edge of the vanity. He held his phone up and mouthed, *For the gram.*

Eli glanced sideways and grinned, popping fake fangs over their canines. "The better to eat you with, my dear."

Zach laughed silently and lowered his phone. "People are gonna think we're canon."

"The Big Bad Wolf and the Beast? What a sexy pair," Eli teased.

Ram horns sculpted in foam and painted matte gray curled away from Zach's temples. His ears were pointed, jaw extended by another prosthesis. His take on the Beast was satanic, to say the least. Fake blood coated his mouth and chin, and his fitted suit was torn at the collar and stained red, as were his cuffs and the shredded bottom of his black dress pants.

"I think so." Zach gave Eli a once-over. "You ready?"

Before Eli could answer, the Makeup Wars volunteer standing at the edge of the stage hollered, "All right, contestants, that's time! Brushes down, let's get lined up for the runway!"

They weren't ready, but they had to be, so they nodded. Zach's playful voice came and went as they shoved their brushes, sponges, and glue into a tote bag. *I think so.* Eli turned the phrase upside down. Repeated it to themself and came to a terrifying conclusion: Zachary Miller, their ex-fucking-boyfriend, was absolutely flirting with them. And Eli had no idea how to *not* flirt back.

Cassie's glittery veil dragged behind her as she stepped into place at the front of the lineup, followed by Beverly, Zach, and, last, Eli. Lights crossed the stage, and applause rang out. They took another long, deep breath and glanced at their phone.

> **Eli Peterson:** bev and zach obliterated me and cassie
> **Eli Peterson:** like . . . one of us is For Sure going home.
> **Bodhi Babe:** YOU SOUND LIKE A DUMBASS
> **Eli Peterson:** i'm serious
> **Bodhi Babe:** Don't psych yourself out. I'm watching the livestream right now.
> **Bodhi Babe:** Stella says "hi my good bitch"
> **Eli Peterson:** tell her i say hi back

A second went by. Three dots bounced in their message bubble.

> **Bodhi Babe:** OOF BABE THE BETTER TO EAT YOU WIIITTTHH?! WOW
> **Eli Peterson:** it was a J O K E
> **Bodhi Babe:** Suuuuureee it was. Don't be breakin his heart again Liz
> **Bodhi Babe:** and use a condom
> **Eli Peterson:** i'm never talking to you again goodbye forever
> **Bodhi Babe:** Byyyyyeeeee ✌️
> **Bodhi Babe:** Okay but seriously good luck. you're gonna kill it
> **Eli Peterson:** ugh
> **Eli Peterson:** ♡

Theresa's voice boomed through the microphone. "Are you ready, Anime Bay?"

The lights dimmed. Their voices echoed, Cassie's, Beverly's, Zach's and Eli's, and the glow from the big screen hovering above the stage played the video they'd shot last night. Once it ended, Theresa called out Cassie's name, and the runway began.

Cassie strutted across the stage. Her mermaid cosplay was inspired by an underhyped anime about sirens and sea creatures. A prosthetic starfish was glued to her cheek, painted to appear as if it had grown out of her skin. Her beauty makeup was on point, as always. Glittery eyelids and perfectly executed scales shone on her throat and forehead. Once she had crossed the threshold backstage, Beverly walked out.

"Yep, this is it," Cassie said through a sigh. "I'm *definitely* going home."

"You don't know that yet." Zach offered a reassuring smile.

She shot him a wilted look, lips pursed, eyebrows raised, and gestured to herself. "I don't need bullshit, Zach. C'mon."

Eli shook their head. "You don't know what they're basing the scores on. You've got this in the bag if they judge us on beauty skills."

"Good thing it's a special effects competition," she said, not angrily but defeatedly.

The audience cheered and hollered for Beverly as she thumped her scepter on the stage and twirled her black cloak.

Zach walked out, shoulders pulled tight, hoofed boots clopping the stage. He didn't wobble—impressive—despite not having heels to balance on, and he shoved his thumbs through the belt loops on his dress pants, cocky and otherworldly. His horns looked perfectly realistic, a harsh contrast to his cartoonish features. Silicone prostheses exaggerated his jawline and accentuated his cheekbones, and dark paint hollowed his eyes. He was somewhere between man and animal, unsettling and demonic, and Eli didn't bother averting their eyes. They followed him across the stage, trailing every step as he turned around and walked backstage again. Zach held their stare.

"Don't forget to howl," he said, grinning wide.

Eli rolled their eyes.

Theresa said their name into the microphone: "Eli Peterson!"

The ballroom ignited. Cheers and applause and whistles filled the air as Eli walked onstage. *Don't trip.* They put one foot in front of the other and lifted their chin, blinking away the sting in their eyes from the overly bright lights. The white wool outerwear Bodhi had crafted turned them into an unassuming sheep: hood covering their face, snap-buttons clasped from their ankles to their chin. They waited until they were at the edge of the stage to rip the cloak open and toss the hood back, revealing their wolf makeup and the tattered costuming underneath.

They bared their fangs in a snarl and curled their fingers, displaying their blood-tipped claws. Even one of the judges gave a surprised laugh. They hated themself for it, but they couldn't help feeling a little relieved. Cassie's makeup was good. Beautiful, even. But it was simple and understated, and Eli wouldn't, *couldn't* go home. They walked backstage, shaking the thought away. They didn't want to be glad about someone doing worse than they did. They didn't want to let this competition, no matter how life-changing the prize was, make them into someone who celebrated other people's defeat. But still . . . somewhere deep, buried in their core, Eli hoped Cassie would be sent home because that would mean they got to stay.

And they *needed* to stay.

Eli halted in front of the full-body mirror. Their breath caught, trembling on a rushed gasp. *No, no, no.* The paint on their wolfish snout had cracked, flaking away from the foam. They leaned closer, studying their reflection. If they tried to repaint, it might muddy the color. If they tried to speckle the cracks, the paint wouldn't dry fast enough, and

Theresa Jenkins could *not* see them in wet paint. Their pulse quickened.

Cassie's makeup might've been simple, but it was still *good*. Completely fucking painted, at least. Eli closed their eyes, forcing air into their lungs. When they opened their eyes again, Zach stood behind them, head tipped, scanning their reflection.

"It's fine," he said, and nodded slowly. "I didn't even notice until I saw you staring at it."

"The judges noticed," they said. "It's literally their job to notice."

"I bet they didn't."

"I bet they did."

Zach heaved a sigh. He'd transformed into a goatlike monster, but his smile was still the same. Quiet and gentle and *Zach*, like something plucked out of a dream Eli had half forgotten. A good dream. The kind they wanted to go back to. Zach took long strides to their side. He'd always been infuriatingly taller than them, but his hooves made him even taller, looking down at them with beastly eyes.

"It's fine," he said again.

"It's not." Eli swallowed around the lump in their throat.

Zach palmed their shoulder.

The stage manager cupped her hands around her mouth and shouted, "Contestants, back onstage in five . . . four . . ."

They got in line behind Zach, curling and uncurling their fingers. Their hands were slick inside the gloves, cheeks hot under their makeup, but they had to keep it together. *Smile.* They had to walk out there and pretend nothing was wrong. *Head high, chin up, eyes forward, back straight.* Applause came and went as the artists took their places, lining up center stage.

"Once again our artists have given us four fantastic makeups and a lot to consider," Theresa said. Her hair was pinned into a bun, eyes lined in electric blue and face dusted with glitter.

The guest judge, Margaret Madness, rested her elbows on the arms of her wheelchair. She tapped her fingers together, giving each artist another once-over. "We were at quite an impasse, to be honest. But I think we know who's winning the Anime Bay Cosplay Runway." Her Dalek dress fanned over her ankles as she shifted, turning to look at Theresa and Scott. "Are we ready?"

"I think so. Anime Bay, are *you* ready?" Scott asked, grinning.

The audience clapped and whooped. Lights crisscrossed the stage. Eli held their breath.

"In third place . . ." Scott paused, offering each contestant a smile. "Eli Peterson! Their Big Bad Wolf makeup was a nod at the classics, and we loved it."

Eli's knees wobbled. They plastered on a smile, waved at the crowd, nodded politely at the judges, and kept their composure. From first place to third place. Just like that. Their scores couldn't have been *wonderful*, but they had the chance to keep going, place higher at the next runway, get more votes on Instagram and a better overall ranking from the judges. Their chest tightened. Third place wasn't good, but it wasn't *gone*. They were still in the fight, and that was all that mattered.

"Second place, Beverly Belle! What a beautiful, set-ready Maleficent cosplay. Well done," Scott said.

Beverly smiled and waved.

Eli glanced sideways. Cassie's throat clenched. She squared her shoulders and blew out a breath, nodding curtly at Zach as they both stepped forward.

Theresa took the mic. "And first place in the Anime Bay Cosplay Runway is . . . Zachary Miller for his rendition of the Beast!"

Applause and whistles filled the ballroom again. Cassie smiled painfully at the ground. They couldn't hear her over the noisy audience, but they saw her mouth form the words *It's okay* when she looked at Zach. Beverly set her hand on Cassie's back.

"Cassie Anne Montgomery, your Siren cosplay was beautifully executed, but unfortunately, we can only take three artists to Oakland, and the judges decided that you'll be going home," Theresa said.

Cassie kept nodding. "It's okay," she said, this time to Beverly. A flashlight blinked to life in the stage wing. She went first, hurrying backstage and knuckling at her eyes. She stopped in front of the vanity where her eyeshadow palette and a bottle of liquid latex sat next to her pink train case. "I don't know why I'm crying. It's fine, it's just a contest. Not a big deal."

Eli shook their head and tried to smile. "Because shit like this is tough," they said, watching her dab a tissue under her eyes. "You did great, Cassie. A ton of brands are gonna be banging down your door to use their product because of this. You'll be a high-end beauty influencer in no time."

Beverly wrapped her arms around Cassie from behind and set her chin on Cassie's shoulder. "Eli's right, you know," she said.

Cassie stripped off her wig and tossed it on the vanity. "Yeah, I know, but..." she said, shrugging. Her mouth wobbled. "I wanted *this*."

Zach appeared next to Eli. His elbow knocked into them. "Sorry," he mumbled, and adjusted, causing their wrists to bump. "There'll be other opportunities," he said to Cassie. "And you probably won't even need them. You and I both know you'll be doing avant-garde runway work by the time this competition ends."

"Yeah, maybe," Cassie said, sniffling through a laugh. "You guys'll keep in touch, right?"

Eli leaned closer to Zach, resting their shoulder against him. "Yeah, of course we will," they said, and took Cassie's hand.

They hadn't won, but they hadn't lost, and everything inside them was at war with how to feel about that. Eli didn't want Cassie to go, but they *needed* to stay. Third place wasn't good enough, but it would get them to Oakland, to the next runway. Closer to Beyond.

And in the end, that was what mattered.

The scholarship. Their future.

Winning it all.

CHAPTER THIRTEEN
Los Angeles

"OKAY, SO LAST WEEK YOU PLACED THIRD, THIS WEEK you'll place first. No biggie," Bodhi said, pinching a sewing needle between her teeth.

Eli straightened their back. "I don't know, Bodhi. Beverly and Zach are the real deal."

She hushed them, a sharp sound, and held a measuring tape against their waist, mumbling around the needle's silver point. "You want this tight, yeah? Like, corseted?"

"Yeah, I'm doing the season three dark magic outfit," Eli said.

"No sleeves?"

"No, I'm doing arm prostheses, so no sleeves. How short do you think it should be?"

"Oh, short. *Real* short." She pushed the needle through a bundle of fabric and dropped the tape measure, stepping back to give Eli a quick once-over. "You'll need thick tights. Are you wearing heels?"

"Yep, they're borrowing my boots," Stella said, tossing the words over her shoulder as she dug through Bodhi's sewing kit. "You think people'll be surprised when you walk onstage as Wych?"

"Probably, yeah," Eli said, looking at themself in the mirror hanging on the back of Bodhi's bedroom door. "It's not like I haven't cosplayed feminine characters before, you know? I just think people expect me to always dress masc." They plucked at the lengthy black skirt, following Bodhi's thumb to their midthigh. Bodhi grabbed another needle and stuck it through the fabric. "That's *short*, Bodhi, like—"

"Hence the tights," Bodhi said. "If you're cosplaying Wych, you've gotta be sexy. You know that."

They chewed their lip. Usually, they'd agree, except putting on a skintight black dress with a pleather corset in front of their ex made them nervous. *Delta Quest* was a ridiculously popular anime, and Wych was the perfect choice for week three's Superhero/Supervillain runway theme, but they already didn't know what to do with Zach. Strutting around in a sexed-up outfit felt like an invitation for more flirting and more weird coffee-not-dates and more lingering feelings they couldn't shoo away. The problem wasn't Zach's attention, the problem was *wanting* Zach's attention. Eli blushed.

They wanted Zach to look at them. They wanted him to want them again.

And that wasn't fair. Not after Eli had stomped on his heart.

They snagged a bit of loose skin with their teeth and flinched. "What time are we getting dinner?"

"Zach's off at five, so around six, I think," Bodhi paused midsnip of the dark fabric. "Oh, shit. That's the issue, huh? You're bein' all shy about this cosplay because—"

"No, that's not it. He has nothing to do with it," Eli snapped.

Stella hummed. She stepped around Eli's discarded clothes and tapped two fingers under their chin, tipping their head to loop a choker adorned with an acrylic crystal around their throat. "The outfit doesn't have to be super femme sexy. You can always wear pants with the corset instead of the skirt."

"No, I know, I just . . ." They huffed out a frustrated breath. "Okay, fine, yes. It's about Zach."

"Called it," Bodhi sang.

Stella smothered a laugh and tucked a black lock behind her ear. "Care to elaborate?"

"We've been, I don't know, getting close again, I guess? Talking a lot, going out for coffee, joking around together. And I just . . . I feel like I'm doing something wrong, like I'm baiting him. Like I'm fucking with his head, I guess? It's awkward and stupid." Eli sighed, watching Bodhi pull a strip of fabric away, leaving a jagged asymmetrical hem above their knee. "I don't get to still want him, that's not how this works."

"Oh, honey," Stella said, laughing, at the same time that Bodhi whistled and said, "Eli, you idiot."

Eli whipped their head back and forth. "What? *What?* I'm serious! You're not supposed to break up with someone and keep flirting with them *years* later. That's shitty."

Stella said, "It's normal, actually. Welcome to dating while queer, sweetheart."

"I'd agree with you if you'd actually *wanted* to break up with him," Bodhi said, scoffing. "We've talked about this. You guys got together in the eighth grade, and you ended things on really . . . I don't know, stupid-as-shit terms. What'd you expect? Poof, feelings gone? Sorry, boo, but that's not how this stuff works."

They wiggled their nose. "I think we've established that already, thanks."

"Like I said last weekend, maybe you two aren't done."

"That's the whole point of breaking up, Bodhi. Finding a way to be done."

Stella sighed, patting them on the rear. "Yes, but sometimes you don't get there. Sometimes a relationship has to run its course even after you thought it was over."

Eli licked their lips, studying their reflection. Maybe Bodhi and Stella were right. Maybe they weren't done with Zach; maybe Zach wasn't done with them. Maybe all this shit—FaeCon, Makeup Wars, Beyond—was fate nudging them together again. They shoved the thought deep, deep down, away from their too-hopeful heart, and winced, jerking as Bodhi's needle pricked their stomach.

"Oh, damn," she exhaled through her teeth, shooting them an apologetic glance. "Sorry, babe. Better not stab someone on set, huh? Watch me lose the only gig I've got before it gets off the ground."

Eli shook their head dismissively, still stuck on thoughts of Zach and this goddamn outfit until they realized what, exactly, Bodhi had said. *On set. Gig.* Eli gasped, pawing at the air in front of Bodhi's face as she pushed the final pin through the fabric beneath their armpit.

"Excuse me, *what*?" they exclaimed.

Stella laughed in her throat and removed the choker.

Bodhi grinned, hands propped on her hips, another silver needle dangling from between her full lips. "Indie film, shooting in Pasadena. They're payin' close to nothing, but I get a Head of Costuming tear sheet and my name in the credits."

"Bodhi, *what*?" Eli barked out a surprised laugh and pulled her into a hug. "That's amazing! When did this happen? *How* did this happen?"

She shrugged, still grinning, and flicked her finger up and down, gesturing to Eli's outfit. "Take that off so I can start the corset."

"Tell me!"

"It just happened, honestly. I heard about a thing through one of the other interns who knew a makeup artist who needed a designer for a zombie movie with a three-figure budget." She hung the dress and corset from the handle on her closet door. "No one else wanted to do it, so I reached out to the makeup artist, and he passed along my portfolio."

"You skipped the part where you Internet-stalked the makeup artist for three days before finally figuring out he was the guy to talk to," Stella said.

Eli laughed harder. "Did you really?"

"Shut up. Of course I did. You would've, too. But yeah, anyway, I did the thing," she said, shrugging on a cropped denim jacket. "I got my first gig."

"I'm proud of you," Eli said, and they were. *Look at us*, they wanted to say. But there was nothing to see yet, not with Makeup Wars, not with Beyond. They were on their way, though. Both of them. Together.

Bodhi cleared her throat. "I didn't mention it because you were doing your stuff in San Francisco, and I didn't wanna derail anything."

"Telling me about the good stuff in your life is never derailing." Eli knitted their brows and pushed their bottom lip out. "Always tell me, always, *always*."

"Okay, fine, yeah, I hear you. It wasn't a big deal until, like, yesterday, when I got the offer, so . . ." She shrugged toward the door, smothering her smile. "You almost ready?"

Eli pulled their boots on and nodded. "Yeah, just a sec. God, I can't believe—I mean, I *can*, but still, holy shit, Bodhi. This is a big deal, like, a huge, gigantic deal."

"I tried to tell her that, too," Stella said, slinging her purse over her shoulder.

"I just really, *really* don't wanna fuck it up," Bodhi said. She wrung her hands, gathering air until her cheeks bulged.

"You won't." Eli stuffed their wallet in their pocket—*thank God for men's jeans*—and glanced at themself in the mirror before turning back toward Bodhi. "You're gonna crush it."

For years, Bodhi had shied away from compliments. Not fun compliments like *Your ass looks amazing in those jeans* or *Your cat-eye is on point*. She ate those up. But weighty compliments about work or school or designing were always brushed over, as if talking about her achievements might jeopardize them. Eli didn't get it; they'd buckle under the heaviness. But maybe that was what made them good for each other, *the best* for each other, knowing Eli would always be proud of the dreams Bodhi kept quiet about, knowing Bodhi would always be there to take the pressure off, to reassure Eli, to understand.

Eli set their hand on her shoulder and squeezed. "Seriously, Bodhi. That film crew's lucky to have you."

Bodhi's smile softened, just for a moment, then she rolled her eyes and shrugged their hand away. "Yeah, yeah, well, anyway, Zach's meeting us at the Noodle Shack. Can we go? Are we ready?"

Eli met Stella's gaze and shook their head. She shrugged as if to say, *I know, I know*, and looped her arm around Bodhi's waist.

"Yeah," they said, and the almost-forgotten thought of seeing Zach again nipped at their ankles.

I hope I'm ready.

♡   ♡   ♡

Eli picked slippery rice noodles out of rich, fishy broth and completely failed at eating tom kha elegantly. Stella was in the seat beside them, and Bodhi and Zach sat across from them, picking through steaming bowls with red chopsticks. They'd shared a plate of crispy spring rolls and battered seafood, and Eli had listened as Bodhi had rambled about the terrible internship she couldn't wait to finish, going on and on about wedding dresses, veil construction, and tulle. Eli had fidgeted with the straw in their rose milk tea. Bodhi had introduced Stella, who'd asked Zach a million and one questions about New York. Zach had answered, but his eyes had flicked to Eli, and he'd chosen his words carefully, skimming descriptions of Times Square and Central Park and the Shockwave workshop.

Eli didn't know how to engage with whatever this was. Zach had just appeared again, out of nowhere, wedging himself into the hollow boyfriend-shaped space in Eli's life. They'd watched him laugh with Bodhi, sip her iced coffee, and steal a fried shrimp off her appetizer plate. It felt like nothing had changed, yet everything had. *Everything.* But here they all were, sitting at the Noodle Shack in a city they'd individually gravitated to, laughing like old times, eating together like old times, talking about jobs and careers and big life choices just like old times.

Zach poked at the last of his tom yum. His shoulders rounded toward his ears, snapback flipped backward on his head. "What's everyone doing after this?"

Bodhi glanced at Eli. Her lips quirked.

Their jaw shifted. *Don't,* they said with their eyes. *Do not.*

"Me and Stella are catching a movie, I think," Bodhi chirped.

Stella immediately nodded. "Yep. Movie night. What about you, Zach? Anything interesting?"

Eli was certain Bodhi and Stella hadn't planned a movie night.

"I was thinking about taking a drive to Griffith." Zach shifted his gaze to them. "Eli, you in?"

Say no. They offered a lopsided smile. "Yeah, I don't have any plans." They hesitated, following Zach's mouth as it curved upward. *Damn it.* "I'll go."

Bodhi checked her phone. "Oh, wow, babe, we should take off."

Stella stood, smoothing her hand over Eli's shoulder as she walked behind their chair. "Good to see you, Eli, and nice to finally meet you, Zach. These two talk about you a lot," she said, and gestured between Bodhi and Eli. "Hope the skies are clear at Griffith."

"Have fun," Bodhi sang, waving over her shoulder before she took Stella's hand.

The bell above the door chimed. A second later, Eli's phone buzzed.

Bodhi Babe: Have fun

Eli set their phone facedown on the table and picked at their thumbnail. "I'm gonna order a tea to go. Want anything?"

"Nah, I'm good. I'll meet you outside?" Zach stood, brushing invisible crumbs from his lap.

"Yeah, be right there."

They walked to the counter and ordered another rose milk tea, extra sweet, while Zach slipped through the door. Their mind spun, orbiting a situation they'd actively hoped for and avoided—being alone with him in the city they both loved, the place they weren't supposed to land. Eli inhaled deeply. Their binder flexed and tightened, and they adjusted their charcoal pencil pants, tucking and untucking their sheer pink top. Once the server delivered their refilled tea, they went still, staring at the counter, hoping a coffee stain might spell out their future. What was about to happen? What the hell were they even *doing*? They gulped in another breath and stuffed a couple dollars into the tip jar before they left.

"Ready?" Zach stood with his hands in his pockets, shoulder propped against a street sign.

Eli nodded and followed him around to his truck, a shiny Toyota given to him by his parents on his sixteenth birthday. They hoisted themself into the passenger seat. Rolled down the window and let the summer air cool their flushed cheeks, listened to Zach's pop-punk playlist, and mouthed the words to a new Beartooth single. They tipped their head against the seat, watching Zach's fingers curl around the gearshift, his elbow propped on the door, knuckles resting on his jaw. Headlights cut through the dark. The freeway was illuminated by red brake lights and glowing skyscrapers.

The last time Eli had been in that truck, they'd broken up. The time before that, Zach had parked on a shady street near the beach and Eli had crawled into his lap, pushed their hands under his shirt, left love bites on his throat. Before that, Zach, Eli, and Bodhi had lounged on a blanket in the bed of the truck, doing tarot readings and smoking shitty homegrown weed they'd bought from a surfer in Venice. Eli licked their lips, turning to look at Zach.

"I'm glad you and Bodhi are okay," Eli said.

Zach sighed, nodding. "Me, too. I probably should've reached out sooner, I just . . . I don't know, I had a lot going on."

"She told me."

His knuckles whitened on the gearshift. "Told you what?"

"Basically, that you didn't reach out because you didn't want her to feel like she had to choose. Because I made it hard—"

"You didn't make it hard. It *was* hard, all of it. Bodhi was here, with you, in Los Angeles, and I was clear across the country. It made sense to give us space. All of us."

He thought I was leaving him, too.

"She never *chose* me. You know that, right? She loves you."

"I know," Zach snapped like a cornered animal.

Eli clamped their mouth shut. They watched the road. Brake lights, broken white lines, guardrails. Listened to the music play low through the speakers. Pushed down the urge to snap back, to fight, to let themselves be angry. A tantrum wouldn't solve anything, and Zach's constant coming and going, like an unruly tide, made them anxious enough. They didn't need to add to the volatility of *whatever this was* by starting an argument.

Zach stayed quiet for a moment, jaw shifting, eyes forward. Distant. "Stella's nice. Think they're good together?" He flicked the blinker and turned onto the winding road that led to the observatory.

"I didn't know at first. Stella's cooler than us," they said, snorting out a laugh. "But yeah, I think so. She's got a job, and she's good to Bodhi. Good *for* her, too, I think. And, well, you know Bodhi. She's confident, but not that confident. Prideful, but has a hard time being proud of herself. Stella's got her shit together, knows what she wants, but she's also, like, really calm and supportive." They offered a playful smile and rolled their eyes, thankful for the subject change. *Minefield avoided.* "They're different, but a good match."

Another moment came and went, quiet and tense. "What about you?" Zach asked. His throat flexed around a swallow, and he moved his hand from the gearshift to the steering wheel, gripping hard. He kept his gaze ahead, but his voice—a little shaky, a lot curious—betrayed the unbothered look in his eyes. "Anyone new?"

Eli wanted to laugh. They almost *did* laugh. They stared at Zach, following the strong slope of his jaw, smooth except for a snag from a razor, and studied the black ink stitched into his skin above his collar. "No," they said softly, and then again, on a laugh, "No, Zach, there's no one new."

Zach's lips lifted. He rested his arm over Eli's seat, looking through the rear window as he backed the truck toward the overlook. He still smelled the same, like that stupid expensive cologne from that stupid expensive beachwear store.

"Anyone waiting for you in New York?" Eli asked.

He barked a laugh and hit the button on the dashboard. The engine died. "Why would there be? I'm not going back," he said, and slid out of the truck.

Eli closed the door behind them and met Zach's eyes over the edge of the truck bed. "You're not?"

"My life's here," he said simply, like Eli should've known better. He pulled the gate down and hoisted himself onto it, feet swinging above the dirt.

The sky stretched, deep and black and splattered with stars. Los Angeles glowed below them, bright blue and neon green, electric yellow and brake-light red. Across the way, over the white dome of the Griffith Observatory, the Hollywood sign's blocky letters cut across a steep hillside. Eli walked on their tiptoes, hugging the scratchy brush dividing them from the overgrown valley at the bottom of the slope. Wild sage and prickly aloe bloomed around them, and bushels of cream-colored buckwheat peppered the dry grass.

"Look at me," Zach said.

Eli's heart skipped, but when they glanced over their shoulder, Zach had his phone chest-high and snapped a picture. They waited for Zach to do something else, *anything* else. To get closer. But he didn't. He lowered his phone and leaned back on his palms, staring at the crescent moon hovering above the city. They took their time, walking slowly from the cliff to the truck, and sat beside him.

"Remember that time we ran from the cops?" Zach asked.

Eli hiccupped on a laugh. "All because you wanted to sit in one of the O's."

"Would've made a sick profile pic."

"And it almost got us arrested."

"It's the Hollywood sign! We had to try," he said, head lolling, eyes pinned on their face.

"Remember when we broke into your neighbor's backyard?"

Zach laughed, bold and bright. "To use the pool? Yeah, I remember."

"Still can't believe their housekeeper saw me naked. Not a little naked, like, entirely, not one stitch of clothes on me, butt-ass naked," they said, and tried not to giggle, but Zach pulled them in with contagious, shoulder-shaking laughter. "Seriously, I'm still embarrassed. I left my clothes there, huh?"

"You did, you totally did," Zach said, howling as he fell onto his back, eyes trained on the stars again. "Didn't your parents give you *the talk* after that? Because you came home in my sweats?"

Eli sighed. "They sure did."

"Won't have to worry about that now. New beach house has its own pool. Chlorine, though, which sucks. I really wanted saltwater."

They rolled their eyes. "Oh, it's not a *saltwater* pool, it's a normal *rich-people* pool? Boo-hoo. Poor Zach—"

"Hey, c'mon, it's a first-world problem, but it's still *my* problem."

Their conjoined laughter echoed, sheltered by the wilderness around the trailhead. Carefully, Eli leaned back until they were flat, legs dangling, shoulder to shoulder with Zach in the bed of the truck. They stayed like that for a long time, breathing, resting, soaked in comfortable familiarity. Eli stared at the sky until they realized Zach had turned to look at them. They didn't know how long they'd been like that— Eli counting stars, Zach studying their profile—but they were too afraid to turn toward him, to look at him, to meet his eyes when they were this close.

Eli was afraid if they did, they would kiss him. Right there, witness to a thousand lights in the hills above a wild city.

"Did Beverly tell you about her big gig yet?" Eli asked.

Zach nodded. "Did you really think I'd stay in New York?"

Eli's chest squeezed. "I don't know. I'm just glad you didn't."

Zach touched Eli's hand, finger curling around their pinkie. "Yeah, me, too."

They stayed there, right there, like that, barely touching, but holding on—*keep holding on to me*—and watched the moon rise a little higher.

CHAPTER FOURTEEN

Oakland-Heroes Expo

CARS PEPPERED THE STREET OUTSIDE ELI'S HOTEL ROOM. From the fifteenth floor, they stared between buildings and watched sunlight scale the estuary. Orange banners fluttered on the sidewalk, and signs across the street pointed to the Marriott, guiding convention-goers to Heroes Expo. They pressed their hand to the glass and thought about the confirmation email in their inbox.

```
Consultation with Dr. Tamura—
September 15, 12:00 p.m.
```

The time from the start of the competition—four entire weeks—had gone by in the blink of an eye. It felt like FaeCon and Makeup Wars had fallen into their life ages ago, but it had barely been a month. They'd moved out on their own in June, July had gone by in a flurry of fast-paced conventions, and August had arrived, unexpected and promising. They had two months left—sixty-one days—until they were approved or denied for top surgery. Eli subconsciously touched the bottom of their sports bra, tracing the tight line below their left breast. No more binders, no more underwire, no more overly baggy clothes to hide in when they were too sore to wear a bra. They sighed, eyes drifting closed. No more days and weeks and months spent living in a body that didn't match the vision they had for themself.

Eli opened Instagram, skimming comments under a selfie of them holding three liquid lipstick tubes from a vegan brand they'd signed with last week. They tapped Cassie's profile and liked a video titled "Swan Eyeshadow Tutorial" that she'd posted a couple hours ago and then scrolled through their dashboard until a promo for Heroes Expo lit the screen.

When conventions took place *inside* a sponsored hotel, everything was a lot easier . . . and a lot louder. People kicked suitcases through the hallway, and laughter echoed from a group of con-goers waiting by the elevators. Downstairs, the lobby was overrun with cosplayers and people searching for the designated badge pickup room. Eli was thankful that the Makeup Wars team had stored their badge at the front desk, along with a Heroes Expo lanyard and two complimentary breakfast tickets.

Eli flicked the app away, tucked their phone into their pocket, and grabbed the Heroes Expo Guide, flipping through pages of panels, booth numbers, and sponsors. They should've worked on their runway makeup, snapped a few influencer shots, or answered emails from their Brand Managers. But Fridays weren't busy, one of their favorite comic artists was selling prints at their booth, and Eli had a total lack of self-control when it came to collecting cute artwork.

They changed into a flesh-tone binder and a loose She-Ra tank, slipped on their Vans, and looped their lanyard over their head, adjusting the strap of their purse as they pulled the door shut behind them. When they turned, their nose smacked a wide, warm chest.

Zach laughed, because of course it was *his* wide, warm chest. *Why does this keep happening?* "Perfect timing."

Eli inched away, cursing the heat in their cheeks. "Sorry, hi. You headin' downstairs?"

Zach gestured to the copy of *Shadow Deliverance* tucked under his arm, the same copy he'd bought at Anime Bay the previous weekend. "Yeah, I saw the writer is in Artist Alley with copies of volume two. Figured I should snag one before he sells out."

"Oh, yeah, that makes sense," Eli said.

Two nights ago, they'd stared at the night sky next to Zach, fingers looped together, hip to hip, and as much as they'd wanted to, as much as they'd thought about it, they hadn't kissed him when he'd dropped them off at their apartment. Every reckless part of them had wanted to, and every practical part of them had said, *wait, stop, don't,* as if kissing Zach was crossing a boundary they hadn't already crossed.

But that was bullshit. Eli was already too close. Their heart was already too hopeful.

"Seen Beverly yet?" Zach asked.

Eli shook their head, stepping into the elevator once the doors slid open. "She shot an Insta-story at some swanky condo in Santa Monica, so I bet she'll get here tomorrow."

"Yeah, I saw that," he said, and raised an eyebrow. "Pretty nice digs, huh?"

Eli snorted. "Says the guy who's living in their dad's Malibu beach house."

Zach grinned bashfully, shaking his head. "Yeah, yeah, but it's not like it's *my* house."

"Does it have a Jacuzzi tub?" Eli teased, pretending to sneer. "I already know about the plain, regular ol' *chlorine* infinity pool. I'm sure there's a fully stocked bar with top-shelf booze, right? Stainless-steel appliances and floor-to-ceiling windows—"

"Come by sometime and see for yourself," Zach said smoothly, like a challenge.

Eli met his eyes on a fleeting glance and immediately looked away. They wanted to ask a thousand questions. *Is the ocean close enough to hear at night? Do you really want me there? What're we doing? Where do we go from here? Can I hold your hand?* But they stayed quiet, thankful for the chime of the elevator as it rocked to a stop.

The conference space on the bottom floor was split between two wings. The East Wing had been repurposed for panel rooms, charging stations, and workshops, and the West Wing was roped off for Artist Alley. The Cosplay Competition and the Cosplay Runway would take place in a ballroom on the fifth floor, and a few other large-capacity rooms were reserved for cosplay repairs, movie showings, and arcade games. Heroes Expo was a smaller convention with a heavy fandom appeal and a focus on local artists, and Eli definitely wasn't mad about the lack of a stuffy Exhibitor Hall.

They moved through the room with Zach one step behind them, slipping between swooning princesses and sidestepping an *Attack on Titan* group. Zach's palm ghosted their lower back. They accidentally knocked their knuckles into his hand as they walked through the open double doors and into a narrow room lined with booths. When they stopped abruptly, he bumped into them, his chest to their back, his breath on their ear, and when they took another step, kept walking, kept moving, he snatched their hand, pawed at them, and then let them go.

What're we doing?

Eli grinned, laughing in their throat. It was like they were fourteen again, trading clumsy touches for smiles.

Eli stopped to snap a selfie for their Insta-story, phone held at arm's length, capturing their grin, head tipped to the side, and Zach behind them, smiling with his Heroes Expo badge dangling from between his teeth. They walked together through the aisles. Zach stopped to buy a bat-shaped pansexual enamel pin and clipped it to his Monsterpalooza T-shirt, and Eli browsed a booth filled with handmade dice and cute, stylized role-playing sheets. They bought a *Chaos Reign*–themed set printed in pastel pink and blue. Clue, the artist Eli had been searching for, was stationed in Aisle E. Holographic prints hung from burlap rope, and their booth was draped in a nonbinary flag.

Eli immediately pointed to a *Voltron* print: a main character drawn with top surgery scars, kissing another character. "Can I get one of these, please? And a mini-artbook?"

Clue flashed a grin, their rich black skin splashed with star-shaped glitter. "Sure, babe. Can I sign it for you?"

"Oh, yes, please. Is it weird to ask for a selfie with you?"

"Pssshhh, Eli Peterson? Taking a selfie with *me*? Hell, yeah!"

They know who I am. Eli tempered their smile and turned around to snap a picture with Clue. They both wore goofy smiles; Clue flashed a peace sign, and Eli held up their new holographic print.

"I'll be rooting for you tomorrow night," Clue said, and handed over the artbook.

"Thanks, I'll need all the luck I can get. Is it okay if I tag you?"

Clue nodded. "Please do. Thanks for stopping by!"

Zach fell into stride beside them. "You look a little star-struck," he said.

"I'm a lot starstruck," they admitted, laughing under their breath. They noticed Zach's hand, still resting on their back, and they reached out to touch his forearm.

He pulled away and wrung his hands, clearing his throat. "Did you see Andrew Daye's booth anywhere?"

They flashed an awkward smile. Maybe hand-holding wasn't on the table. "Aisle A, I think? Against the back wall?"

Zach bumped his shoulder against theirs and shoved his hands into his pockets. "Think he'll have enamel pins this time?"

Eli sighed, keeping pace beside him. "Maybe."

They should've left his hand on their back. Should've kept him there, touching them like he used to. They pulled their shoulders back, feigning confidence, and waited near the edge of Andrew's booth while Zach bought the next volume of *Shadow Deliverance* and a crimson pin that said

Bloodsucker! in block letters. After they walked Artist Alley twice, Zach pointed through a window to a smoothie truck parked outside the hotel. They wove through the crowded lobby and stepped onto the sidewalk. Balmy air hit their faces. City smells drifted around them.

At the smoothie truck, Eli ordered a tart raspberry, guava, and blackberry mix. Zach went with something impossibly sweet, as always, filled with strawberries, banana, and mango. They took shelter under a tree in the courtyard where cosplayers posed for photographers. A few con-goers sat in a patch of grass, picking at dumplings in a cardboard to-go container, and a couple read manga together on a bench.

Eli put their back to the tree and sipped their smoothie. Mottled sunlight beamed through the branches and scaled Zach's face. A breeze pushed leafy vines back and forth. Zach tilted his head, eyes heavy on them.

"You ready for tomorrow?" he asked.

Eli chewed on their straw. "Yeah," they lied. "You?"

Zach nodded. "Your parents gonna watch you on the live feed? Bodhi said she's tuning in."

"Oh, no. Probably not. You know how they are. They don't think any of this shit is real, like, real as in 'sustainable.' Dad's still convinced I should be an architect."

"Still?"

"Still. What about you? How's your mom and dad?"

"Busy, like always. But good, I guess. Dad's working a lot, Mom's out with friends a lot. Same shit, different day."

Eli heaved a sigh. Zach's parents were nice the way associates at high-end stores were nice. Because they had to be. Georgina had never fussed when Eli spent the night, and Paul had always called them *sport*, which was, despite his condescending tone, delightfully gender-neutral. But when it came down to being accepted, Zach had brought Eli home like a puppy he'd found in the gutter, mangy and unkempt and a little too nippy for their tastes.

"They never liked me, huh?" Eli asked without meaning to say it aloud.

Zach's brows knitted. "My parents? Sure they did."

"I just . . . I wasn't what they imagined, right? For you?"

He blinked, lips parting for an irritated exhalation. "I didn't give a fuck about whatever they imagined for me, Eli. If I did, I would've followed in my father's footsteps, taken business classes, and married a pretty girl who'd drink schnapps with my mom on the weekends. I would've, I don't know, learned to *golf*," he said, scoffing. "Trust me, I'm not what they wanted for me, either."

"What do they think of Makeup Wars?"

"They think I'm doing a hell of a lot to hang out with the person who dumped me on my ass." He laughed, toeing meanly at the ground. When he met Eli's eyes again, his smile softened. "I'm kidding, sorta. But yeah, my parents are lukewarm about the whole thing."

Eli's heart lurched. They pushed away from the tree and stepped toward him. "Zach, I—"

"Don't," he said. That single, cutting word sliced Eli to the bone. Zach inched backward, running one hand over the back of his neck. "Anyway," he sang, laughing again, "I think there's a makeshift movie theater somewhere inside. Supposedly they're doing a Miyazaki marathon. Wanna check it out?"

Eli sighed. They tried to smile, but their lips barely curved. The back-and-forth between the two of them, the roller-coaster, the lingering feelings and restlessness . . . it all felt too big for them. Big and bright and ugly and dishonest, settling like an anchor on their chest. *What do you want?* The question sparked and died on the tip of their tongue.

Zach steered his gaze to the sky, breathing slowly. "Look, can we just not talk about this? I shouldn't have said anything. Today's been good—*really* good—and I don't want to ruin it, so . . ."

"No, I get it. Let's go find the theater," Eli said.

Zach smiled again, nodding.

Awkwardness gave way as they waded into the crowded lobby. Eli slid behind a *Gundam* cosplayer and said, "Excuse me," as they stepped around an *Air Gear* group on roller skates. Fingertips touched their knuckles, briefly at first, before Zach looped his index finger around theirs, allowing them to guide him through the busy hotel. In the elevator, Zach kept their fingers linked, and as they walked down a nearly empty hall on the fourth floor, he still didn't let them go. It wasn't until they found the theater, a large ballroom filled with folding chairs, comfy sofas, and people sprawled across blankets, that he pushed his palm into Eli's hand.

The room was dark except for the projector playing *Princess Mononoke* on a giant roll-out screen and the occasional phone illuminating in someone's lap. Eli didn't know how tightly they should grip Zach's hand. They wanted to squeeze, to dig into his skin and hold on, but they kept their grip loose and easily escapable. They glanced around before settling on an unoccupied loveseat in the back row and tried not to hold their breath when Zach's thigh pressed against theirs.

"You okay?" Zach asked. His fingers were still curled intimately around their palm, resting on their leg.

"Yeah, I'm fine." Eli plastered on a smile.

Ashitaka, the main character, had just left his hometown with his elk, Yakul, and was in search of a cure for the deadly demon mark spreading through his body. Eli had watched this movie a thousand times, but they still stared at the screen, keeping their eyes trained on Moro, the wolf god, and Princess Mononoke's bloodstained face. They felt Zach like a heat wave beside them. Every time he shifted, they tried not to fall into old habits. Whenever he stretched his foot or rolled his heel against the floor, they imagined easing closer, draping themself across his lap like they used to, and pressing their cheek to his chest like they used to, and opening their mouth over the tendon in his neck like they used to.

When he let their hand go and trailed his fingers along the grooves between their knuckles, they swallowed hard, ignoring the fiery knot below their belly button and the urge to turn toward him, to kiss him, to snatch his bottom lip between their teeth and push their hand between his legs. Eli wanted to make him gasp like they used to. Right there in that dark room, at that goddamn convention, during that fucking competition they desperately needed to win.

Eli turned their hand over. Zach traced the lines on their palm, his eyes still fixed on white wolves and forest sprites.

"You're not here because of me, are you?" Eli whispered.

Zach's mouth tensed. He dragged his fingers over their wrist before folding his hands neatly in his lap. "Isn't this your favorite part?" he asked and jutted his chin toward the screen.

Princess Mononoke pressed the tip of a blade against Ashitaka's neck. She hollered, "I'll cut your throat! That'll shut you up!"

Ashitaka, dazed and calm, said, "You're beautiful."

This is a terrible idea, they thought. *A monumentally awful idea.*

Still, Eli nodded and took Zach's hand again, lacing their fingers between his knuckles. "Yeah, it is."

CHAPTER FIFTEEN

Oakland-Heroes Expo

AFTER THE MOVIE ENDED, AFTERNOON SLIPPED INTO EVE-ning, and the panels at Heroes Expo took a sharp turn from family-friendly to eighteen-plus. People clustered at the hotel bar, a line formed outside the "Rated E" fan-fiction panel, and laughter echoed from behind a cracked door where Marvel-themed speed dating took place.

Eli wrung their hands, leaning against the back of an unoccupied chair in the lobby. "How hard do you think it'd be to find weed around here?"

"Not hard," Zach said, and laughed under his breath.

Eli bumped their shoulder against his and made for the front door. Zach fell into step beside them. Cool air hit Eli's cheeks, and the smell of hot asphalt filled the parking lot, still peppered with wandering con-goers nursing vape pens and cigarettes. Once the credits had rolled in the makeshift movie theater, Eli had unlaced their joined fingers and stretched their arms above their head. They hadn't touched after that.

Hadn't linked pinkies or clutched softly at each other. But the feeling stayed—Zach's hand in theirs, his thumb passing over their knuckles, his fingertips tickling their palm.

Now Zach's hands were stuffed in the front pockets of his jeans, and Eli was too shy to reach for him. They walked through the parking garage, where a few people stood around a car, passing a vodka bottle back and forth, then ventured onto the sidewalk. Finally, Eli caught wind of familiar-smelling smoke drifting from the back side of the hotel.

"I bet there's a dispensary around here. We could just ask someone to buy it for us," Zach said.

Eli shook their head. "Too complicated. C'mon."

They followed the sour smell until they found two cooks sharing a stubby joint by the back door. Eli didn't hesitate, even when Zach paused behind them. "Got another one of those? I'll double what you paid for it," they said, and Zach hissed—*Eli, seriously?*—while the guy holding the joint, a lanky white kid with a rose tattooed on his throat, gave Eli a quick once-over.

The guy glanced at Zach and lifted a brow. "Well, you're obviously not cops," he said, snorting. "Thirty."

Eli scoffed. "For a *preroll?* Fifteen."

"Twenty-five."

"Twenty," Eli said, and pulled a folded green bill out of their back pocket.

The other cook snatched the smoldering butt and smothered it under his shoe. "Just do it, man. Break's over anyway."

"Fine, twenty," the guy said. He dug in his apron and pulled out a simple white-wrapped joint. They traded, and the cook walked inside without another word.

"You just paid twenty bucks for catnip," Zach said matter-of-factly.

Eli rolled the joint under their nose. "Doesn't smell like catnip, asshole."

"Do you even have a lighter?"

They paused, glancing from the concrete to Zach's face. *Shit.* They tried to stay quiet, but as soon as Zach snorted, attempting to halt his laughter, they doubled over and laughed, too. They both cackled until their sides cramped, until Zach was heaving and Eli was swiping at their watery lashes.

Once Eli caught their breath, they tucked the joint behind their ear and grabbed Zach's wrist, tugging him toward the parking garage. The people sipping from an almost-empty vodka bottle were also smoking spicy cloves and lent Eli a lighter. After that, Eli and Zach wandered around the dark parking lot, passing the joint back and forth. Car horns blared in the heart of Oakland's city center. Muggy heat thickened the night. Eli sucked smoke into their lungs, sinking into the fuzzy warmth spreading from their head to their toes. Their pulse slowed. Bravery taunted them, daring them to take Zach's hand again. They didn't. Instead, they tipped their head back and searched for the moon.

"I'm getting top surgery," Eli said. They parted their lips but didn't breathe. Just kept their eyes on the sky, walking, waiting.

They'd known Zach for long enough that losing him had felt like losing a piece of themselves. Like Eli had severed their own shadow or pried out a rib. They'd missed him mercilessly, but they'd never, not once, mentioned surgery to him. He'd always loved them pretransition. He'd fallen for Eli *before*. They didn't know if he could ever love them again, and they certainly didn't know if he'd love who they were *after*.

Their shin clipped a bumper and they stumbled, knocking into Zach. They blurted, "Sorry, that was weird."

"Top surgery?" Zach asked. He took another pull off the joint and handed the stub to Eli. He stopped to lean against a darkened streetlamp.

Eli fit their mouth around the pinched butt and inhaled until the weed ignited close to their fingers, singeing their lips. They squatted to stamp it out, exhaling gray plumes. "Yeah, it's when—"

"I know what it is, Liz."

They clamped their mouth shut. Their thoughts were too loud. *What if he hates you now, what if he'll never look at you the same, what if he's confused, what if he doesn't understand, what if, what if, what if.* Eli grasped their elbows, folding their arms around themself.

"Do your parents know?" Zach asked. He touched his thumb to the tip of each finger, a nervous fidget.

Eli met his eyes. "No, not yet," they said quietly and then quickly added, "but I'll tell them—I'm *going* to tell them, I *plan* on telling them, just not . . . not yet."

A worry line creased Zach's forehead. "Who's gonna take care of you?"

Eli held their breath again. When they exhaled, they didn't speak, but their lips formed the word *What?*

"Bodhi's got that film gig and her bullshit internship, and your parents are thirty miles away, and, I mean, I know it's at least a two-week recovery, so who'll take care of you?" Zach tilted his head, cheeks suddenly flushed, hands lacing and squeezing and nervously wringing. "You'll need help with your bandages and drains and—"

"How do you know so much about this?" Eli interrupted, a little too loudly.

Zach blinked. His green eyes softened, flicking around Eli's face. "I wanted to make sure I knew everything in case you ever decided to go this route."

"Knew what, exactly?"

"How to take care of you," he said, frowning, as if Eli should've known that.

Eli gripped their elbows tighter. They didn't understand at first. Couldn't put the *how* and *why* together until they repeated Zach's words back to themself, slower, each syllable sticking like molasses.

Zachary Miller had researched top surgery. He'd prepared for this; he'd done the work. And like so many times before, Eli suddenly remembered that Zach was the best thing that had ever happened to them.

Eli took a breath and threw their arms around his shoulders. They hadn't realized what they'd done until it was too late. Their face was already buried in his neck. They were already pressed against him, holding on to him, inhaling the scent of his eucalyptus shampoo. Zach didn't react at first. His chest stilled and he went rigid, but after a strained, suspended moment, he wrapped his arms around them. His palms followed Eli's spine to their nape. One hand cupped the back of their head, holding them carefully, tightly, like he used to.

Seconds stretched. Eli closed their eyes as Zach feathered the shorn hair behind their ear. Laughter rasped in his chest, quiet at first, then louder. "Your head feels weird," he mumbled, running his hand over Eli's hair again. "Like, a really soft blond tennis ball."

Keep touching me. Eli nodded and rested their cheek on his shoulder, staring at the upward tick at the corner of his mouth. "Good weird or bad weird?"

"Good weird."

"I thought you'd be mad," they said, and closed their eyes again.

"What? About your hair?"

Eli huffed a laugh. "About my surgery."

Zach tightened his hold on them. "Is that why?"

"Why what?"

"Why you bailed on New York?"

Eli peeled their eyes open and stared at the taut tendon in Zach's throat. Their chest clenched, fighting against the sleepy weightlessness filling the rest of their body. They shouldn't—*couldn't*—have this conversation while they were high. They'd fuck it up. The truth would come out jagged. *We're from different worlds. I'd hold you back.* Not now, not like this.

"I bailed on New York because I was scared," they said, and it wasn't a lie.

Zach sighed. "Scared of what?"

Eli stepped back. Zach tipped his head, gaze lingering on their lips until they cleared their throat. He met their eyes. "Everything," they said, and laughed, blinking away an uncomfortable sting. Sadness sneaked into their voice, snaring their laughter like a fishhook. If Zach had wanted to, he could've reeled them in, could've demanded answers, could've convinced Eli to spill the truth. Every inelegant bit of it.

I refused to be your downfall.

"Everything," Zach echoed under his breath. His blood-shot eyes swept to the ground, brows pulled together, lips pressed into a pale line. He winced like Eli had struck him and went back to wringing his hands. "I could've kept you safe, though," he added, as if Eli needed convincing. "Unless it was me—"

"It was never you." Eli swallowed around the lump form-ing in their throat. "It had everything to do with me, Zach. My mess, remember?" They looked at the sky again and forced an awkward grin. "Anyway, we have food vouchers for room service. We can split a pizza, maybe? If you're hungry?"

Zach tried to smile, too. The way his lips barely curved, how he looked lost and undone, made Eli's heart drop into their stomach. Their fingers brushed his knuckles as he pulled away, tucking his hands into his pockets.

"I'm actually pretty beat. Maybe tomorrow?" Zach attempted another feeble smile.

Eli nodded. "Yeah, no, I'm tired, too."

They walked through the lobby and stood together in the elevator. Eli thought about Artist Alley, the cozy convention-style movie theater, and how right it had felt to hold Zach's hand. The bell chimed. Eli stepped out. Zach touched their lower back again, gently steering them around a *Chaos Reign* group in casual cosplay.

"Thanks for the, um—*today*, for everything," Eli said, and scrubbed their hand over the back of their head. "I mean, for hanging out with me. Artist Alley, smoothies, the movie. It was really nice. I had fun."

"Felt like old times," Zach said. He glanced at them over his shoulder, taking long strides to a room two doors down. "Good night, Eli."

Eli wanted to follow him. They wanted to kiss him, and order greasy, overpriced room service with him, and crawl into bed with him. They missed him horribly, terribly, relentlessly.

"Night, Zach," they said, and watched the door swing shut behind him.

♡ ♡ ♡

The makeup trailer at Heroes Expo stretched across seven designated spaces in the crowded parking garage. Muffled chatter leaked through the thin walls. Car doors slammed, and laughter and footsteps echoed.

Eli, who had succumbed to nagging anxiety and arrived ten minutes early, stood alone in front of the middle station, staring at their reflection. Their kit was open, palettes stacked neatly on the counter next to paint tubes and spiny forearm prostheses. They gripped the sleeveless to-go cup they'd grabbed at the breakfast bar, pressing heat into the center of their palm. Yesterday still clung to them. Wandering through Artist Alley, holding Zach's hand, sharing a joint with him in a quiet parking lot. The two of them were crawling back to each other, somehow, some way, and Eli didn't know if they had the courage to let him go again. They remembered how he'd winced last night, how pain had bloomed behind his eyes when they'd said *everything*. They remembered burying their face in his neck and feeling his hand curl around their nape.

How could they possibly let him go after that? How had they ever let him go before?

The door swung open.

Beverly flew into the trailer. Her split-colored blond wig sat catawampus on her head, one teal ponytail high on the left, the adjacent pink ponytail low on the right. She flashed a grin and rolled her makeup kit to an empty station next to Eli.

"I was *this* close to missing my flight," she said, pinching her fingers together. "How're you, sweetie, you—whoa, excuse me! Sexy, *sexy*! Is this your runway outfit?" Beverly gasped and slid in front of Eli, plucking at the corset strung on a velvet hanger with their matching microskirt. "Holy shit, you're totally cosplaying Wych, huh?"

Eli blushed. "Think it's too much?"

"Uh, no," Beverly said, gaping. She swatted them playfully on the arm. "But Zach is going to—"

"Shhhhh, don't go there." They batted at her like a cat and pouted. "I'm already, like, puke-nervous as is, can we not?"

Beverly arched an eyebrow and pinned them with a teasing look. "Fine, fine," she whispered and made a playful show of turning her hand in front of her mouth, locking her lips. "But no, it's not too much. It's winning material. Are you doing . . . ? You totally *are*," she whined excitedly, dancing her palms across the arm prostheses laid out on Eli's station. "You've got this in the bag. Seriously."

Eli crossed their fingers. "We'll see. It's down to the wire."

Beverly smiled, but the movement fractured. Something sad and sudden sparked behind her eyes, as if she had more to say. She plastered on a toothy smile and righted her wig. "Sure is. I went with Harley, obviously."

"*Obviously,*" they parroted and tugged on a ponytail. They had absolute faith in Beverly's ability to create a fantastic cosplay, but Harley Quinn was really, *really* simple. Especially this late in the game.

The trailer door opened again, and Zach walked inside, sunglasses lowered over his eyes, black Pokémon tank snug on his broad chest. He took the empty station opposite Beverly on the other side of Eli and paused to assess their Wych cosplay. His eyes shifted over the edge of his glasses, landing on them.

Eli swallowed hard. "What?"

"That's a whole lot of leg," he purred.

Beverly screeched through laughter.

Eli's blush deepened. "Nothin' you haven't seen before," they said, and turned toward their station, arranging their brushes from small to large. They shot Zach a narrow-eyed smile, tempering the heat in their belly. "What'd you choose, huh?"

Zach smiled crookedly. He opened his kit and unearthed a foam face piece, dropping the prosthesis onto the blank counter. *Of course.* He arranged tubes of red, black, and white paint on his station. The unfinished rendition of the crimson symbiote, Carnage, stared at the ceiling. He met Eli's eyes and huffed out a laugh. "You ready?"

Eli held his gaze. For a moment, they forgot how to speak. Forgot how to breathe. Forgot how to do anything besides stare at Zachary Miller.

Beverly pumped her fist in the air. "Round three, *fight!*"

As soon as the timer started, Eli went to work prepping their prostheses, spreading Pros-Aide onto the back of a silicone application. Halfway between beauty and horror, Wych wasn't an easy character to cosplay. But they'd practiced the makeup twice in their apartment, and Bodhi had tailored the costume to their exact measurements. As long as they pulled off Wych's unsettling gothic vibe, they'd be fine.

Hopefully.

They carefully pressed the first prosthesis to their forehead, blending the edges with a cotton swab soaked in alcohol to melt away the excess silicone. When they lifted their fingertips away, the prosthesis jutted from their brow, carved in the likeness of the Wych emblem from *Delta Quest*. They made a mental note to remember coagulated blood gel—the grooves in the silicone would look too shallow without it. Next, they applied the extravagant prosthetic chest piece and concealed the silicone with a layer of beige paint to match their skin tone. *Okay, steady.* They placed a precise sweep of shadow on their eyelid, carved knife-sharp liner from the corner of their eye to the tip of their eyebrow, and glued down a pair of spidery lashes.

Next to them, Zach hurriedly dabbed paint onto his mask, swapping out a paint-soaked sponge with a hair dryer between layers of crimson, maroon, and black, and Beverly rapped along to a hip-hop song booming from her Bluetooth speaker while she peeled a fake tattoo sheet away from her cheek.

"Careful with those," Zach teased, eyeing the jagged black spines Eli was gluing to their forearm.

Eli grinned and set each prosthesis, holding them in place until the glue dried and the thin, blackish extensions fanned away from their arm, creating the illusion of spikes. "Scared I'll put a spell on you, Carnage?"

Zach chewed his bottom lip and faced the mirror, tugging his mask into place over his face.

Eli couldn't see his expression, but they heard his deep, raspy laughter.

♡   ♡   ♡

Eli tugged at their skirt behind the privacy screen. Music boomed from the speakers and the audience chattered, awaiting the Heroes Expo Cosplay Runway. They grimaced as they assessed their reflection. Prosthetic tendrils jutted from their cheekbones, scaled their arms, and curved away from their knuckles. Black sclera lenses shadowed their eyes, and a dark, sultry wig spilled to their waist. They smeared a bit more blood gel into the prosthesis stretched between their collarbones—creating the illusion of complicated, rune-shaped scarification—and did the same to the matching piece on their forehead, tapping the finishing touches into place with a spatula.

It had been a *long* time since they'd seen themself in a feminine outfit. They exhaled shakily, tucked the spatula into their brush belt, and tightened the clasp on boots they'd borrowed from Stella. *Here goes*, they thought, and stepped into the staging area.

Beverly gawked, draped in a colorful confetti jacket and skintight shorts. "That's a damn makeup artist," she said, gesturing to Eli. "Like, *daaammmn*."

They glanced at themself in a vanity mirror: black-lipped, draped in a floor-length cape, spiked like a lionfish.

Zach adjusted the cuffs on his suit jacket. His Carnage was low-key and finessed, but a monstrous foam mask still shielded his expression. He looked at Eli for a long time, studying the extravagant black claws perched on their arms, their chest stuttering on unsteady breath, their waist cinched into an hourglass. Eli smiled, attempting confidence. They basked in Zach's stare until Beverly wrung her hands and stepped between the two of them.

"So, I'm leaving." She bared her teeth in a half cringe, half smile. "Like, *leaving*, leaving. As in the competition."

Eli shook their head. Disbelief speared them, surfacing in a loud gasp. "Wait, what?"

"Yeah, whoa, hold on," Zach said, voice muffled behind serrated teeth and a gelatinous tongue.

"It's for a good reason, I promise, I wasn't supposed to say anything. I just couldn't *not* tell you when I know the judges are announcing it tonight. I got a gig. Like, a giant, life-changing gig, and I couldn't pass it up," Beverly said. She scraped away a bit of fiery lipstick with her teeth. "I mean, c'mon," she mumbled, and swung her oversized foam hammer, "you think I'd really go with *this* version of Harley if it wasn't for a reason?"

For a moment, Eli didn't understand. Then the microdetails fell into place, and *everything* clicked.

"Holy shit, you got a job with DC? Like, a film gig?" they asked, pitching themself toward her.

Beverly's grin widened and she bounced on her toes. "I can't say anything else, but . . ." She swung her hammer again, laughing joyfully.

"That's fucking incredible, Bev," Zach said. He pulled her into a one-armed embrace, unable to actually hug her with the huge prosthetic mouth stretching away from his jaw.

Eli hugged her, too, hopping in place as the volunteer for Makeup Wars called them to the queue. The overhead lights in the Main Hall dimmed. Theresa Jenkins announced the beginning of the Makeup Wars runway, and Beverly slid to the front of the lineup. She walked first, swinging her hammer, grinning and laughing. Eli walked second, their cape billowing behind them, stomping in Stella's heeled pleather boots. They rested their hands on their hips and smiled at the crowd, but their thoughts still raced.

Beverly exiting Makeup Wars meant Eli and Zach were the only two competitors left. The last artists in the race for Beyond. Beverly Belle signing a contract with a famous studio meant Eli would have to face off with Zachary fucking Miller. Their throat burned, but they forced a fanged grin and stood proudly, listening to the crowd whistle and applaud. Once they exited the stage, Zach walked. His Corporate Carnage cosplay was perfectly executed, but the paint job had been a bit ambitious for a two-hour window. The colors weren't as crisp as they could've been, some cracked, others muted. Zach's makeup was beautiful, but Eli hoarded selfish hope. They wanted to win, desperately. But they wanted Zach, too. Just as desperately. Those two desires collided behind their ribs. Crashed and combusted.

Beyond. Zach.

Eli could sink their fingernails into that scholarship and hold on for dear life. They'd given themself Zach before— loved him, let him go, loved him still—and they didn't know if life would let them have their cake and eat it, too. That didn't stop Eli from wanting to win it all, though.

The competition. The guy.

"Good job," Eli said, nodding to Zach as he took his place behind them in the queue, waiting for the judges to call the top three back onstage.

Zach straightened in place. "Not good enough."

They couldn't see his eyes or the set of his mouth. They didn't know if anger lingered beneath the foam and latex on his face or if sadness cinched his brows. But they knew defeat, and they knew distance, and they recognized both in his muffled voice.

The music swirled to a crescendo, and Scott Brant spoke into the microphone. "Contestants, please make your way to the stage!"

Beverly skipped to her designated spot. Eli followed, taking their place beside her, and Zach stood to their right. The trio faced Theresa, swathed in a pink suit embroidered with golden constellations, Scott, dressed down in a muscle tee and jeans, and the guest judge, Jayson Rue, sporting a beautifully crafted Princess Serenity cosplay. The audience hummed and chattered as Jayson brought the microphone to her smiling mouth and stood, curling her fingers around a golden ponytail.

"All right, all right," Jayson said. Her soft laughter echoed through the large room. "I'm so, *so* excited to be the guest judge tonight, especially since I've been given the honor of making an extraordinary announcement. Are you ready, Makeup Wars?" The audience in the Main Hall cheered and clapped. "This is a competition, of course, but instead of an elimination, we're overjoyed to say goodbye to a contestant and give our heartfelt congratulations to the new makeup artist on set for DC's next woman-led superhero film—Beverly Belle!"

A spotlight illuminated Beverly, and she stepped forward, folding into a bow in front of the judges, then turning to bow for the audience. When she straightened, Jayson approached for a polite hug, as did Theresa. Scott grasped Beverly's hand and grinned. His mouth shaped the words *Congratulations, good luck.*

Theresa took the microphone. "Beverly, your talent will be missed onstage, but we wish you nothing but success. Now, this is *still* Makeup Wars. Consider this a plot twist, if you will. An impromptu quest!" The Main Hall erupted into cheers. "While *both* our finalists will be competing during next week's runway at FanEx in Portland, Zachary and Eli will be scored using a new point system. Each competitor will be judged in specific categories that will influence our overall decision at the Cosplay Runway at Sea City, Seattle, where one artist will be crowned the winner. But tonight . . . who's taking home the bragging rights?"

Beverly bounced in place, glancing between Eli and Zach.

The lights dimmed. Eli held their breath. Zach's paint wasn't on point, and they'd done *a lot*. Prosthetic spines, silicone cheekbone pieces, latex wounds and scars. But Zach still had the size, the grandeur, the immediacy that most special effects were known for—

"Eli Peterson!" Theresa hollered.

The room erupted into applause and wolf whistles.

Yes, they thought, and their chest emptied on an exhalation. *I did this. I can do this.*

Zach bumped his claws against their hand. "Not good enough because you were better," he rasped. "I didn't stand a chance against all that leg."

Heat bloomed in Eli's chest. They beamed for the audience. "No, you didn't," they said, and curtsied in their microskirt.

CHAPTER SIXTEEN
Oakland

"**I CAN'T BELIEVE YOU ACTUALLY THOUGHT YOU WOULDN'T** win," Beverly said, passing a lukewarm fifth of vanilla vodka to Eli.

They tipped the bottle against their mouth, winced, then shook their head. "C'mon, I didn't know if the judges were looking for size or detail. Zach still had a crazy-good piece."

"Your execution was perfect. Like, totally, completely *perfect*. I knew you had it in the bag the minute I saw your costuming. Did you do that yourself, by the way?"

"Oh, no. My friend Bodhi designed the outfit. I borrowed her girlfriend's boots, too," Eli said.

Zach walked out of the hotel bathroom, scrubbed clean of Pros-Aide and latex. "That's cheating," he teased, and plopped into a floral chair across from the bed where Eli and Beverly sat. "Using Bodhi like a secret weapon."

Eli gestured to Zach with the half-empty bottle. "You could use a designer if you had one. *No application help* doesn't mean *no creative help*. Rules are rules."

"Uh-huh, sure. Rules with *loopholes* for *cheaters*," he teased.

"*Not* cheating, just smart," Eli said.

Beverly cackled. "Okay, so there's a club, like, two miles away, I think. We can share a Lyft. I've got a . . ." She stuck her tongue between her teeth and pulled a silver flask out of her fringe purse. "So we can spike the shitty watered-down soda or kombucha or *whatever* they've got at the bar."

"You sure it's not twenty-one-plus?" Zach asked.

"Nope, eighteen. It's a queer club called Solar. They're sponsoring the convention, so we get a discount at the door if we show our badges," she said, glancing between Zach and Eli. "Oh, c'mon, you can't bail. We're celebrating my gig, Eli's win, you two being the Makeup Wars finalists!" She pouted her shell-pink mouth. "C'mon," she whined, "it's my last hurrah!"

Eli stole a cautious glance at Zach. They were already too warm. Too brave and eager to be alone with him. *But we won't be alone*, they thought, justifying the promise of a dark dance floor, more booze, and Beverly's nonexistent chaperone role to keep them away from their ex.

All they could think about was pressing against him and finding his hand like they'd found him in the theater and in the bed of his truck. After last night—wrapping their arms around him in an empty parking lot—and after watching him pause backstage before the runway, assessing Eli like a prize, they couldn't help themself. For weeks and months, they'd tried to tear themself away, but Eli Peterson simply didn't know how to *not* want Zachary Miller.

"You down?" Zach asked.

Eli nodded. "Yeah," they said, and took another vanilla-flavored swig, "if you are."

♡ ♡ ♡

Heavy bass shook the dark-paneled walls at Solar. The crowded nightclub was tucked above a high-end strip mall, blaring hip-hop and EDM into the empty boutiques and eateries below. Half-dressed con-goers and casual cosplayers prowled the room. People wearing yellow wristbands sipped cocktails and beers, while bartenders tossed cherries into clear soda for the underage attendees. Some furries danced at the edge of the DJ's raised stage. Eli pushed their thighs together, standing near the bar in yet another mini-skirt—*Bold choice, self*—and plucked at the slouchy *My Hero Academia* shirt tucked into the high-waisted denim. They scanned the undulating crowd while Beverly ordered three sodas with lime. Beside them, Zach folded his arms across his chest, eyes darkened by charcoal liner, neon flashing across his lightly stubbled cheeks. He was devastatingly handsome. Gorgeous and different and exactly the same.

"You okay?" Zach asked.

Eli tore their eyes away from his sharp clavicles, jutting beneath the collar on his button-down, and blinked. Startled. Fucking *caught*. Zach smirked, and Eli huffed, thankful their burning cheeks were hidden in the dark.

"Yeah, fine. Why?" Eli challenged.

He tipped his head and arched a brow. "You were staring."

"I wasn't, actually."

"You were, but okay."

"What's that supposed to mean? *Okay*?" Eli dared. They grinned and straightened their spine, posturing confidently.

"Doesn't have to mean anything," Zach said. He reached out, closed the space between them, and flicked Eli on the nose. "You have my permission. Stare away."

They swatted his hand. "I don't remember giving *you* permission backstage."

Zach smirked. "Did I make you uncomfortable?"

Eli darted their tongue across their bottom lip. *Calm the hell down.* "No, not at all."

"Do I have your permission now? I'm happy to look elsewhere if—"

"*Shut up*," Eli said, tripping into laughter.

Beverly knocked a dewy cup against Eli's arm, pressing the boring-soda concoction into their hand. "C'mon, let's go, I don't know, somewhere crowded," she said, nodding toward the dance floor.

Eli appreciated the chance to look away from Zach, to temper the flutter in their chest. They followed Beverly into the crowd, hyperaware of Zach's presence behind them, stepping where they stepped, palm ghosting their waist. In the center of the thrumming crowd, Beverly slid the flask out of her purse and dumped vanilla vodka into each cup, stealing paranoid glances over her shoulder.

"Okay, okay—cheers!" Beverly exclaimed, and tucked her flask back into her purse, tapping her cup against Eli's and Zach's. She gave a high-pitched whoop. "To my first fucking gig and the Makeup Wars finalists!"

Eli laughed, hollering along with Beverly and Zach. They gulped their spiked soda, crunched a cherry under their teeth and sighed, relieved, when a burst of sweetness dulled the bite of the vodka. They exhaled hard and twirled, guided by Beverly's hand on their wrist, throwing them into a playful spin. The trio sipped their drinks, chewed limes and swallowed cherries, linked hands, swayed playfully and innocently, and sang along to the remixed anime theme songs blasting from the speakers.

A pink laser flashed across Zach's face. Deepened the shadows beneath his cheekbones and turned his grin violet. Blue glinted on the hoops punched through his ears, and Eli had to look at him. Couldn't stop themself from following the pearlescent light strobing across his inked skin, illuminating him like a villain, like an enchantment, like something from a past life. And maybe he was, maybe he wasn't. Maybe Eli had never let him go, even when they'd sent him off alone and kicked his heart in the ass.

They gnawed on their numb lip, enjoying the syrupy thickness filling their skull. *Get closer*, they thought, watching Beverly loop her arms over Zach's shoulders. *Touch me, you idiot.* But Zach just laughed, and Beverly swung herself playfully from his broad frame, and Eli didn't know what the hell to do.

Someone nearby caught Beverly's attention—a friend or a peer—and squealed delightedly with her, hopping in place. "I'll be right back," Beverly called, and was swallowed by a sea of moving bodies.

Eli licked soda droplets off their lips. Across from them, Zach shifted awkwardly, toeing at the sticky cement floor. Someone's shoulder bumped Eli, feet shuffled past them, and they opened their mouth to say something. *Dance with me. Come here. Please, Zach, can we—*

"Think I'll grab another drink. Want anything?" Zach asked, projecting his voice over the music.

"I'm good, actually." They sipped their half-full soda.

His smile drooped. "Come find me, then, yeah?"

"Yeah, sure. Um, actually, wait, Zach—"

But he was gone, drifting toward the bar.

Eli heaved an aggravated sigh. *You gigantic coward*, they thought, and stared at the place where Zach's shape had faded. Maybe it was for the best. Maybe the two of them just . . . didn't have a shot. Maybe Eli didn't deserve another chance. But they couldn't help jolting onto their tiptoes, wanting to chase him, to take his hand and pull him close. They said *Sorry* under their breath when another person knocked into them and ducked through groups dancing nearby, grinding and smiling, palms coasting sweat-dampened clothes.

They skirted the edge of the dance floor and let their weight go heavy against the wall, staring at the ceiling, listening to everything shake. Their heartbeat stampeded. Lightness filled their limbs and gathered behind their kneecaps, loosening their spine, causing their head to buzz.

Go find him. Tell him. Fuck, just kiss him.

Eli lolled their head and searched in the direction Zach had gone. The bar was two people deep, cocktail and mocktail orders flying from thirsty customers. A couple cosplaying Pokémon Gym Leaders leaned against the bar top, kissing lazily while a bartender stirred their drinks. *Where are you?* Eli flicked their gaze across the crowd again, snagging lace-trimmed maid skirts, Heroes Expo lanyards, fluffy boot covers, and pointy elf ears. *There.*

They stared at the upper half of Zach's tattoo. His arms, loose and relaxed, face crinkling midlaugh. A petite hand rested on his elbow, stacked with gold bands and tipped in trendy acrylics. Eli's throat constricted. They gave the person standing before Zach a drunken once-over. Pretty—*really* pretty—with a dazzling smile, golden Cinderella curls, and perfect fucking bone structure. A gorgeous femme wrapped in a glittering red sequined dress, making Zachary Miller laugh. Eli looked away.

Ouch.

They should've known better. They should've expected it. Should've prepared for exactly *that*—Zach being touched by someone else.

"You're Eli Peterson, aren't you?"

Eli whipped toward the voice, taking a clumsy half step sideways. They glanced from a tapered chest to round cheeks and kind eyes. They recognized him, maybe. Rich umber skin. Swathed in a striped vest; hips strapped with empty holsters. Eli blinked, searching their memories.

"Yeah, I'm—*oh*," they said stupidly. Their eyes widened. "Vance," they blurted, hiccupping on a surprised laugh, "you're Vance Johnson."

"That's me. He, him. You use they, them, right?"

"Yeah, wow, sorry, I just . . ." They laughed again, gutrich and genuine. "You're the comic artist who started that slice-of-life *Chaos Reign* fanzine, right? I backed that project, like, four minutes after it launched."

"The one and only." Vance offered a coy smile.

"And you're cosplaying, let's see . . ." They studied his elaborately detailed outfit. "Jesper from *Six of Crows*?"

He bowed, laughing in his throat. "If Eli Peterson, cosplay royalty, recognizes my costuming, then I guess I've done something right."

Eli trailed their bottom lip across the edge of their cup. "I highly doubt I'm royal *anything*, but thank you."

"You are," Vance said. His smile split into a grin. "And I've got my money on you for Makeup Wars. Zach doesn't stand a chance."

Eli finished their drink, mentally expunging Zach's name from the conversation. "Have you had a successful con? It's my first time at Heroes Expo. Been pretty awesome so far," they said, exhaling through the vodka burn.

"Oh, yeah. Sold out of the fanzine halfway through day one, almost sold out of prints on day two. This is my fourth year in a row. I'll definitely be back."

Eli nodded and stopped themself from searching for their ex-boyfriend and red sequins. Instead, they spoiled their lonely heart, enjoying undivided attention from someone else. Vance Johnson, comic extraordinaire, lifted his chin and assessed Eli's face, confidence radiating from his comet-dark eyes and full-lipped smile.

"Need another drink?" Vance asked.

"I'm good."

Vance opened his mouth to speak, but Beverly leaped from the dance floor and slung her arms around Eli's neck. "Hey! What're you doin'? Where's Zach—oh, hi," she untangled herself from Eli and shot her palm toward Vance. "I'm Beverly."

"Vance," he said, grasping her palm. "Saw the big announcement. Congrats on the DC job."

"Thanks, yeah, It's pretty unreal, honestly." She flashed a toothy grin, swiveling to face Eli. "I'm callin' it a night before I get too sloppy," she said, giggling cutely.

"Oh, yeah, okay." Eli glanced toward the bar. "I'll go with you—"

"No, no, I'm fine. A few fan-artist friends are sharing a taxi with me. Stay and have a good time," she said.

Eli glanced from Vance to Beverly. "You sure?"

"Yeah, totally. We're still riding to the airport together, yeah?"

"That's the plan."

"Awesome. Tell Zach I'll see him in the morning." She hugged Eli and waved to Vance. "Nice to meet you!"

Beverly bounced away, linking arms with a Gwen Stacey cosplayer hovering near the packed bar.

Eli wrung their hands. They gave Vance a tiny smile, anxious and too warm under his watchfulness.

"So," he said sheepishly, and nudged his shoulder toward the dance floor. "Do makeup artists dance?"

Excitement spiked through them. It had been a long, *long* time since Eli had danced with someone. Bravery stoked by an embarrassing bout of jealousy needled their heart. They thought about Zach—*He's probably still flirting with blond Jessica Rabbit*—and nodded, spinning toward the crowd.

Vance followed them onto the dance floor. He tested a touch to their fingertips, then snatched their knuckles and chuckled, melting into the pack. Eli swung their hips, shimmied their shoulders, laughed and teased and enjoyed flirtatious touches—Vance's hand on their waist, his mouth crossing their cheek, their waist pressed against his for one, two, three seconds—but the moment Vance tried to keep them close, to hold on to them, Eli shied away.

Steadied themself and faked a smile, swallowing against the urge to say, *I'm sorry* or *I need to go* or *I'm still completely, one hundred and fifty percent in love with my ex.* They teased at closeness. Allowed Vance to place his hands on their hips. Draped their wrist lazily over his shoulder and kept their jaw angled away from him, unkissable and unattainable.

At one point, Eli peered through the undulating bodies around them and found Zach, standing still in a moving labyrinth, watching them from the edge of the dance floor. His mouth was set, shoulders held tightly, fingers buckled into fists. They stumbled and blinked, pulling away from Vance as Zach moved through the crowd.

Suddenly, Zach was there, his palm a solid weight on Eli's lower back, his mouth tucked against their ear. "I'm leaving. Have fun," Zach snarled.

Eli had known him long enough to recognize the angry prickle in his voice. They tried to catch him, but he yanked away and made for the exit.

"Whoa," Vance said. He cringed and lifted his eyebrows.

"Yeah, I'm sorry." Eli stumbled backward, smiling apologetically. They bumped into a gyrating furry and yelped. "This was fun, I just, I gotta go," they said, and chased after Zach, abandoning a very confused, very handsome boy on the dance floor.

They saw him dip around a group doing shots and picked up their pace, loping through the exit. Sticky air hit their face. Eli swiveled back and forth, searching the patio outside the club. They rounded the corner and found Zach stalking down the sidewalk.

"Hey," Eli barked, storming after him. "Zach!"

Zach stopped and glanced over his shoulder.

They snatched his wrist and tugged him around to face them. "What the hell was that about, huh?"

"Go back inside, Eli," Zach said, refusing to meet their eyes.

"No, not without an explanation."

He snorted out a mean laugh and asked, too quietly, "What do you want me to explain?"

"We can start with your bullshit on the dance floor," Eli said. Their voice cracked.

His mouth twitched, tongue darting over his bottom lip. "I didn't come out with you and Bev to watch you grind on some . . . some *guy*, all right? That's not what I signed up for. That's not—"

"No, you don't get to do that. You don't get to act like you weren't flirting with someone at the bar."

He barked out another laugh. "I wasn't," he said, eyes darting past Eli. He mumbled *Excuse us* under his breath, clasped Eli's elbow, and shuffled them into the alley alongside Solar, making room for a wobbly group to stumble down the sidewalk.

"Like hell you weren't," Eli growled, unable to conceal the emotion thickening in their throat. They wrenched away from Zach, standing on tiptoes to meet his gaze. "I saw you, and I saw her, and—"

"She was asking about *you*." Zach sneered the last word close to Eli's slack mouth. "She makes anime-inspired stick-on nail art and asked if I could introduce you to her so you two could do a cross-promo, platform-boost livestream, *whatever*." He arched an eyebrow, snaring Eli in an amused glare. "Her shop is called Tipped by Annie. She gave me her Instagram handle, and she's real fuckin' nice."

Eli blinked. Processed. Swallowed hard and clung to the anger boiling inside them. "If that's the case, then why act like an alpha-male asshole when you saw me doing, literally, nothing? I was just dancing."

"I told you I was leaving. I didn't *act* like anything."

"We both know that isn't true."

"What do you want me to say, Eli?"

"The truth, for starters," they said, too loudly.

Zach pursed his lips, saddling them with a hard glare. "You think I like watching you dance with someone else? You think I enjoy cuddling with you in a movie theater again and laughing with you again and being near you *again* and then seeing another person put their hands on you? Trust me, I know how it sounds," he said, words clipped and heated. He furrowed his brow and scoffed sadly, weakly, before anger, or something like anger—defeat, maybe—filled his voice. "I know how it looks, okay? Why do you think I walked out?" He stopped, eyes wide, lips parted, and heaved a sigh. "It's pathetic to want someone who doesn't want you back."

Their breath caught. "What?"

Zach's lips twisted into a snarl. "Look, I can't do this."

Eli couldn't help themself. They couldn't ignore the painful lurch in their chest, couldn't stop their body from jolting forward. They grabbed Zach, palm secure on his rough cheek, and tugged him closer. Their lips collided. Zach exhaled through his nose and almost fell into them, crowding them against a chilly brick wall. Shielded by the dark, Eli hiked their leg around Zach's waist, clutching his face, prying at his mouth, tasting his gasp, and swallowing the small, wounded sound that bloomed in the back of his throat.

Their heart thundered. *I've missed you.* They kissed him hard, drowning in Zach's hot breath and soft lips, turning bold and courageous against his body. Zach scooped one hand around their thigh while the other settled like a collar at the base of their neck, holding them tenderly, possessively. Zach kissed Eli with a hunger they'd never known, and when he pulled away, when he leveled Eli with a haunted, shaken look, they guided him back to them.

"Zach, I *miss* you," they whispered, lips grazing his mouth.

Zach followed their jaw with his thumb. "Come here," he said, as if they weren't tangled together, as if Eli wasn't already weightless in his arms, and kissed them again.

CHAPTER SEVENTEEN

Oakland

ELI WOKE TO SUNLIGHT BEAMING THROUGH THE BLINDS. Distantly, they heard cars rush along the street, and nearer, water pelting tile behind the closed bathroom door. They blinked, shifting beneath a white comforter, before their thoughts sharpened and memories from last night surfaced in a rush. *Solar. That alley. Making out with Zach. Stumbling into—*

They gasped, shooting upright, and searched the floor for their clothes. "Shit," they whispered, rubbing their temple with the heel of their palm.

Last night, Zach and Eli had hailed a Lyft. Linked hands in the backseat. Crashed together in the hotel elevator, stumbled through the hall, and landed in Zach's room. Eli remembered leaning against the door after Zach had eased their shirt away. How he'd put his teeth to their neck, collarbones, belly, unzipped their skirt and worked a hickey on their inner thigh. They'd laughed

251

together. Tumbled into bed. Undressed each other. Eli swallowed hard. They touched two fingers to their mouth and thought of their lips on Zach's sternum, his hand between their legs, how he'd silenced their breathless sounds with a rough kiss.

"*Fuck.*" They pulled their knees to their chest, clutching the sides of their head.

So, that had happened. Like, *really* happened.

They shifted their feet around the foot of the bed and snagged their underwear with their toes, slipping the lace-trimmed fabric over their hips. Their skirt was next to Zach's shoes, shirt crumpled in front of the door. They hunted for their sports bra—clinging to the edge of a half-open drawer—and got dressed as quickly and quietly as possible. They found their phone on the nightstand and silently rejoiced when their room key slid from inside their phone case, smashed between their ID and debit card.

For a moment, they considered crawling back into bed and waiting for Zach to find them. But staying meant talking, and Eli wasn't ready to say a goddamn *thing* to him about last night. They crept into the hall, carrying their shoes under one arm, and inched the door shut. They fumbled with their key as they crossed the hall, scampering away like an unwelcome tomcat, and put their phone to their ear. *Steady*, they thought. *Inhale. Exhale.* They shouldered into the dark room and made for the bathroom, flicking on the light as Bodhi's sleepy voice came through the speaker.

"Hello?"

"I slept with Zach," Eli said, just like that. They stared at their reflection. Eyes pitted and smudged with charcoal, throat marred by a mouth-shaped bruise, cheeks flushed. They licked their sour teeth and took a shaky breath. "Sex, Bodhi. I had sex with Zach."

"Yeah, no, I heard you, babe," Bodhi said. She blew out a breath, lips flapping. "You okay?"

They blinked at their reflection, eyes hot and watery. Their chin dimpled and their mouth wobbled. "I don't know," they croaked. As soon as Bodhi sighed, Eli broke, hiccupping over a weak sob. "This is a disaster," they wailed, and sank to the floor. "I had *no* idea how to compete against him before, so how the hell do I compete against him now? I've fucked everything up—*everything*—what am I even doing?"

"I mean, technically, you haven't fucked *everything* up. You just fucked Zach," Bodhi said.

Another wail echoed through the bathroom. "You're not helping!"

Bodhi laughed through a yawn. "Where are you right now?"

"Back in my room. He was in the shower when I left. I'm just..."

"Sitting on the floor?"

"Bathroom floor, specifically," Eli said, sniffling.

"Okay, so, first off, explain to me how you *didn't* see this coming."

They frowned, flopped on the cool tile, and knuckled the speaker icon. Their phone clattered on the floor beside their head. "What do you mean?"

"Don't play dumb," Bodhi barked.

Eli swiped at their nose with the back of their hand. They'd anticipated holding his hand. Kissing him, maybe. "Fine, I was prepared for, like, a single smooch, not missionary position."

"Missionary? *Really?* That was the front-runner for your angsty makeup sex?" Bodhi made an unimpressed noise.

"Can you not? It was fine, by the way. Great, actually." Eli's face burned. They pawed tears off their cheeks and huffed. "It wasn't just sex. It felt like more than that."

"You still have feelings for him? Like, *real* feelings?"

"Yeah," they whimpered. "Am I that obvious?"

"Oh, yes. Abso-fucking-lutely. But it's still polite to ask."

Eli whined.

Bodhi continued, "And I'm guessing he still has feelings for you? I mean, I pretty much *know* that, but."

"That's what he said last night. We'd been drinking, though. Maybe it was just a fluke. Like, maybe we were just drunk and messy and . . . and fuck, I don't know."

"I know you both pretty well, and no offense, but drunk and messy is your thing, not his. I doubt he'd sleep with you if he wasn't goin' all in. Especially since, you know, *you* broke up with *him*."

"No, you're right. He was sweet, too," they said, hardly above a whisper. "Tried to be a gentleman."

"Tried?"

They chuckled through another ugly sniffle. "Yeah, I didn't let him."

"See! You were totally a messy little bitch—I called it," Bodhi teased, laughing, too. "You used a condom, right?"

Eli squeezed their eyes shut, ugly laughing, but stopped the moment Bodhi's question registered. They shot upright, smacking their forehead on the underside of the sink. "*Ow*— what? Yeah, I mean, I think so." They rubbed the blooming sore spot above their eyebrows and stared at their phone. A text flagged the top of the screen.

Zachary Miller: where'd you sneak off to?

"Liz," Bodhi said, exhaling their name like a warning.

Eli chewed on their bottom lip. They remembered every-thing—Zach mapping their body, his hips between their thighs, sweat-slicked skin pressed against them, his mouth dusting their shoulder—but they didn't remember seeing him put a condom on, and they didn't remember putting a condom on him.

"We were a little busy," Eli snapped. "I'm sure we did. I mean, I don't think he would've, *you know*, if we didn't have one."

"But you're not sure?"

"I'm pretty sure!"

"Okay, pretty sure isn't *sure*," she said.

"I'm, like, eighty-five percent sure."

"Oh, my God, you need to figure this shit out pronto," Bodhi said.

"I know," Eli groaned, wheezing through another pitiful whine. "What if I just walked into the ocean?"

"Eli."

"Or shacked up with Sasquatch."

"*Liz*."

"Or—"

"Listen here, my good bitch. Everyone *oopsies* into bed with their ex at least once. You got it over with, done, bingo, dicking complete. Now, you're gonna stop crying, you're gonna wash your face—on second thought, wash everything—you're gonna wear something cute. I said *cute*, not slutty."

"*Hey!*"

"Listen!" Bodhi bellowed. Her voice careened through the bathroom. "You're gonna go talk to Zach, make sure you used a goalie, and then you're gonna win Makeup Wars. That's it. Done deal. Say *Yes, Bodhi.*"

"I—"

"*Yes, Bodhi!*"

Eli heaved a sigh. "Yes, Bodhi," they said, and snatched their phone. They stood and faced their water-logged reflection again, all tear-streaked skin and reddened nostrils. "I look like shit."

"Good thing you're a makeup artist," Bodhi said. "Text me, okay? Love you."

In the background, Stella hollered, "You rocked the runway in those boots!"

Eli swallowed another laugh and ended the call, turning their gaze to the mirror.

Their breath still trembled. Anxiety opened like a pit in their gut. They weren't crying because they regretted last night. They were crying because last night had been too good. Felt too right. Made an already complicated situation a lot harder to navigate. Eli wanted Zach. Wanted to be with Zach.

But they needed to win Makeup Wars. They *needed* that goddamn scholarship.

"What the hell are you doing?" they whispered. Another stray tear curved down their cheek. They slapped the droplet away.

They remembered Zach's lips hovering above their mouth. His nose tapping their temple, his lashes brushing their cheek.

Don't, they wanted to say to their heart. *Don't you dare.*

But it was too late. Eli was done. Completely, utterly lovestruck.

♡   ♡   ♡

After a scalding shower, Eli color-corrected the hickey on their neck with green primer, beige concealer, and sheer powder and cut heavy black wings across their eyelids. They sculpted their brows, contoured their cheekbones, dotted fake freckles on their nose, and snapped a selfie for Instagram. Lazy grin, tongue out, winking at the camera. The caption said,

Finalist. #MakeupWars

They posted the picture and gave the room a sluggish sweep, checking for forgotten socks and toiletries. Once they were satisfied that they hadn't left anything behind, they took a deep breath, grabbed their makeup kit and suitcase, and made for the lobby.

So, how, exactly, were they supposed to ask Zach about last night? It wasn't like they hadn't slept with him before—they'd slept with him for, literally, years—but confronting him about a stupid fucking condom after their stupid fucking breakup at this stupid fucking hotel made Eli's insides unsteady. Last night had been *amazing*, and Eli didn't know how to process being with Zach again and being in competition with him, too. They didn't know how to reconcile being unequivocally in love with Zach and knowing they needed to beat him.

Squeaky wheels rolled to a stop beside them. Eli glanced at familiar black combat boots and flicked their eyes upward, landing on Zach's handsome face. He gazed at them over the edge of his bat-shaped sunglasses.

"You ghosted me," he teased, voice low and hushed. "*Again.*"

Well, shit. Eli's cheeks flared. "I went to my room to get ready," they said, which was barely the truth. "I had to pack and brush my teeth and—"

"I get it, Eli. It's fine," he said. His smile faltered but didn't break. "Is everything . . ." He paused to clear his throat. The elevator doors slid open. "Are we okay?"

Eli stepped into the elevator. Their tongue stuck to the roof of their mouth. They steeled their expression, hoping their sharply applied makeup hid their nervousness. "Yeah," they said, nodding vigorously. "Yeah, of course. I just . . . I actually had a question, because I can't really remember—not that I *don't* remember, because I do—but . . ." They gnawed on their lip and waited for the doors to close.

Zach hit the lobby button. "But?"

"We used a condom, right?" Eli whispered, cringing through embarrassment. They wrung their hands. Their binder felt tighter.

A rosy blush tinted Zach's fair cheeks, and his jaw slackened. "Yes, yeah, of course," he said, nodding quickly. "I would never—"

"No, I know. I might've had a bit of a meltdown because I wasn't sure, and—and yeah." They blew out a relieved breath as the elevator dropped. "*Jesus.*"

"Meltdown, huh?"

Eli pinched their fingers close together. "Little bit."

"We used a condom, but I haven't been with anyone. Like, I haven't had unprotected sex with, like, *anyone* in . . . I mean, not that it matters. I just figured you might want to know—"

"No, yeah, it's fine. I haven't been serious with anyone, either."

"Good."

"Good?"

Zach snorted out a chuckle. "Great," he blurted. Laughter shook his shoulders.

Eli laughed, too. Stared at the mirrored ceiling, grinning sheepishly. "Awesome."

Moths or bats or fucking *porgs* were darting around in their rib cage. Zach touched their knuckles, just barely, fingertips teasing at their palm. *What the hell are we doing?* The elevator rocked to a stop, the doors opened, and Eli grasped the handle of their suitcase, stepping into the claustrophobic lobby. Heroes Expo guests wandered around, paying tabs at the concierge, waiting for taxis, and standing outside the hotel restaurant.

"Hey," Zach said, nudging Eli with his elbow. He held his phone out for a selfie. "Top two," he whispered, and flashed a grin.

"Top two," Eli parroted, smiling for the camera.

Across the lobby, Beverly bounced in her orange sneakers and waved her arm. "Eli, Zach, hey! Our table's almost ready!"

Zach ran his hand along Eli's elbow. "Hungry?"

Eli wanted to memorize that touch. *Every* touch. They nodded and resisted the urge to kiss him, right there, in front of everyone. "Starving."

CHAPTER EIGHTEEN
Portland-FanEx

ELI WAS GIVEN A GRAND TOTAL OF THREE DAYS AT HOME, and they were stuck at the diner for two of them. It wasn't *great*, but they needed tips to fund their last two cosplays, and they couldn't let their day job slip, either. Having a supportive manager and curious teammates was a plus, but if Eli didn't win, they'd need their stability back. *Stability* meaning double shifts, overnights, and hopefully—fingers crossed—more sponsorships. Even though they'd tried to trick themself into the idea of a peaceful transition back to their boring, basic life, Makeup Wars still pulsed with the promise of a future, of their dreams manifesting, of Beyond.

But getting to that future cost money, and money cost time. The extra cash was nice, yeah. But they could've done without the exhaustion.

They slid out of the airport taxi, thanked the driver, and hauled their suitcase onto the sidewalk, wincing through the dull ache in their right arm. Waiting tables never *didn't* suck, but the worst part had to be the balancing act—propping heavy trays on their smallish limbs. *You're too young to sound like a creaky staircase,* their mom had said, rubbing at a stubborn knot that had taken root beneath their shoulder blade two weeks after they'd started at Denny's. *Seriously, honey. You can stay home, take classes at Saddleback, transfer to a four-year when you're ready.* But Eli had transferred to the Denny's in West Hollywood instead and moved to Los Angeles.

Four months seemed like a lifetime ago.

They heaved a deep, tired breath and tilted their head, scanning the windows peppered on the Marriott's curved towers. FanEx banners speared the garden area outside the automatic doors, and a shuttle idled in the drop-off area, waiting to collect cosplayers and convention attendees. Eli wanted to get some goddamn sleep. They wanted to take a bath, smoke a joint in their underwear, and hibernate like a grizzly bear. But unlike the other conventions in the Makeup Wars circuit, FanEx had scheduled the Cosplay Runway on Friday night. Day one, not day two.

Stage-ready in *t* minus five hours? Yeah, they needed an energy drink. Like, a *huge* energy drink.

A car door shut. Footsteps hit the sidewalk behind them.

"Weird, huh?" Zach said. He appeared at their side, wearing torn black denim and a Star Wars tank, and pushed his sunglasses to the top of his head. He met their eyes on a smile. "Being the final two."

"I always thought it'd be you and Beverly," they said, and it was the truth. They'd always *hoped* it would be them standing next to Zach in the semifinals, but the reality still felt distant.

"I didn't."

Eli smiled, just barely. They had to guard themself against Zach's ability to bulldoze into their heart. Had to remember every overnight shift and hard-won sponsor, every penny pinched, dollar saved, and ramen packet cooked. Still, they couldn't look away from his quirked lips and jade eyes. *Damn him.*

"You okay?" Zach nudged their ankle with his boot.

"I worked the midnight shift, and made an extra pair of fangs when I got home, and *then* I had to pack, and LAX was a nightmare, and . . ." They blew out a breath. "I'm just *really* tired."

"Checked in yet?"

"Yeah, I did the online thing. I've just been." They gestured to themself, the sidewalk, the hotel. "Standing here, doing this."

"Set an alarm, text me your room number, and go take a nap."

"Why, so you can let me sleep through the runway?" Eli teased. They tugged their suitcase into the lobby. "Claim the Makeup Wars crown and run off to Beyond?"

"Can't win if I'm not competing against the best," Zach said.

Eli snorted. They swayed into him. Shoulders bumped, fingers linked and loosened, and they imagined curling against his chest, dozing through the afternoon, ordering room service, staying in bed, and making out until evening darkened the Pacific Northwest. But they had a cosmic-themed makeup to execute, and they couldn't keep daydreaming about the stupidly beautiful, grossly talented ex-boyfriend they'd accidentally hooked up with.

"Seriously, Liz. Get some rest. I'll see you in a bit," Zach said. His thumb clipped their chin, a simple, intimate touch. He smiled again and walked to an unoccupied space at the check-in counter.

Eli hadn't seen Zach since they'd parted ways in Los Angeles. They still regretted not inviting him upstairs when the taxi had dropped them off at their apartment. Eli had video chatted with their parents, covered a shift for Max at Denny's, and met Bodhi for coffee the next morning. They'd texted Zach, though. Sent him a picture of the perfectly good waffle someone had sent back for being too sweet—one cheek stuffed full, fork dangling between their lips—and got a picture of the Miller beach house in return. Moonlight skating the infinity pool and, most importantly, Zach's bare upper half reflected in the sliding glass door.

The two of them hadn't talked about what had happened in Oakland. But Zach would send things like *Are you okay, are we okay*, and Eli would answer with *Yeah, we're okay, can't wait to kick your ass in Portland*. They sent each other sleepy selfies, talked about the new graphic novel Zach was writing, and liked each other's posts on Instagram, laughing at comments from viewers and fans.

> **Glow_Beam:** omfg zach and eli are totally back together
> **MKEUP:** RIGHT!?!?!
> **Cindy_babe016:** My ship is seriously sailing
> **AnimeArt_:** are you guys dating again?

Neither one of them asked the hard questions, though: *Are we doing this? Do we want to be together again? Do you trust me with your heart? Will you stop running?*

Eli got their key from the concierge, found their room, and stood at the window, watching the Willamette River ripple in the sunlight. Their phone buzzed incessantly, lit with a flower emoji and the name "Mama."

"Hey, Mom," Eli said, tapping the speaker icon.

"Hi, honey. How's it goin'? Was your flight okay?" She sounded tired, too. Like she'd finished another fifty-hour week.

"Flight was fine. I worked an overnight, so I'm kinda beat, but everything's good. Got checked in, saw Zach in the lobby."

Claire laughed a little, the sound all mothers made when it came to heartache, heartbreak, anything heart related. She hummed into the speaker. "Zach, huh? And how is *he*?"

"Fine," they said, too softly, then again, "He's always fine."

"I bet it's a bit," she paused, considering, "*odd* doing this with him. Is everything okay between you two?"

They watched geese skim the river and thought about lying. Thought about the truth, too. "It's hard," they said. "I still . . ." Their throat hopped, turning their voice froggy. "You know, I still—"

"Oh, baby, it's okay to still feel something. Breakups take time." Claire clucked her tongue.

"I still feel *everything*," they admitted, and cleared their throat. "I just want to win this. I really do, like, bad, Mom. I know you and Dad don't get it—*I know*—but I want this more than I've ever wanted anything." For a minute, they didn't know which *want* they were talking about. Beyond or Zach. They sniffled, pawing at their damp lashes. *No more crying,* they vowed. "Did you get the pictures?"

"I did," she said enthusiastically. "That last one was a little much."

Eli snorted out a laugh. "Yeah, I know, I know."

"You looked amazing, *obviously*." She heaved a sigh. "I have to remind myself that you're almost twenty, you know. Keep walking into your old room and forgetting you're gone."

"I'm not *gone*, Mom. C'mon."

"Living on your own, traveling on your own, starting a whole life on your own . . ." She gave a playful whine. When she laughed, Eli did, too. "I know you want this, honey. I just worry, that's all. You're so, *so* talented. I don't know where the hell you got it from."

Eli laughed harder. "You, probably."

"Well, certainly not your father." Laughter traveled through the speaker, echoing from her to them, them to her. "Just keep your eyes open, okay? Be smart, and vigilant, and tenacious. Makeup isn't exactly stable, but it's paying off, right?"

"Little by little, yeah." Sorta. *Almost.* "Beyond can help make it happen. *Really* happen."

"Then kick his ass, baby," their mother said, whispering into the speaker. "I love you, okay? Call me tomorrow."

They smiled. "Love you, too. Bye."

For the first time, Eli felt the worry-shaped anchor their parents had placed on their chest lift. They breathed. Closed their eyes and chuckled to themself. Their mom wasn't thrilled, but she was happy for them. Encouraging them. Rooting for them. And that was all they'd ever wanted.

They tapped Zach's message bubble.

> **Eli Peterson:** Room 806. Don't let me sleep past 4.
> **Zachary Miller:** Got it

They didn't take off their makeup or get undressed, just flopped onto the puffy comforter and closed their eyes. They tried to think of the latest anime they'd watched or book they'd read, tried to fool their brain into drifting somewhere new.

It's okay to still feel something.

But as always, Eli dreamed about movie sets, stage lights, handmade monsters, and Zachary Miller.

Much like Heroes Expo, FanEx was a lively show with a loyal following and a local fan base. Eli had expected a small audience, but when they peeked around the door of the designated Makeup Wars green room, a line for Hall A—where the Cosplay Runway took place—snaked along the wall and wrapped around the escalators. They pulled themself behind the door before anyone glimpsed the glittery fins glued to their face.

"Crowded?" Zach asked. He leaned over the counter at his station, holding a horn against the center of his bald cap.

Eli nodded, glancing over Zach's jagged red-and-black paint job. They should've known he'd jump at the chance to showcase a *Star Wars* cosplay for a celestial-themed runway. Donning wicked bone-colored horns and traditional Zabrak markings, Zach became a fearsome Sith. His coloration was on point, prostheses perfectly placed, costuming immaculate. *Damn him*, they thought. *Damn him, damn him, damn—*

"Earth to space mermaid," he said, grinning at their reflection. "We've still got thirty minutes. Chop-chop."

They rolled their eyes. "It's so quiet in here. Like, way, *way* too quiet."

Zach flicked around on his phone. Pop punk music played, as always. "Better?"

Eli remembered zooming down the 101 last spring break, their bare feet propped on the dash. Bodhi's surfboard was strapped in the bed of Zach's overpriced truck, and she was sipping a joint in the backseat while Eli drank spiked iced tea, one hand wrapped around their cup, the other settled on Zach's knuckles atop the gearshift. Zach was singing.

They blinked the memory away and nodded. "Yeah, much better."

Despite their two-hour nap, Eli still felt feeble and fucking *tired*. They should've rested more. Should've put some energy on reserve instead of picking up another shift. They walked back to their station and gave their makeup a once-over, testing the tacky Spirit Gum on their throat. Hopefully their makeup didn't showcase their exhaustion. They'd decided on a flashy design inspired by a character from *Planetary Bounty*, a space-set anime about a gun-slinging bounty hunter and his crew of misfits. LoLo Locke, the quirky cosmic mermaid, a botanist with luminescent scales, sparkly gills, and exaggerated fae-like ears, was the perfect candidate for the runway.

Eli placed gill-shaped silicone prostheses on top of the sticky gum and held the pieces against their neck, smoothing the edges with a bit of alcohol. Their reflection shone opalescent, dusted finely with pearl-toned powder. Tiny cheekbone prostheses exaggerated their eye shape, and white mascara turned their lashes transparent, making them appear alien and otherworldly. Last, they speckle-painted the silicone, put in their white contact lenses, and made sure their costume was ready for last looks. Beside them, Zach finished applying his horns and draped a black cloak around his shoulders.

A Makeup Wars volunteer cracked open the door and said, "Two minutes 'til last looks, finalists."

Eli sighed. They should've bought another energy drink. They stared into the mirror, looking over their makeup—violet contour, abalone scales, pointed ears, blocked-out eyebrows, and blue-tinted lips. *It's not enough*, they thought, stealing a glance at Zach as he clipped a fake light saber to his purposely tattered belt. *I should've skipped that shift and sculpted a bigger face piece.*

But it was too late. Zach had preemptively demolished them.

"Ready?" Zach asked.

They swallowed, nodding tightly. "Yeah, let's go."

The volunteer guided the pair through a door labeled STAGE CREW and gestured to separate stations lined with exposed bulbs and a foldout privacy screen. Eli set their bag down and watched the volunteer stare at his white-banded watch. "And last looks begins . . . now," he said, and dropped his hand like a race had started.

Honestly, this *was* a race. It had just already been won.

Eli hurriedly worked another layer of shell-pink freckles onto their nose and cheeks, adding depth to their paint job. Masked by the privacy screen, they squeezed into the skin-tight jumpsuit, fastened fake gold chains around their waist, and buckled thick bracelets to their wrists, minding the fin prostheses glued to the backs of their hands. They touched the glowing teardrop-shaped net filled with faerie lights arcing away from their forehead, dangling like an anglerfish's lure. When they stepped out from behind the screen, Zach turned toward them, swathed in black, looking powerful and *perfect*.

"Cast the anchor," Zach teased, and winked.

They blushed terribly. "Fish jokes. Wonderful."

"Oh, c'mon. What'd you expect?" He stepped closer. Gently touched his thumb to the delicate finlike appendages, made of plastic wrap and acrylic, glued to their foam ears. "This is gorgeous, by the way. One of your best."

They tilted their chin upward, gazing at Zach's intricate paint job and yellow eyes. "Yeah, but you'll still win."

"We'll see."

"Finalists, it's time to queue up. Zachary, you're first," one of the volunteers said.

Zach dropped his hands, and Eli immediately wished he'd touch them again. They tried to shove the thought away, to focus on the runway—*the goddamn semifinals*—but they couldn't stop thinking about that night in Oakland. Zach pinning them to the wall outside the club, his thigh snug between their legs, falling backward onto his hotel bed and pulling him down with them. They wanted to relive that, to have Zach again, to be with him again.

"You good?" Zach asked.

Eli snapped into the present. "Yeah," they said, nodding like it was the truth. "I'm fine."

Theresa Jenkins rallied the crowd as introduction music filled Hall A. "It's officially the semifinals. Are you ready, Portland?" The crowd hollered and clapped. She continued, "Please welcome our first finalist to the stage—Zachary Miller!"

Eli and Zach had been given the opportunity to send stage presence requests for the semifinal and final runways to build ambience for their cosplays. Zach had chosen darkness, of course. He stalked onto the stage, black cloak billowing behind him, horns concealed, and illuminated his red light saber while the room was pitch black. A second later, spotlights beamed, and he pushed away his hood, spinning his light saber for the audience.

When he loped into the stage wing, he didn't speak, but he touched Eli's trembling hand.

"And our second Makeup Wars finalist is . . ." Scott Brant's deep voice filled the room. "Eli Peterson!"

The lights dimmed, and smoke machines sent fog skating across the stage. LoLo Locke's ocean-world music from *Planetary Bounty* played over the speakers, and Eli darted out, creeping through the artificial mist, lit by its lure and the glow-in-the-dark paint splattered across their skin. The audience clapped and whistled. Slowly, the stage lights brightened to full strength and Eli did their typical runway walk, slinking across the stage, standing still for the judges, and then disappearing into the wing.

They knew they could've done more. Could've made larger prostheses. Could've exaggerated their features, done a better paint job, constructed LoLo Locke's botanical lab coat or attached flowers to their costume. But they'd been too busy at the diner, hoarding funds for the finale, and daydreaming about Zach.

"Givin' me a run for my money, Liz," Zach said, glancing over his shoulder as the pair waited for their cue.

Eli clenched their jaw. "Yeah, we'll see."

The audience yipped and hollered when Zach and Eli walked back onstage and stood before the judges. As always, two spotlights shone down on them, and the judges assessed their cosplays from the table. The guest judge, María Love, smiled. She was cosplaying La Muerte— fake candles glinting on her wide-brimmed hat, face painted like a calavera—and rested her skeletal glove on the microphone.

"Welcome to your second-to-last runway, finalists. Tonight, we scored your cosplays in different areas. Those scores will help determine who will be crowned the winner in Seattle, but for now, we'll be using them to highlight strengths and weaknesses. Our winner in the Set Ready category goes to . . . Zachary Miller!"

Of course. Eli forced a smile, thankful no one was *losing* but still upset about generally lacking in the professionalism department. *I should've focused.* They squared their shoulders. *I wonder what they wrote on my scorecard.*

Scott leaned toward his mic. "Zach, your Sith cosplay is stunning. Camera ready, set ready, and completely badass."

Zach grinned and tipped his head politely.

Theresa turned her eyes to Eli. "Eli Peterson, you're our Creative Development winner! You've executed an imaginative design full of originality and technical skill."

Relief washed over them. They nodded thankfully and waved at the crowd.

"All right, Zachary Miller, Eli Peterson, I hope you're ready for the Makeup Wars finale because it's only two weeks away! We want to see big, beautiful full-body cosplays with over-the-top costuming and incredible special effects. Utilize your overall talent," Theresa said, gesturing to Zach with a wave, "and use your technical skills to fine-tune your design," she shifted her open palm to Eli, "and remember, you're fighting for a scholarship at Beyond!"

Hall A roared with cheers and applause.

Eli stood beside Zach, listening to wolf whistles and laughter and clapping, and silently promised to kick his ass in Seattle.

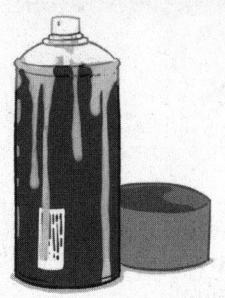

CHAPTER NINETEEN

Portland

Zachary Miller: are you too tired for doughnuts and books?

Eli blinked at their phone, standing in the bathroom surrounded by makeup remover wipes and dirty towels. They'd planned on ordering something greasy off the room-service menu and watching whatever Hallmark movie was on TV. Notifications flagged their Instagram and TikTok, and a few comments on their Weblog channel remained unanswered. They rolled their bottom lip between their teeth and reread Zach's text. Within seconds, another message appeared.

Zachary Miller: don't make me go to the world's biggest bookstore by myself
Eli Peterson: I'm exhausted
Zachary Miller: we'll be lowkey

They frowned. *Wow.* Blew out a breath. *Stupid, hot, ridiculous man-child. We're not doing this, self. We're not making this shit a habit two weeks before—*

Zachary Miller: please. i'll buy you tea
Eli Peterson: Fiiiinnneee

The sun threw gold into the summer sky. People crowded around food trucks, holding leashes and shopping bags, while skateboards scraped the sidewalk. Restaurants and bars were packed with families, couples, and polycules, and boutiques propped their doors open with chalkboard signs, inviting tourists inside to shop during the last few hours of the day.

Zach held the door for Eli at Powell's City of Books. "I've heard this place is pretty cool," he said.

Cool was an understatement. Books filled giant shelves throughout the huge, multilevel building, featuring an array of genres and subgenres sorted into color-coded rooms. Eli ran their fingertips across well-loved spines and plucked a poetry paperback off an end cap, flipping through pages while Zach loomed behind them. The runway still haunted them, disappointment clinging to excitement that sparked whenever they stood close to Zach. A part of them lashed out, insistent that they get back to work, brainstorm their final cosplay, grind until they'd perfected every piece. But a softer part took shelter in the simplicity of a bookstore and Zach's chin resting on their shoulder.

"Rumor has it they've got rare books on the top floor," Zach whispered.

"Remember when we used to sit in the manga section at Barnes & Noble?" Eli asked. They leaned against Zach's chest. Warmth sank through their T-shirt. "Ditch last period, stop by the spicy mango cart, read as much as we could until the booksellers made us move."

"We used to take the train up to Small World in Venice all the time, too. Chilled with the bookstore cat."

Eli laughed in their throat. *Yeah*, they thought, *until we almost got caught making out in the science fiction section*. But they weren't brave enough to mention that.

"C'mon," Zach said. He dusted his palms along their waist, dropped away, and grabbed their fingertips.

They kept his hand in theirs, took the stairs to the top floor, and walked into the private room, where autographed books were propped on stands behind locked cases. A collection of signed first-edition Anne Rice books filled one shelf. There was a limited-print-run copy of *Fight Club* by Chuck Palahniuk, old Oregon cartography hardcovers, poetry with faded text, and signed comics. Eli wandered from one dimly lit case to the next, skirting sallow pages and cracked spines.

"You still working on *your* book?" Eli asked.

Zach followed the cliff of their knuckles with his thumb. "A bit, yeah. Influencing steals a lot of my time, though."

They nodded. Being an influencer was fun but stressful on a good day and completely paralyzing on shitty days. Everything in between fell somewhere on a sliding scale, usually close to *fun*, sometimes hovering in the *anxiety alert* area right before *shitty*. "You could always take a step back and work on your graphic novel. People might like to read it one day. You never know."

"I don't want to blend whatever makeup brand I have with my nonexistent writing career. It's hard enough being a mannequin; I don't need to invite a bunch of strangers into my writing life, too."

"Scared people might ship you with a rival writer?" Eli teased, pausing in front of a leather-bound Tolkien.

"Pretty sure my viewers already have someone in mind," Zach said. He tucked his mouth close to their ear. "And I can't *step back*. I've got a competition to win."

Eli snorted. They turned, nose to nose with the boy they couldn't stop chasing, and said, "Didn't you mention tea?"

His smile sharpened. "I might've. Want to grab a book or two on our way out?"

They shook their head. Embarrassment squirmed under their skin. They didn't need to check their banking app to know they had enough spending money for a book or a bottle of SFX cold foam. They had two hotel vouchers for a convention-sponsored dinner and a twenty in their wallet for airplane snacks, and that was all. "I'm on a book-buying freeze," they said. "Still got a whole series I need to get through."

They'd been stuck in this loop for years—lying to Zach by omission even though he was savvy enough to figure them out—but they had no idea how to break the cycle. Money was a monster Zach had been comfortable with since he was a kid. A constant, nonthreatening presence he was aware of but never had to worry about. Meanwhile, Eli slept with one eye open, waiting for the day a sponsorship ended and their account went dry.

Zach didn't press. He nodded and held the door, trailing Eli through the bookstore and back onto the sidewalk. Stars blinked through the darkening blue, and streetlamps stretched the shadows. Dingy city scents lifted into the air as Eli fell into step beside Zach. Once again, their fingers inched toward him, barely brushing his knuckles, curling tenderly around his thumb. Zach's map app guided them to a tea shop near Voodoo Doughnuts. Eli ordered matcha with tapioca pearls. Zach insisted on sweets, too. They leaned against exposed brick outside an abandoned theater and stole bites from each other's pastries: a joint-shaped doughnut and a strawberry-filled vanilla bar.

Zach caught the side of Eli's mouth with his thumb, swiping at stray rainbow sprinkles, and Eli tried not to blush when they pushed the last piece of doughnut between Zach's lips.

What the hell are we doing?

"Good?" Eli asked, clearing their throat.

Zach sucked sugar from his pinkie and flicked through his phone. "Very. Where to next?"

They rocked from heel to toe, considering. They could walk by the river and talk about Oakland. Eli could tell Zach the truth. *I never stopped wanting you. What is this? What are we? Do you still—*

"Oh, check it out," Zach blurted, flipping his phone around. An online flyer for an arcade café filled the screen, flagged with the FanEx logo. "Free tokens for con attendees. Got your lanyard?"

They tugged the strap on their mini-backpack. "In here, yeah."

Zach nudged them with his shoulder. "C'mon, it's right down the street from our hotel."

We should talk. Eli felt the words flounder in their mouth. *We need to talk.* But they smiled and nodded, and their lungs spasmed when Zach took their hand.

They walked together while evening fell over the city. The neon stag sign glowed yellow, green, and blue, and music tumbled onto the street whenever a bar door swung open. Much like Los Angeles, Portland peppered the night with the distinct sound of glass clanking, raucous laughter, and hurried footsteps. Eli stayed close to Zach, rounding the corner with his hand still linked around their palm, and dropped their empty cup into a trash can before slipping into an arcade café called Coin Toss.

Vintage consoles and noisy pinball machines flashed and whirled, lined against the wall across from high-top tables. The person at the door gave Eli and Zach five tokens each and gestured to the barista station, rattling off a scripted two-for-one latte deal. Con-goers shared apple muffins and sipped cold brews, and someone at an oval booth jutted their chin at Eli and Zach. Hushed chatter came and went. Eli felt eyes on them, tracking their long strides toward the game consoles.

Eli Peterson and Zach Miller. Yeah, they used to date, I think. Head-to-head in that cosplay contest.

"Okay, so, Bubble Time, Pac-Man, or Frogger?" Zach asked. He pitched his body toward Pac-Man.

"You be the hungry little blob, and I'll shoot bubbles," Eli said. They angled the joystick and fired lasers at pixelated bubbles. Beside them, Zach hissed at the screen, running from a pack of colorful ghosts as he hunted for a bouncing berry. They switched after the first round, then moved on to Frogger, cheering each other on as their frog hopped across busy highways.

"Is this a date?" Zach asked suddenly.

Eli blinked, startled, and sent their frog crashing into a high-speed truck.

"That was weird. I'm sorry, I just—"

"No, it's fine. I hadn't really thought about it," they said. *Bullshit.* It was the only thing they'd thought about since they'd left the hotel. They stepped away from the console, hiding their furrowed brow and confused expression, and gripped the sides of a pinball machine, staring at the colorful display beneath the glass. "Do you want it to be?"

Beeps and pings filled the room, battling with alternative rock and low chatter. Eli slipped a token into the pinball slot and took a quivering breath. *Can it be a date?* They wanted Zach to say *Yes.* They wanted him to kiss their cheek, and start over, and pick up right where they'd left off. Before the heartbreak, before New York, before they'd let him go. Eli pulled the toggle and sent a silver ball bouncing around the machine.

Zach placed his hands on the pinball machine, bracketing Eli's hips. His breath hit their ear, chasing goose bumps along their arms. The fine hair on the back of their neck stood on end.

"Question is, do *you* want it to be?" he asked. Laughter sneaked into his voice. "I'm not the fickle one."

Eli stopped breathing. They hit the buttons on the machine. Felt their chin dimple and their mouth wobble. "Yeah, I know," they whispered.

"I wouldn't want to make you feel trapped," he teased, running his lips along their jaw. "Like I've got you on a leash."

The silver ball went careening past the guard, and the words *Uh-oh! You Lose!* blinked on the rectangular screen.

"It's not . . ." They craned away. "It was never about that."

Zach went rigid. He froze behind them, tension ratcheting. "I thought we were joking around, I—"

"I can't do this." Something cracked behind their binder. Broke wide open and spilled into their body. Eli's eyes went hot, their throat clenched, and they brushed past Zach's outstretched arm, face pointed toward the floor.

"Can't do what—Eli, wait!"

Eli hurried through the café, pushed open the door, and ran. Their feet kicked hard against the concrete, carrying them through the warm summer night, around a couple holding hands and a person in a wheelchair, past smokers loitering outside a grungy bar and someone carrying an oversized bouquet. *I never felt trapped. Is that what you thought? Is that what I made you believe?* They hiccupped on a soft sob and darted into the Marriott. Their shoulders shook and their stomach jumped, coaxing the tightness in their throat to worsen and their lungs to burn. *It wasn't your fault*, they thought. *It wasn't your fault. It was never your fault.* They jabbed the elevator button over and over again.

Footsteps beat the polished floor behind them, and Zach grabbed their elbow. "Eli, what—" He paused, panting to catch his breath. He tried to meet their gaze, but they stared at the floor. "What's goin' on? What's wrong? Did I say—"

"No," they said miserably. "You didn't say anything wrong. You didn't *do* anything wrong."

The elevator doors opened. Eli stepped inside. Zach followed. He took Eli's shoulders, then their face, thumbs working at wet cheeks.

"What happened? What'd I do?" Zach asked. His brows pulled and his lips slackened. Worry etched lines into his forehead.

What'd I do?

Their face crumbled, chest heaved, and they shook their head. The truth bubbled up and out of them in starts and stops. "You didn't *do* anything. Not now, not then. I never felt leashed, Zach. It was never about space or . . . or feeling *trapped*. I wanted you *so* bad," they said, coughing through a hitched breath. Their voice was froggy and weak, soaked with emotion. "But Shockwave was expensive. It was so, *so* expensive, and you had the money—you *have* money."

They lifted their face and met his eyes, searching his sad, soft expression for any signs of anger. Nothing. "If I would've gone with you, I would've used all my savings, and I didn't have much. And top surgery is expensive, too. It's really expensive. You've never had to want, you've never had to worry about money or stability or bills, but I did. I *do*. And I want . . . I need to change." They gestured loosely to their upper half as the elevator rocked to a stop.

"And I knew if I told you I didn't have enough money to go, that it was Shockwave or surgery, you would've canceled everything. You would've skipped a workshop you'd been dying to go to and a city you wanted to live in, and you would've stayed. I couldn't let you do that, okay? I couldn't be the reason your life stopped moving. That's the truth. It was never about not loving you. I loved you. I *love* you," they blurted, and sucked in sharp, panicked gasps. "I'm sorry," they said, hardly above a whisper, and their face tensed into another sob. When the doors opened, they said it again, "I'm sorry," and rushed into the hallway.

Zach didn't follow. He stayed in the elevator, still as a corpse. Eli opened the door to their hotel room and braved a glance over their shoulder. Watched him lift his face and turn toward them. His mouth made the shape of their name—*Liz*—and the elevator closed.

♡   ♡   ♡

The shower ran hot on Eli's shoulders. They stood beneath the high-pressure water with their forehead resting on the tile. *I love you.* Their voice ricocheted in their mind, fluttering like a bird against a window. They'd said it accidentally, but it was the truth. Everything else, though? Yeah, the rest had been a fumbled attempt to make him understand why they'd broken both their hearts. They inhaled damp steam and let water flow over their face, rinsing away salt.

They wished Bodhi was with them. Wished they could've crawled into their mom's lap and let her stroke their hair. Wished they were at the diner, focused on food-running and taking orders, and not stuck alone, dwelling on being in love with someone who probably thought they were totally fucking pitiful. They soaped their body, shaved, scrubbed their face with milky cleanser, and stepped out of the shower. Took their time with their skin-care routine, dabbing moisturizer given to them by an ambassador—a brand they could never afford—onto their face and neck.

All the nice things they had, luxury makeup and organic skin-care products, bargained for by a platform and a following. Earned because Eli had learned how to sell themself and their skills, because they were *queer* and *new* and *fluid* and *fresh*. Sometimes reality chewed through the comfort their influencer status usually gave them, and they wondered if their skill had anything to do with their success. They shook the thought away, scolded themself for even thinking it, and aimed their phone at the sleek white bottles stacked on the silver bathroom tray: rose-hip serum, Moonbeam moisturizer, collagen eye cream. The lighting was a little off, but they snapped a picture anyway, tagged Sunbeam Skincare, and added the image to their Instagram story.

They stepped into a pair of underwear and pulled a loose T-shirt over their head, remembering Zach standing at the end of the hall, saying their name before the elevator shut. They tapped his text bubble and sighed, toothbrush stuck between their lips, thumbs hovering over the keys.

Can we

Backspace.

Do you think we could

Backspace. Backspace.

I know I kinda freaked out I'm

Knuckles rapped the door. Eli startled, whirling toward the sound. They rinsed their mouth and glanced at their reflection, eyes still puffy, cheeks still pinkened. Glanced at the time—12:01 a.m.—and knew it couldn't be anyone else. They walked into the entryway, curled their toes against the carpet, hand hovering over the knob, and angled their bare legs behind the door as they eased it open.

Zach was dressed in denim and a black shirt, his eyes heavy on their face. He raked his hand through his hair, lips parting and closing, searching, until he finally said, "You're right," and nodded curtly. "I would've stayed."

Eli rested their temple on the door and pulled, allowing him to step inside. Moonlight sneaked between the curtains and lit the dark room, and yellow light from the bathroom poured into the hallway. Shadows reigned everywhere else.

"I would've skipped Shockwave and stayed with you," he said, almost defensively.

"Or you would've tried to pay my way to New York," Eli said. They wrung their hands, watching him through their lashes. "And I couldn't let you do that."

For a moment, Zach went silent. His throat flexed. "I just wish I understood *why*."

"Because you've never had to worry about what other people might think of you if you can't do something yourself. You've always had the means, you've always had the support, and there's nothing wrong with that, but I didn't. I've always had to be my own safety net."

"But *I* could've been your safety net, Eli. I could've loaned you—"

"And then I would've *owed* you," they said, gentling their voice. "And that wasn't an option."

"Okay, but I would've *stayed* with you. We could've put off the workshop, you could've moved into the Malibu house with me. I would've taken care of you," he said, reaching for their hands. "I'll still take care of you."

Eli tried to smile. "I need to take care of myself, Zach."

"Okay, sure, but not when you're recovering from *surgery*, Liz." He sighed over their name.

They gripped his palm. "Surgery was a long way off. It's *still* a long way off. But I couldn't put a stop to your dreams and your future and your whole life, Zach."

"You were the most important part of my life," he said, exasperated. "You. *Us.* Fuck Shockwave, fuck New York. We mattered more."

Eli blinked away the sting in their eyes. Because they believed him. Because they regretted everything. Because they wished they could unbreak his heart. Because they couldn't believe he was standing in front of them, holding their hand, saying *us*.

"I'm sorry," they whispered. "I didn't know what to do. I thought letting you go was the right call. We had all these plans, and these huge dreams, and everything felt too . . . too perfect. It felt *real*, and anything that goddamn good had to be impossible because nothing *good* in my life has ever been easy. Except for you," they said, and folded against his chest. "Except for us."

Zach wrapped around them. He pressed his lips to the top of their head and hummed when they snaked their arms around his shoulders. "I wish you would've told me," he whispered, nosing at the soft dent behind their ear. "I knew you had issues with money, but we never talked about it. You could've told me about that, about your surgery, about everything."

"I didn't want to scare you," they confessed. "I didn't want you to think I was, like, radically changing even though I *am* radically changing. And the money stuff is just . . . it's really hard, okay? It's hard, and embarrassing, and there's no way to make you understand. I know that's harsh, but—"

"Look, I don't live your life, I don't walk in your shoes, but that doesn't mean I wouldn't have listened." His hands settled above the lace trim on their underwear. He met their eyes, gaze stern and unyielding. "If it's run from me or drop a truth bomb, I want you to tell me the truth. Even if you think I won't understand, even if you tell me in a text or a letter or *whatever*. I want you to tell me, all right? Hit me with the harshest shit you've got. I can take it."

"You never have to worry about anything, ever," they mumbled.

"That's not *exactly* true, but I hear you."

"When it comes to money," they clarified.

"Okay, fair."

"You didn't tell me you'd researched top surgery."

"Uh-huh, and you didn't tell me you were *considering* top surgery."

"Yeah, okay, that's fair, too." Eli closed their eyes and sighed. Zach's forehead tipped against their own. "Your parents hate me," they said.

"No, they don't." Zach laughed under his breath.

"They act like I'm a possum digging through their trash."

"Am I the trash?"

Laughter jumped into their throat. "Yeah," they said playfully. "Trash who lives in a Malibu beach house."

"Eli," he sent breath across their mouth. "C'mon, look at me."

They opened their eyes.

"I'm still here," he whispered.

"Yeah, you are. And I don't know why." They pushed their fingers through the trimmed hair at the base of his skull.

"Because I love you," Zach said, like someone would say *obviously.* "Because I've always loved you."

Eli exhaled sharply through their nose. "Hurting you was the hardest thing I've ever done."

"I wish you hadn't felt like you needed to."

"Me, too."

"New York sucks, by the way. Garbage everywhere, rats the size of Pomeranians," Zach said.

They laughed again. "Did you go to the Met?"

"No, museums were a me-and-you thing. I just latched on to Cassie, who told me everything about her husband and then babied me when I got sad-drunk and told her everything about you."

"Oh," Eli said, tripping into another surprised laugh. Zach laughed, too. They felt like a dick for disliking Cassie in the beginning, when jealousy had wormed into their heart. Felt like an idiot for not thinking Zach had missed them. They felt so, *so* much. "I'm sorry for everything."

"I'm sorry, too. For everything," he said, and kissed Eli firmly on the mouth.

Eli wanted to kiss him for hours. Wanted to kiss him until sunlight beamed through the window, and kiss him well into the morning, and kiss him in the shower, and kiss him, and *kiss him*. But despite the heat thrumming at the base of their spine, Eli was bone-fucking-tired.

"Stay with me," Eli mumbled, catching his lips in another kiss.

Zach nodded. He stripped down to his briefs and slipped under the comforter. Eli followed, tucking themself against Zach's solid chest. They traded slow touches. Zach traced patterns along their spine, and Eli thumbed at his collarbone.

I missed this, they thought, and linked their ankle over his foot.

"You were crying when you said you loved me," Zach whispered, voice hushed in the nearly silent room. "Which wasn't *exactly* how I pictured getting you back."

Eli tilted their face toward him. "I love you, Zach," they said, and brushed their nose against his. "I've loved you the whole time. When I let you go, when I saw you at FaeCon, when we drove to the observatory—I've loved you every day."

Zach kissed the side of their mouth.

They fell asleep with their palm on his chest, heartline to heartbeat.

♡   ♡   ♡

Eli woke to the blue hour casting a silver glow on Zach's shoulder. He slept on his side with his back to them, chest rising and falling. They watched him for a while. Traced his tattoo with their index finger and curled their arm around his waist, aligning their smaller body against him. He hummed pleasantly, clutched their wrist, and brought their hand to his sternum. They held on to him, dipping in and out of sleep, until city noises woke them a second time two hours later.

Zach rolled over, pawing cutely at his eyes. "Mornin'."

Eli smiled and pushed their face against the pillow. "Hi."

"Sleep okay?"

"Yeah, you?"

He nodded, hair askew, lashes fluttering, gorgeous and half awake. "Almost forgot you wake up like this," he said, and grabbed his phone off the nightstand, aiming at Eli. "Nobody's supposed to look good in the morning."

"Sorry," they teased.

"You should be."

Eli snatched his phone and crawled closer, sweeping their legs over his waist. Zach lifted one eyebrow and rested his knuckles on the pillow beside his head, gazing at them as they snapped a picture. His offered a lulled smile, and Eli blushed, capturing a streak of light bent across Zach's stubbled jaw. They tossed the phone onto the bed beside them and braced on their palms.

"We have the whole day to do whatever we want," they whispered. Their mouth hovered above his chin. "Any ideas?"

"Room service." He angled his smile upward, kissing them chastely. "Could go to the convention for a bit, come back here, sketch out some ideas for Sea City, find a sushi restaurant nearby, walk by the river. We've got options."

"Or . . ." they purred, and kissed him harder, deeper. Morning breath be damned. "We could stay here."

Zach ran one palm along their spine. Their shirt pooled around his wrist, exposing inch after inch of bare skin. Fingertips played on their navel, higher, tickling their ribs, *higher*, and slid between their small breasts. "Right here?"

Eli's breath hitched. "Right here."

They kissed him slowly. Pried at his mouth and welcomed the soft pass of his tongue behind their lips. Tasted his quivering breath, felt his thumb on their nipple, knew the eager arch of his hips, pushing between their thighs, searching for connection.

"Tell me you have a goalie," Eli mumbled.

Zach barked a laugh. He clutched their waist and rolled them over, framing their pulse with his teeth. "Yeah," he said, breathless, and bit their throat.

"*Thank God.*" They craned into his mouth, raked their fingers through his hair, and held on to him, hands growing urgent, bodies glowing hot, memorizing every sinuous movement and quick gasp.

Distantly, Eli thought, *Beyond*, but nearer, rising from somewhere deep in their core, they thought, *Fuck, I've missed this. I've missed you. I want this. I want it all.*

Zach left a bruise atop their skipping heartbeat.

Eli said, "Come here," and kissed him again.

CHAPTER TWENTY
Los Angeles

LOS ANGELES BURNED.

Wildfires charred the dry hills surrounding the city, chasing rabbits, deer, birds, and coyotes closer to cars and buildings. Eli changed the water in the oversized bowl behind Denny's and dumped a few cans of cat food into a silver saucer. Four pairs of eyes peered at them from beneath a nearby dumpster—a raccoon and her babies. They nudged the food toward the furry family with their foot.

"You'll get to go back home soon," Eli said, glancing at the brutal red sky.

In the kitchen, Eli took off their apron and tossed it into the laundry hamper next to the back door. They clapped Max on the shoulder as he scooted bacon around on the grill and squeezed through firemen and first responders in the dining room. Linda stood behind the register, counting bills back to a firefighter.

"Banana cream or key lime, honey?" Linda asked.

The firefighter pointed to the banana cream.

Eli grabbed a preboxed slice and handed it to her. "Stay safe out there."

"We'll do our best," the firefighter said, and walked into the hazy afternoon.

"Thanks for bein' here. I know you've got a lot going on with your wild-ass makeup stuff," Linda said. She heaved a tired sigh and tucked wiry silver strands behind her ear, squinting at the preboxed pie slices in the refrigerator. "Firefighters don't like key lime even when it's free, I guess."

"Need me here tomorrow?" Eli asked.

Linda tipped her head, considering. "I might. For the dinner rush, at least. Five hours, maybe. Could you swing it?"

Five hours of time and a half plus tips? They couldn't really say *No*. "Yeah, I can make it happen. I'm still good to take tonight off, yeah?"

Linda batted at the air in front of her. "Yeah, yeah, you've got Sunday and Monday off, too, and *yes*, I approved the vacation time next weekend. Juana is gonna beam your runway thing onto the big screen with her fancy tablet." She jabbed her finger at the blank TV hung in the corner, usually reserved for football and game shows. "Go on, get out of here. Pray these fires do the same."

Eli nodded and waved over their shoulder. "Fingers crossed. See you tomorrow."

Linda shooed them away and turned her attention to the ticket machine as it spat out another receipt.

Eli put their earpods in and stepped outside, sunglasses lowered over their eyes, bag slung over their shoulder, and made for the sidewalk. The Makeup Wars final was five days away. They had their design sketched, prosthetic molds carved and cooling on their bathroom counter, latex purchased, and silicone ready to heat and pour, but their cosplay still felt too big for them. From extended claws to stilts stuffed into hooves, full facial reconstruction to a pelvic attachment, it was bigger than anything they'd ever done, and Eli just . . . didn't know if they were ready to wear something completely, utterly extravagant, and they *really* didn't know if they had the skill to pull it off.

A car horn blared, and tires scraped the sidewalk beside them. They jumped like a cat, whipping toward the vehicle with their mouth open in an angry snarl, ready to shout, *Watch where you're fucking going—*

"Get in, dumbass," Bodhi hollered, flashing a toothy grin.

"You almost ran me over," Eli snapped, and flopped into the passenger's seat, tossing their bag by their feet. "Thanks for the ride, though. How's the new gig goin'?"

"I was on my way to your place anyway. Figured you could use a lift." She stuck her arm through the driver's-side window and flipped off the Mercedes behind her, inciting another string of annoyed honks, then yanked the wheel, pulled into traffic, and sped through the yellow light at the intersection. "I mean, it's an indie gig, so it's not great, but I'm getting paid, and the crew is cool. How's Firefighters Eat Free Friday going?"

"More like Firefighters Eat Free *until the Fires Are Gone.*" Eli sighed. They sank against the torn seat cover and kicked their heels onto the dashboard. "Which is awesome—I get it—but there's a lot of tired first responders in the city right now, and Denny's only has so many coffee pots."

Bodhi cringed. "Yeah, yikes. Busy, then?"

"*Very.* Did you get a chance to look over my stilt attachments for Sea City? I'm almost finished with the hooves, but I need to make sure the stilts'll fit the same way stilettos do. Otherwise, I'll have two big dents where my shins should be."

"Oh, yeah, as long as we've got a layer of foam between your feet and the fur covers, then it should look naturally tapered. Did you finish the headpiece yet?"

"I'm still working on the horns, but I'm almost done."

"*Niiiiice.* So, what're we ordering tonight? Chinese? There's that new Ethiopian place by Santee Alley, too. *Oh!* What about the Southern Shack on Sunset? Apple-butter biscuits sound—" She pinched her fingers near her mouth and smooched the air.

"No doubt I could go down on some barbecued chicken and fried green tomatoes," Eli said, eyeing Bodhi with an impish smile. "But I demand fried okra and those little jalapeño cornbread appetizers, too."

"Done!" She pulled into an empty space along the street outside Eli's apartment.

Bodhi ordered delivery from an app on her phone, trailing Eli up the staircase and into the air-conditioned apartment.

She toed off her sneakers. "Holy shit, you *cleaned*."

"Excuse me, I always clean," Eli exclaimed defensively.

"You do *not*. You, like, never actually—oh, wait, wait, I get it. You did the dicked-down deep clean, didn't you? Zach's totally been over here." She shimmied her shoulders and thrust her hips toward the bed. "Keepin' you busy, huh? Are you guys snapping nudes to each other yet? Officially rivals-to-lovers on Instagram?" She pitched her hips forward again, crudely gesturing at Eli. "Is there a *ship* name?"

"I'm going to throw you out the window," Eli said, far too calmly. It was true, though. Eli had unpacked their books and filled the bookshelf against the wall, organized their clothes, and dusted the coffee table.

"Who sent the first mirror shot?"

They rolled their lips together, suppressing a grin. "I did," they confessed.

Bodhi heaved through belly-shaking laughter and dropped her shawl on the floor. "*Of course* you did. Okay, so, tell me about Portland. What happened? What's goin' on? Are you two, like, *together* or?" She plopped on the floor next to their bed and prodded them with a pointed acrylic fingernail. "You've been working nonstop since you got back. Spill."

Eli sat cross-legged on their bed. They remembered ordering room service and thumbing powdered sugar off Zach's chin. Holding his hand, walking through Artist Alley at FanEx, kissing him on a bench facing the Willamette and mapping his body in their hotel room. They remembered coming home, Zach arriving at their apartment, jacket halfway down his arms, kissing them fiercely in the doorway as they pulled him inside. They'd touched each other like they were making up for lost time, like the plane ride and Eli's night shift had put too much distance between the two of them.

"I don't know if we're together, but we're definitely something," Eli said. They swallowed hard, smiling sheepishly, and pulled at the webbing between their fingers. "It feels good, obviously. But I don't know. It's hard—"

"I bet it is," Bodhi teased.

"Shut up," Eli hissed. "I want to win Makeup Wars—I *need* to win—and now me and Zach are," they swung their hands dramatically, "a *thing* again, and he's literally the only person left standing in my way, and I know he wants it, too, but . . ."

"But nothing," Bodhi interjected, and smacked her palms together. "You can be all up in Zach's business and still fight tooth and nail to win this competition."

"Sure, yeah, but it's *Zach*. Can I even win?"

"Yes." Bodhi channeled confidence, as always. "Look, just because you two are hooking up again—"

"We're not just hooking up," Eli said.

Bodhi cocked her head, lifted her eyebrows, and waited.

A knock sounded at the door, hitting *pause* on the conversation. Bodhi retrieved their takeout and thanked the delivery person before she sat back down, arranging Styrofoam containers on the floor around them.

"So the whole ugly-snot-crying in Oakland wasn't an *Oh, no, I had drunk escapades with my ex* tantrum?" Bodhi tossed a plastic fork at them.

"No, it was an *Oh, no, I still love my ex* tantrum," Eli said, and heaved a defeated sigh. "And then I freaked out, gross-cried in Portland, and kinda told him that."

"Kinda?"

"Yeah, I just, like, yelled it at him."

Bodhi forked okra into her mouth. "Okay, hold up, let me get the boning-to-breakdown timeline straight. You had sex with Zach in Oakland at Heroes Expo." She jabbed her fork at them. Eli nodded, and she continued, "And then you went to the convention in Portland, started gross-crying, and told Zach you're still in love with him?"

"Missing a few beats, but yeah, basically."

"And he did what?"

"Came to my room. We talked for a while, he told me he loved me, we spent the rest of the weekend together, and . . . Yeah, I don't know." Eli stabbed their chicken breast and brought the whole thing to their mouth, tearing a bite out of it. "It's like we're back to bein' *Zach and Liz*. Like nothing changed, except everything *did* change, everything is still changing, and I just . . . I don't know. I should've stayed away from him, because now he's back, and I don't know what he wants, and I know what *I* want, but I don't know if I'm allowed to want that."

"Chew your food," Bodhi blurted, flashing her palm.

Eli glared but chewed their food and swallowed. "I don't know how to go back to being how we were before I broke his fucking heart, Bodhi."

"Apparently, you didn't break him bad enough to keep him away. You hurt him, yeah. And now you're, like, self-flagellating to make yourself feel better instead of accepting what happened. You made a mistake; he didn't *accept* your mistake—lucky you—and now you two are workin' it out." She pushed the cornbread biscuits toward them and opened a container of apple butter. "To be completely honest, I don't think he flew all the way back to California just to win a scholarship he doesn't really need to begin with."

"Then why come back? And what does that even mean, he didn't *accept* my mistake?" Eli stuffed chicken, then cornbread, then a green tomato into their mouth. Barbecue sauce smudged their cheek and chin, and they blinked, watching Bodhi roll her eyes. They slurred, "What?"

"Are you serious?" Bodhi threw a handful of napkins at them. "Zach isn't the type of guy to put himself out there for the entire ding-dang world to see unless he's fighting for something, and I highly, *highly* doubt he needs to fight for Beyond. I mean, maybe I'm missing something, but it seems like he came back to shoot his shot with you, babe. That's what not accepting your mistake means. Coming back to get *you* back."

Eli scooped a blob of butter onto a biscuit and shoved the cornbread into their mouth. Their chest tightened painfully. They thought back to every moment spent with Zachary Miller: their heartsick argument in the makeup trailer, counting stars as they lay together in the bed of his truck, holding his hand in a makeshift movie theater, smoking a joint with him in a dark parking lot, kissing him hard outside a crowded nightclub. All those instances, every single touch, had been a choice. Zach had placed himself directly in front of Eli. He'd followed them, reached for them, returned to them, and, regardless of how hard they'd tried to stay away, they'd spent every second reaching back.

"What should I do?" Eli whispered.

"Do you want to be with him?" Bodhi asked.

"Yeah, I do. I really do."

"Can you be with him and beat him, too?"

They met her eyes and nodded reluctantly. "I don't have a choice."

"If he loves you, he'll be expecting that," she said, and lifted her brows.

Eli nodded, casting their gaze to the half-finished headpiece draped over stacked sci-fi paperbacks on their nightstand. "Yeah," they said, and thought about Zach and Beyond and their future. "I hope so."

Bodhi and Eli idled outside the Miller beach house. Firelight stained the night Mordor red and reflected off the rippling black water, gilding the square two-story building. Eli inhaled steadily and nodded, studying the wide windows and gray garage door.

"Well, at least it isn't a mansion." Bodhi laughed sarcastically.

"Close enough," Eli said. They gave her a smile. "Thanks for the ride."

"Anytime. We're still on for a costume design session, right?"

"Yeah, I'll have the hooves ready for a test run. Headpiece, too."

"Oh-kay," she sang, nudging her chin toward the sleek, shoebox-shaped house. "Well, good luck with the *talk*."

Eli slid out of the passenger seat and slung their backpack over their shoulder. "See you tomorrow."

"See you," Bodhi said, and pulled away from the curb.

Breathe. Their binder stretched tight across their chest, a comforting squeeze. The beach house Zach called his home away from home—the place his parents typically reserved for high-paying tourists—looked entirely normal in this neighborhood. Every house was unique, some modern, some vintage, all fixed with a price tag Eli couldn't imagine. High six figures, probably seven. Mostly rentals, cutely labeled *summer chateau* or *getaway house*. They followed the path from the sidewalk to the porch, lined with chunky aloe plants and trimmed grass, and traced the bronze numbers next to the door: 1349. When they knocked, the porch light blinked to life.

They waited. Knocked. Waited. Anxiety knotted in their stomach. They rang the doorbell.

Zach opened the door wearing sneakers and navy joggers. Sweat slicked his chest and arms and beaded on his forehead. He panted, plucking the wireless headphones from his ears. "Hi," he said, bewildered.

"Hey, sorry," Eli said, glancing at his collarbones and veined forearms. "You said I could come by anytime." They flicked their eyes around his biceps and finally landed on his loose smile. *Damn him.* They shrugged, offering a lopsided grin. "Surprise."

"You weren't out here long, were you? I was on the treadmill."

Of course you were. "Just a few seconds."

"Good," he said, and propped the door open.

Eli stepped inside, tipping their head back to take in the high ceilings and stark white paint. A floating staircase led to a loft, and a beautifully assembled leather sofa filled the living space in the center of the ground floor. It was everything Eli had expected—*unreal.* The entire rear wall of the house was glass paneled, facing an infinity pool surrounded by baby palms. Stone stairs led to the beach, where waves rolled over golden sand. A high-end treadmill sat at an incline next to the couch, angled toward a flatscreen hung above a modern fireplace.

They laughed in their throat and placed their backpack on the kitchen island. "Nice place, rich kid," they said, leveling a teasing smile at Zach.

"Can't complain." Zach scrubbed his palm over the back of his head and gestured to the stainless-steel appliances in the airy kitchen. "There's juice and iced tea. I was gonna . . ." He trailed off.

Eli hoped he was blushing and slack-jawed, watching them peel off their shirt. They shimmied out of their denim shorts and kicked away their boots, hopping on one foot toward the back door as they tugged at their sock. They left their clothes on the smooth wood floor and glanced over their shoulder.

"Go swimming with me," they said, rallying confidence and trusting themself to be desirable, or playful, or sexy— *whatever*. Hoping Zach would see them as Liz, the person he wanted to be with, and Eli Peterson, the makeup artist who fully intended to kick his ass next weekend.

Eli could be both people. They *had* to be both people.

They left their second sock on the concrete and leaped into the water. Zach followed, ditching his clothes and diving into the pool. He snagged their ankle. Eli yelped, barking out laughter, and splashed him when he surfaced.

"How's your final cosplay comin' along?" Eli asked. They circled him, gliding through the water, tasting ash and brine and chlorine. The pool lights glowed, submerged in the slippery tile, casting a green glow on Eli's beige binder and Zach's pale skin.

Zach spit water at them and said, "I don't think we're supposed to share trade secrets."

They dropped, kicked, and twirled through the water. Breached in the shallow end, trapping Zach against the lip of the pool. "True." They kissed his wet mouth. "You still haven't told me why you entered the competition. You have Shockwave under your belt, you could pay for Beyond. Why bother?"

"My *parents* could pay for Beyond," he corrected, and took their lip between his teeth.

Eli hummed. "And?"

"And I wanted something for myself. My mom and dad were completely against Makeup Wars. Shocking, I know," he said sarcastically. "I've never done anything for me. Shockwave was our thing, and that," he searched their face, "didn't go as planned. Makeup Wars was something I could do on my own, for *me*, and then you showed up at FaeCon and—"

"And?"

"And I couldn't look anywhere else."

"You really didn't think I'd enter the competition, too?"

"I didn't know what you'd do, honestly." He thumbed at the strap on their soaked binder and ducked around them, swimming toward the deep end of the rectangular pool. "I know I've got it good, but my family wants me to go to a fancy four-year college, same as yours, and they're pushing me to do literally *anything* except makeup, same as yours. Winning Makeup Wars and getting this scholarship is my way to prove I can do this on my own if I have to."

Eli slunk closer. Zach floated like a crocodile, eyes just above the water. For so long, they'd assumed Zach would get his way, carve a path for himself in the industry regardless of his parents' disapproval. They'd imagined he'd swipe a credit card with the family name stamped into the plastic and do whatever he wanted. With access to money and comfort, why wouldn't he?

"So you're telling me your parents wouldn't help you if you made it clear makeup was your thing? They wouldn't send you to the best school? Get you the best kit? Buy you the best product?" Eli asked.

Zach gave a mean smirk. "They wouldn't *want* to."

"But they would, because they *can*."

"I'd never hear the end of it."

Eli nodded. If they drove their point any deeper, they'd hit a nerve. They sighed through their nose, gaze steady on Zach's face. Their heart panged, and even though they knew how it felt to hope for recognition, for trust in their passion, for faith from people who had never believed in them, they steeled themself against the urge to wilt. Pride might've been

Zach's driving force, as it was for Eli. But unlike him, Eli had nowhere soft to land and no one to catch them if they fell. They had to be their own damn safety net. They had to work twice as hard with half as much to make a name for themself.

In the end, Zach had the promise of a secure future whether his parents liked his career choice or not, and Eli didn't.

Zach scooped his hands under Eli, steadying their thighs around his waist beneath the water. "I know you want this," he said, nosing at their cheek. "I know Beyond is your dream."

"I have a few dreams," they said. They met his eyes, palm coasting from the band on his briefs to the center of his chest. "You're my dream—me and you—we're my dream, too."

He kissed them, lips slippery against their mouth. "Are you sure?"

"I've never been unsure about you. About wanting to be with you, about wanting to make a life with you. But I was scared, and I'm not anymore," they said and clutched his jaw, kissing him deeper. Chlorinated water sloshed around their shoulders, and Eli inhaled a campfire-scented breath through their nose. "It's me and you, right? No matter what. After the competition, we still have us."

Zach nodded, pupils blown, lips catching Eli's chin as he spoke. "Yeah, it's always me and you."

"Don't take it easy on me, Haunt Master," they said, tracing his ears with their thumbs. "I want to win because I beat the best. Not because my boyfriend gave me a head start."

Zach flashed a wolfish grin. "Don't worry, babe," he teased, stealing another kiss. "You won't beat me." He latched his hands around their waist and tossed them into the deep end.

Eli swam to the surface and gulped in a deep breath, coughing through loud, hiccupping laughter.

Zach snatched their foot and dragged them back to him.

"I'm gonna kick your ass next weekend," they said, blushing and hopeful and disastrously in love.

Zach smiled. "You're gonna try," he whispered, and kissed them again.

CHAPTER TWENTY-ONE

Seattle–Sea City Comic Con

SEATTLE BROUGHT SMOKELESS SKIES AND PANDEMONIUM. Lime-green banners—SEA CITY COMIC CON!—hugged the skywalk between the convention center, situated on one side of a busy downtown street, and the conference center on the other side. Beneath it, rippling in a cool breeze, another sign stretched across the glass skywalk. On the left, Zach smiled crookedly, on the right, Eli grinned, and between the two of them, MAKEUP WARS: THE FINAL RUNWAY filled the center of the banner. Eli stood on cement steps, staring at their massive face on display in the middle of the city. *That's me.* They reminded themself to breathe. *Holy shit, that's us.*

"Damn, this is the real deal," Bodhi said. She rolled her suitcase to a stop and glanced over her shoulder, fingering ink-black hair away from her face. "Baby, you got that?"

"Yeah, I just packed *way* too many shoes," Stella hollered, and *click-clacked* across the sidewalk, hauling a bulging suitcase. "Way too much everything, to be completely—oh, my

God, Eli!" She flung her arm toward the banner, pointing excitedly. "You're con-famous!"

Bodhi scrunched her eyebrows together and lowered her sunglasses, following Stella's index finger. "Holy fucking hotcakes!"

Eli hadn't looked away. They watched light play on the laminated sign, noticed a tiny imperfection in their razor-edged cat-eye, studied their own smile, and remembered what they were there to do.

Take home the Makeup Wars crown. Win the scholarship. Don't eat shit in their stilted hooves onstage. *Definitely* don't let their stupidly handsome high school sweetheart distract them.

They lifted their phone and snapped a picture of the banner, then handed their phone to Bodhi.

"Okay, ready?" they asked.

Bodhi bounced in place. "Yes, okay, so . . . little to the left. Good, yeah—oh, you goofball, c'mon—one more . . . aaaaannd cool. I took a bunch." She slapped their phone into their palm and gave an exaggerated nod. "That's you, dude," she whispered, nodding toward the banner. "And your whole-ass boyfriend. You two are, like, literally the *worst* at staying broken up, by the way. A cutthroat contest couldn't even—"

"I know, I know," Eli said, swatting her arm.

"I'm just messing with you." She grabbed the handle of her suitcase. "Can we get this stuff to wherever it's supposed to go? I'm seriously starving."

They nodded. "It's on the fourth floor, I think. Right outside one of the Exhibitor Halls in the," they opened the instructional email and squinted at their phone, "Atrium Lobby."

Eli, Bodhi, and Stella dragged their suitcases and makeup kits through the doors and into the lobby, following stacked escalators to the fourth floor. Across the narrow room, a gaping doorway punched a hole in the wall, leading to one of two Exhibitor Halls. Signs topped brightly lit booths. Plushies, comic books, and memorabilia filled shelves, and collectible items were placed safely in locked cases. The trio took the path adjacent to the escalators. They flashed their badges for security and walked into the Atrium Lobby, a sunny room surrounded by an outdoor garden where cosplay photographers arranged camera flashes and tripods.

"Is that it?" Stella asked, pointing at a door labeled GREEN ROOM—MW.

"Yeah, it's gotta be," Eli said. They wheeled their case toward the room and propped the door open with their foot. They almost dropped their kit, shocked by the familiar face smiling in front of a half-filled makeup station.

Cassie Anne Montgomery winked. "Hey, finalist," she said. "Long time, no see."

"Of course," Eli blurted, laughing gleefully. "You're Zach's assistant, huh?"

"Obviously," she said. Her nose wrinkled above a bright grin. She tipped onto one foot, glancing around Eli. "You must be Bodhi."

"That's me." Bodhi rolled her suitcase to a stop next to the unoccupied station.

From the doorway, Zach's raspy voice sounded. "Hey, Stella," he said, earning a friendly response, and walked into the room, palm skimming Eli's nape as he passed by. "You finally made it."

"Airport was a hellhole," Eli said. They gestured at Stella, who raked her fingernails through her long locks and waved. "Cassie, this is Stella, Bodhi's partner. Stella, this is Cassie."

While the women exchanged introductions, Zach leaned against the counter attached to Eli's newly claimed station. He was dressed in torn denim and a fitted black *Castlevania* shirt, arms folded casually across his chest.

"Did you see the Makeup Wars memo?" Zach asked. His boyish smile was wry and confident.

Eli furrowed their brow and pulled their phone out, hurriedly switching off airplane mode. "What memo?"

"The one about the final promo video. We're supposed to meet a videographer in the penthouse at the Sheraton in an hour."

"An *hour?*" Eli gaped, whipping from Zach to Bodhi. "Is it full-face or do they want us in cosplay or—".

"Makeup, yes. Cosplay, optional," Zach said. He jutted his chin toward Bodhi, Cassie, and Stella. "If you three don't mind setting up the stations, it'll give us some extra time to get ready for this video thing we have to shoot."

"For sure. We're good here," Cassie said, nodding.

"Yeah, we've got this. Text me when you're done and we'll meet for dinner," Bodhi said.

Eli stuffed a few things into their travel case and followed Zach into the Atrium Lobby. Zach brushed his fingers against their knuckles. He didn't take their hand until they were outside the convention center, walking toward one of the con-sponsored hotels. Eli gripped his palm tightly.

"Can you believe we're here? In the finale?" Eli asked.

Zach huffed out a laugh. "Yeah, I can. Can't you?"

"Still a little surreal, honestly."

The pair took long strides down the crowded sidewalk and dipped through the double doors into the Sheraton Hotel. The bar was bustling with con-goers, writers, directors, and special guests. People streamed into the lobby, waiting in front of the concierge to check in. Zach steered Eli toward the elevators. Once they were inside and the doors had slid shut, he kissed them.

"Are we really supposed to keep this a secret until after the runway?" he asked, nibbling their jaw.

"When *this* comes to Instagram and TikTok, yes. It's not like we have to pretend not to be together in front of our friends, I'd just rather avoid random people on the Internet hinting at one of us letting the other win. It'd be a shit show, and you know it," Eli said.

"Oh, you mean *you* letting *me* win, since I'm *going* to win," Zach purred, and stole another kiss.

"Uh-huh, sure." Something fierce and fiery shot through their chest. They snapped their teeth around his lip before the elevator opened to a single door at the end of a short hallway.

Zach unlaced their linked fingers and stuffed his hands into his pockets.

Eli immediately missed the weight of his palm, but they lifted their fist and knocked.

The door was flung open. Eli startled. Zach jumped, too. A person with short ginger hair wearing tight denim overalls and a striped crop top stood before them. A Makeup Wars volunteer badge was clipped to their lanyard, and they regarded Eli, specifically, like a hawk.

"Genevieve Saxon. Ze, zir," ze said.

Oh. Eli nodded. "Eli Peterson. They, them."

"Zach. He, him, and his," Zach said.

"Great. I'm your videographer. Feel free to touch up before we start. I've got a green screen against an empty wall, and we'll do some shots outside on the balcony, too," Genevieve said, and gestured to a table stocked with refreshments. "Soda, water, tea, we've got it all. Help yourself."

"Thanks," Eli said. They glanced at Zach and shrugged toward the bathroom. "Want any eyeliner? Contour?"

"You wanna do my makeup for the promo video broadcasting our epic cosplay duel?"

"It'll be our secret," they said.

He laughed and followed them into the bathroom, plopping down on the closed toilet lid. "Nothing too heavy. Gray eyeliner, maybe. Just cheekbone contour."

"No falsies?" They took his jaw between their fingers and angled his chin upward.

"Not today," he said, grinning sheepishly.

Eli sharpened Zach's cheekbones with flat brown powder and smoothed a smoky pencil along his lash line. "Mascara?"

"Yeah, probably a good idea," Zach said. He traced the inside seam of Eli's jeans, sending a hot arrow down their spine.

They coated his lashes in black mascara and dabbed balm on his lips. He opened his mouth and caught their thumb with his teeth.

"You're distracting," they mumbled, and fought back a feverish blush.

"I could say the same about you." He met their eyes and stepped away, leaving them red-faced and alone in the spacious bathroom.

Damn him. They ignored their too-warm skin, calmed the flutter in their belly, and went to work on their own face. Smoothed cream-based violet shadow on their eyelids, created an angular look with contour and highlight, and penciled their brows into beautiful arches. Their nerves grew. In twenty-four hours, they'd be standing onstage in front of the judges, hoping their biggest cosplay to date won them the opportunity they'd always dreamed about. Hoping they'd executed their skills to perfection, hoping they'd done enough, hoping they *were* enough.

"Eli, we're ready for you," Genevieve called.

They gave their reflection a once-over. Brows, on point. Lips, glossed. Highlight, subtle but effective. They blew out a breath and walked into the suite, following Genevieve's outstretched arm toward the green screen.

"Okay, no vocals for this one. All I need you two to do is stare each other down, then turn toward me and give the camera nice big smiles. We'll shoot a few versions of this so the marketing team has options, all right?" Ze waited for Eli and Zach to nod before ze nodded, too. "Good. You two look gorgeous. Let's get this thing going!"

Eli faced Zach. *Seriously, damn him.* He was so handsome it hurt.

"Okay, and," Genevieve paused, nudging zir hands together in the air. "Can we get a little . . . ?"

Zach's brow ticked upward. He stepped into Eli's space, chest to chest, hands parallel. Eli tipped their head and met his eyes, and their heart skipped. They wanted to slide their finger through his belt loop and tug him even closer.

"All right, good, good. Let's do a countdown. On three, face me. One . . . two . . ." Genevieve held zir hand in the air and nodded, holding up three fingers.

Eli tilted their head and turned to face the camera. Zach did the same, except Genevieve laughed.

"Eyes on *me*, Zachary," ze said.

"My bad," he said under his breath, and flicked his gaze from Eli to the camera.

Ze nodded curtly. "Again."

Eli and Zach went through the motions—facing each other, sweeping toward the lens, smiling confidently—until Genevieve had enough material to send to the marketing team. Then ze ushered the pair onto the balcony and took individual shots. Eli rested their elbows on the railing, shoulders loose, ankles crossed, lolling their head in a lazy motion. They watched Zach watching them. Let their lips gently part, felt their heartbeat quicken, and inhaled deeply against their constrictive binder. Eli met his hungry eyes and smiled for Genevieve's camera. Being wanted by Zach like *that*, dressed in men's clothes, presenting as a masculine person, thinned their skin and made everything feel closer to the bone. Raw and electric.

"Perfect, thanks, Eli," Genevieve said. Ze pointed at the round garden table. "Zach, do you mind sitting on that?"

Zach crossed the balcony and hoisted himself onto the table, seated with his arms resting on his thighs, looking at the camera, then at Eli through his doe-like lashes. He stared at them, flexed his hands, arched his back, and looked powerful and curious and *different*.

Eli wanted to tear him apart. The thought made them blush.

Genevieve finished snapping photographs. "Nicely done. You'll see these hit social media sometime tonight." Ze bowed zir head politely. "Thanks for being easy models."

"Thank you for the shoot," Eli said. They grabbed their travel cosmetic bag out of the bathroom and waved to Genevieve, stepping into the elevator as the suite door swung shut.

At the click of the latch, Zach took them by the face. He framed their cheeks with his palms, tugging until their mouths met in a hard kiss. Eli dropped their bag. Their eyeshadow palette was probably cracked, and their compact might've broken, too, but they didn't care. The elevator closed and Zach crowded them against the cool silver wall. His breath trembled between their lips, palm trailing their throat, their sternum, clutching their rib cage. Zach kissed a fever into them. He kissed them until their lips were swollen, until they were light-headed and needy, until the elevator dinged and Zach detached from them, stepping backward.

The elevator opened. Zach panted, face flushed, staring at Eli. "We could be late for dinner," he said, voice hoarse.

"Yeah," they said, nodding aggressively. "Let's be late for dinner."

CHAPTER TWENTY-TWO
Seattle

THE BUSY KITCHEN AT PHO MADNESS SENT HOT AIR BIL-
lowing into the dining room. Eli sat between Bodhi and
Cassie, across from Stella and Zach. They tried not to think
about what they'd done in their hotel room an hour ago and
distracted themself with a rose-gold Magical Girl ring they'd
bought at Heroes Expo. They rolled the warm metal between
their knuckles and thumbed at the key-shaped gemstone set
in sharp prongs.

Cassie laughed, and Bodhi said, "No, no, I'm serious—
weddings are the worst," and cooks hollered in Vietnamese
behind the pickup window. Eli couldn't focus. Anxiety
and excitement bubbled inside them like a witch's brew,
stoked by a fast, clumsy hookup with their ex-new-*whatever*-
boyfriend and the finale looming on the horizon.

Zach knocked his boot against Eli's shoe under the table.
"No more secrets. What're you cosplaying?"

"No, nope, do *not* answer that," Bodhi bellowed, stretching her arm between him and Eli. "No sneak peeks for the enemy."

"Oh, c'mon. Enemy? *Really?*" Zach rolled his eyes. "It's not like I can steal their idea. We've been working on prostheses and costuming for two weeks."

"Uh-huh, so you can wait a whoppin' twelve hours to see what they're gonna beat you with," she said smugly.

Zach met their eyes, swinging their conjoined ankles back and forth. "Fine," he said through a groan, and winked.

Eli couldn't place how they felt in that moment. Loved, yes. But they felt something else, too. Underestimated, maybe. Okay, not *exactly* underestimated, but delicate. *Treated* delicately. A part of them warmed under Zach's tenderness, but a bigger, meaner part of them wanted Zach to fight for Beyond. They wanted him to scratch and bite and brawl for it, because that's what they would've done. That's what they *were* doing. But there was Zachary Miller, sweet and talented and hidden in their heart, disgustingly calm on the eve of a life-changing day.

Their phone buzzed in their pocket. They stood, swiping their finger across the screen. "Hold on a sec, we're at a restaurant." They ducked around the fish tank next to the host station and stepped into the cool evening. "Okay, hi," they said, sighing, and held their phone out, smiling at their parents.

The screen blurred, but both of their faces appeared. "Hey, honey," Claire said, and at the same time, Gary asked with a laugh, "How's Seattle? Have you been to the big needle thing yet?"

Eli leaned against the wall next to the window and shook their head. "Seattle's good. No, we haven't been to the Space Needle yet. We found a Vietnamese place with a pho-eating challenge, though. Biggest bowl in the city, I guess."

"Well, that sounds fun. Bodhi's with you, right?" Claire asked.

"Yeah, she's inside with Stella and Zach. Cassie's here, too. She competed with us for a while."

"I still need to have a talk with Mr. Miller," Gary said, raising his brows at the screen.

"Dad, *stop*," Eli crowed. "He's fine, we're fine."

"Let the kid live a little," Claire said, and swatted Gary on the chest. "The catwalk is tomorrow, right? At six?"

"Runway," Eli corrected, chuckling.

"Same thing," Claire and Gary said in tandem.

They missed their parents. Right then, all they wanted was to link their arm around their mom's elbow and explore the convention center with her. Take their dad by the wrist and show him the extravagant prostheses waiting in the green room. *Yes*, they'd say, *I made this, I did this, I'm doing this.*

"You're gonna beat him, baby," Gary said. "That guy doesn't stand a chance."

Claire swatted him again. "*Guy?* Be nice! This is Zach you're talking about. He's their . . ." She narrowed her eyes at the screen. "Boyfriend? Partner? Are you two back—"

"Yes, Mom, we're back together. 'Boyfriend' is fine," Eli said, tempering their grin. "I miss you guys. Wish you were here."

"Us, too, sweetheart," Claire said. Sadness tinged her voice, but she smiled, eyes creased with fine lines. "Go eat your soup. Call us before you get onstage, okay?"

Eli nodded, but their smile wobbled. "Will do," they said, and cleared their throat. "I love you."

"Love you, too," Claire said.

Gary leaned toward the phone. "Love you, kid. You've got this."

For the first time, Eli felt *elated* after talking to their parents about something makeup related. They painted on a grin and waved at the screen. "Thanks, Dad. Bye."

Their parents waved, then the call ended. Eli caught the outline of their reflection in the screen. Zach's flat-billed hat flipped backward on their head, high-necked shirt circling the base of their neck, violet makeup still flashy despite rolling around on the floor with Zach after the video shoot. They blew out a breath and blinked away the sting in their eyes.

You're not alone. Realistically, they knew that. Bodhi was waiting for them. Stella was, too. No matter what, they came out of Makeup Wars with Zach at their side. But somehow, for some reason, they wanted Claire to tell them everything would be okay. They wanted mom comfort and familiar perfume. They typed out a text.

> **Eli Peterson:** do you think I can do this?
> **Mama 🏵:** OF COURSE I DO!!
> **Mama 🏵:** ♡ 👍 🐎

Eli gave a short laugh and thumbed wetness from beneath their lashes, doing their best not to smudge their eyeliner. *Finally*, they thought, *a little parental fucking faith.* They'd waited years for that, and now, right there, after weeks and months of work, their life was coalescing into something they'd never, ever imagined.

I can do this. I have to do this.

"Eli, hey!" Cassie leaned around the open door. She tucked her short honey-brown hair behind her ears and smiled, tilting her head suspiciously. "You good? We got spring rolls."

"Yeah, just," they wiggled their phone, "talking to my parents."

She nodded, but her eyes narrowed. "Is everything okay?"

"Oh, you know, just goin' though the motions," they said, wincing around a forced grin. "The motion right now is internal meltdown in case that wasn't obvious."

"Don't worry, it was," she said, and walked over to them.

"Great, awesome. Love that for me." Eli sighed and tipped their head against the pockmarked wall. Of course, Cassie could sense whatever bullshit was going on in their head. She was fun and skilled and intuitive and, most of all, Zach's friend. Maybe his *best* friend. They peeled their tongue off the roof of their mouth and met her gaze. "I'm scared," they confessed, smiling thinly. "Like, run-into-the-woods-and-become-an-Ewok scared."

Cassie snorted out laughter. "Of what, exactly?"

"Losing."

"What makes you think you'll lose?"

Eli gestured wildly to the window. "Well, Zach is, literally, the best makeup artist I've ever met, so—"

"So?"

"If it's me or him, the judges will probably choose him." *And my heart will be completely broken.* They inhaled a quaking breath. "I think we all know that."

"According to Zach, he already won," Cassie said. Her eyebrow lifted, freshly punched with a silver hoop. "But I don't think he was talking about Makeup Wars."

Eli chewed their lip. "I don't know, Cassie. I just, I thought I'd made peace with all this, the competition shit, but I *love* him," they said, chasing the last three words with laughter. "And I want to take something from him, something he wants, too. What does that make me?"

Cassie flicked her eyes from their sneakers to their face. "Ambitious," she said, nodding. "Passionate enough about something and some*one* that you're driving yourself crazy wondering which great love of your life you deserve to have even though you've already got one in your pocket. You being successful won't hurt him, Eli. No doubt, his cosplay is good, *really* good, but it's that good because he's positive he's competing against the best."

"I'm bringing my best, I'm aiming to win, I *have to* win," they said, hushed and low. "But I don't want to hurt him again."

Cassie sighed through her nose. "Sure, fine, but would you be hurt if *he* won? Really, seriously *hurt*?"

The thought made Eli pause. Being successful shouldn't hurt the people they cared about. Logically, they knew that. Jealousy? Fine, it happened. Disappointment? Sure. But . . .

They stared at the sky, then at the cement, and finally at Cassie. "No," they said. "I'd be devastated about losing Beyond—not because he'd won. I'd be happy for him, obviously. But it wouldn't hurt me, it wouldn't change our..." They shrugged, circling their hands. "*Us*. It wouldn't change us."

"Then what the hell are you so worried about? Zach's been about you and *only* you since I met him. Like, he's completely obsessed with you, dude. Sorry, is 'dude' okay?"

Eli laughed. "Yeah, 'dude' is fine."

Cassie took a step backward and pointed over her shoulder with her thumb. "So can we eat dinosaur-sized bowls of pho, or should we tackle another internal meltdown?"

Eli pushed away from the wall and slung their arm over her shoulder. "One meltdown is enough for me," they said, and stumbled into the restaurant. "Thanks, Cassie."

She took their hand. "Anytime."

♡   ♡   ♡

Midnight came and went, and Eli couldn't sleep.

They lay awake, shifting their attention from the ceiling to their dimmed phone screen, doom-scrolling through Instagram. They watched a few closed-captioned makeup tutorials with the sound off and turned onto their side. After arranging a pillow between their knees, flopping around like a dolphin, and kicking uselessly at the sheets, they gave up and slipped out of bed.

Bodhi and Stella slept soundly, curled together on the other bed, and didn't stir when Eli toed on their shoes, pulled a hoodie over their head, and crept into the hallway. They knuckled at their eyes and trudged toward the elevator. Exhaustion filled their body, fighting against excitement they couldn't quiet. *Makeup Wars. Beyond. Zach. Their future.* Everything bounced around inside them, shaking and buzzing.

Where do I go after this?

What happens if I lose?

They stepped into the elevator and hit the top button. They could enroll at a junior college, take bullshit classes, study a bullshit major, get a bullshit job doing something they hated. They could keep working at Denny's, save as much money as possible, choose between scheduling top surgery or financing one of the short-term programs at Beyond. They could move back home, maybe. Or limp into Zach's beach house like a stray and let him take care of them, pay for their things, spoil them.

Abso-fucking-lutely not.

The elevator dinged, opening to a glass-walled room with an empty liquor station. The stools were flipped on their seats, lined neatly atop the bar. Past the patio doors, people gathered on the rooftop in small groups, lounging in wicker chairs and hovering around tables. Eli pulled their hood up and walked into the night. The moon curved like a white scythe, stars sprinkled the sky, and Seattle glowed, peppering the darkness with neon signs and luminescent windows. They walked to an empty table near the thick barricade around the edge of the roof and propped themself on their elbows, looking out over the city.

If anything, Eli had experienced something beyond their imagination. They'd competed with the best amateur makeup artists on the scene. They'd risen to the top of the pack, made a name for themself, stood onstage in four different cities, and showed the world their work. If they didn't win, at least they would always be Eli Peterson who'd placed *second* in the very first Makeup Wars.

Behind them, Zach said, "Hoot hoot, night owl." His voice was bedroom-soft, and his palms were gentle on Eli's shoulders, announcing his presence before he wrapped his arms around their waist. "Can't sleep, either?"

"How're you always finding me?" Eli asked, smiling as Zach nuzzled their nape.

"This time was purely coincidence." He rested his chin on their shoulder, body pressed against their bowed spine and wide hips. "I was prepainting. Needed to get away from the fumes for a minute."

"Last-minute prepainting," they teased, drawing out each word. "Zachary Miller, you procrastinator."

"Yeah, yeah." He sighed and turned to look at them. "I guess my parents aren't coming tomorrow. They've got a thing with an energy-drink rep for whatever yacht party they're planning. I'm pretty sure they could've rescheduled, but," he trailed off, frowning, "I'll just cancel their flights and send pictures."

"Yeah, my parents aren't coming, either. I couldn't find any round-trip tickets for under, like, four hundred, so." Sadness panged in their chest, but they forced a smile and bumped their nose against his cheek. "Guess it's just us."

"You nervous?"

"Yeah, aren't you?"

"Little bit."

"I'm cosplaying Saint Harlow from *Chaos Reign*," they said. "Don't tell Bodhi I told you."

Zach smothered a laugh against their neck. "The faun wizard, nice," he said appreciatively. "I'm doin' Del Toro's Angel from *Hellboy*."

Eli blinked, taken aback. "That's a lot of work."

"It'll be fun. Saint Harlow won't be a walk in the park."

"Yeah, no, stilts are scary," they said.

Zach tipped his face closer and kissed them on the lips.

According to Zach, he's already won.

Eli smiled against his mouth. "I'm gonna kick your ass with my faun wizard," they whispered playfully.

"Not a chance," he rasped, and kissed them again.

Maybe Eli had already won, too.

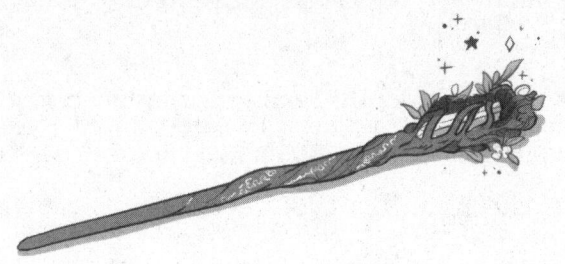

CHAPTER TWENTY-THREE

Seattle-Sea City Comic Con

ELI CHECKED, RECHECKED, AND TRIPLE-CHECKED THEIR station in the Makeup Wars green room at Sea City Comic Con. They were trembling—not great for makeup application—while two volunteers and Genevieve, the videographer, stood next to the door. Bodhi arranged paint tubes and glue cups, plugged in the hair dryer, and primped each flower strewn through Eli's detached headpiece. Across the room, Zach and Cassie hung the massive black wings Zach had built for his cosplay on temporary wall hooks.

One of the volunteers clapped. "All right, finalists! You have three hours to complete your cosplay and thirty minutes for last looks. The judges will arrive backstage for prejudging before you walk the runway. After that, you'll be given two hours to take off your cosplay—completely optional—and rejoin the judges onstage for the final announcement. For transparency, the Makeup Wars marketing team prefers you to be camera ready for the final announcement, so please try to look your best with or without makeup."

Zach chuckled. "Don't look completely fuckin' haggard. Got it."

"We'll begin the challenge with Eli and Zachary seated," the other volunteer said, gesturing to the studio chairs. He waited for Zach and Eli to take their seats, glanced at his watch, and nodded to Genevieve.

Panic bloomed white-hot in Eli's veins. They clutched the armrests on the tall studio chair, staring at their reflection. They hadn't slept much. They had nibbled a granola bar to calm their stomach in the morning and drunk a prepackaged protein shake for lunch. Their insides were tippy and too light.

This is it.

They shifted their gaze sideways and met Zach's eyes in the mirror attached to his station.

The volunteer nodded. "Your time starts ... now!"

Eli threw themself from the studio chair and dumped cleanser onto wadded cotton. They cleaned their face, scrubbing remnants of mascara and eyeliner away, and smoothed primer over their cheeks and forehead. Three hours to apply a full-body makeup. Three hours to make sure their edges were perfect, and their paint job was perfect, and their costuming was *perfect*. Three hours to glue down five large-scale prostheses. Three hours to squeeze their feet into stilted boots and not fall on their ass in front of the judges. *Three hours. Three hours. Three—*

"Eli, breathe," Bodhi snapped. She took their elbow and turned them around. Her earthy eyes locked with theirs. "I'm here. You're here. We've got this. What's first?"

Eli inhaled, exhaled, inhaled again. "We need to get the forehead prosthesis on first, then glue down the headpiece," they said, mustering confidence. "After that, I'll have you work on getting the bodysuit ready while I finish the silicone face pieces. Paint comes last, right before hooves."

She grinned. "Hell, yeah, let's do this."

"Can I turn on music?" Cassie hollered.

"Yeah," Eli called, glancing over their shoulder. "As long as it won't distract your artist."

Zach furrowed his brows, watching Eli in the mirror as he dabbed glue onto his temple. "Nice try, babe, but you can't psych me out."

"Shut up and avert your eyes," Bodhi said, cackling. She shooed Eli toward their makeup station. "I seriously can't deal with flirting across enemy lines right now."

Zach barked a laugh. Cassie laughed, too, and music boomed through the Bluetooth speaker she parked on the counter between their two stations. Genevieve prowled around the room, shooting video and snapping photographs. Eli actively ignored zir and tried their best to ignore Zach, too. They dabbed Pros-Aide onto their forehead with a sticky sponge and aimed the hair dryer at their face, half drying the glue until it was tacky enough to hold the prosthesis in place.

"Hand me one of those," Eli said, jabbing at a stack of clean popsicle sticks. Bodhi handed them one and nodded as they worked the edges of the prosthesis into place.

Their forehead piece bubbled away from their natural brow, accentuating their temples to create space for the extravagant headpiece they'd apply next. They melted the foam with alcohol, blending the edges of the prosthesis into their skin, and blew out a relieved breath. *There.* They feathered their fingers across the piece, checking for droopy corners. *Done.*

"Ready for this?" Bodhi asked. She lifted the headpiece, which was sculpted to fit over Eli's skull and mounted with huge curved horns, and tipped her head, nodding toward the studio chair. "Oh, shit. Wait, should we have done a bald cap?"

Eli froze. Yeah, they definitely should've, but the glue was dry, their forehead prosthesis was in place, and they didn't have time to fix their mistake. Panic needled their throat. They glanced at Bodhi in the mirror and chewed hard on their lip. If the headpiece was too heavy, and it was *really* heavy, then it could slip and tear the foam on their forehead.

"I can do it without one, I think," they blurted. *I hope.* "We'll layer latex over the edges behind my ears and on my neck. It'll hold."

"Are you sure?" Bodhi asked, eyeing them skeptically.

"Yes, I'm sure." It was a risk they had to take. *I don't have time to be unsure.* "C'mon, get the hair dryer."

Eli applied a generous amount of Pros-Aide to their hairline and behind their ears and trusted Bodhi to smear the white glue on the back of their neck. She aimed the hair dryer, blowing warm air on the wet area around their buzz cut, and touched her finger to a few different places.

"You're good," she said. "Ready?"

Eli stole a glance at Zach, assessing his progress: face pieces applied, collarbones sharpened, brownish paint streaked on his face. He was ahead by a mile.

"Hey, no, none of that. Look at me. Are *you* ready?" Bodhi said, steering their chin in a pinched grip.

Their throat flexed. "Yeah," they said, too softly, then again, "Yes, I'm ready."

Carefully, Bodhi lined the headpiece over their skull. She lowered the hollow prosthesis, inching closer, closer—

"Wait!" Eli ducked, squinting at their vanity mirror. They whipped around. Bodhi's purse slouched against the far wall, zipper open, displaying her phone, a liquid lipstick tube, and unused chopsticks from Pho Madness still wrapped in white-and-red paper. "Chopsticks!" They floundered, swatting at the air. "Give me those chopsticks!"

"Chopsticks?" Cassie pulled a confused face.

"Yes, chopsticks," Eli said, exasperated, and almost knocked the chair over as they loped across the room, snatching the wooden sticks from inside Bodhi's purse. Bodhi blinked at them, still holding the horned headpiece in both hands. Eli cracked the chopsticks apart and fit one stick to the side of their face, parallel to their ear. When they popped the stick beneath their forehead prosthesis, Bodhi made a horrified noise. "It's fine—*totally* fine. These'll reinforce the forehead and cheekbone pieces and help redistribute the weight of *that*," they said, nodding at the headpiece. They dabbed Spirit Gum and Pros-Aide on the chopsticks, followed by liquid latex, and exhaled sharply. "Okay, go."

"You've either ruined your entire makeup or you're really goddamn brilliant. Don't ask me which yet," Bodhi mumbled, and fit the prosthesis to Eli's hairline.

"Yeah, don't ask me either," they said.

The piece pushed on their skull, heavy and awkward and secure, hopefully. They held it while Bodhi smoothed the edges and applied another layer of glue and latex. When she stepped back, lips squirming into a thin cringe, Eli lifted their hands away.

Stay, stay, stay.

The headpiece wasn't as sturdy as it could've been, but the prosthesis stayed put. Intricately carved horns curved away from their temples, framed by tree roots cut into the pinkish foam. They'd attached premade silk flowers to certain areas, providing a textured map for the rest of the makeup construction. With the crowning piece in place, Eli went to work applying the silicone face pieces. Their jawline extended, their cheekbones stood higher, and their ears rounded into deerlike ovals.

Bodhi said, "We need you out of this shirt."

Eli shimmied their spaghetti straps over their arms and let the garment fall, exposing their tank binder. Bodhi wrapped the binder in one layer of Ace bandage to provide a barrier for the costume—binders were expensive, and Eli couldn't afford ruining one of the only *two* they owned— and fit the beautiful, hand-sculpted foam chest piece to their body. Roots snaked into the shape of collarbones, gaping flowers bloomed on their upper half, and little caverns waited for gemstones.

"The bottom half of your outfit comes with the stilts, so we'll wait on that. Can I help you paint?" Bodhi asked.

"Yeah, can you get me some water first, maybe? My Hydro Flask is in the suitcase, I think."

"Got it." Bodhi rummaged through Eli's bags.

They finished applying the silicone and started dabbing latex over the punched-out places where the chopstick had torn their forehead foam. The result wasn't perfect, but it wasn't butchered. *Hopefully.* They could cover it with some floral accents or fake moss. *Paint. I need to paint.* They checked the timer attached to their station. One hour.

"Shit, okay . . ." They mixed paint together on the back of a well-used eyeshadow palette and layered green, beige, gold, and reddish-brown onto their face and headpiece.

Across the room, Cassie and Zach glued shiny eyeballs to the black wings hanging on the wall. His prostheses were almost completely painted.

"Water," Bodhi said, and handed Eli their Hydro Flask.

Eli took a few sips and nodded. "Thanks. The silk flowers, moss, and cotton are in that craft-store bag. Let's glue those down and finesse the paint. We'll get the pants and boots on in last looks."

"You sure we'll have time?" Bodhi grimaced.

"I can't risk walking around in those stilts until I absolutely have to. If I fall, everything is destroyed. The bottom half of the cosplay's done anyway; all we'll need to do is get me into it and make sure the paint matches," Eli said.

Bodhi sucked her teeth and forced a nod. "You know your shit, Eli. It's your call."

"We'll be fine," they assured her, and handed her a paintbrush. "One layer, hair dryer, second layer, hair dryer, speckle paint, hair dryer, then we do a final edge check. Got it?"

"Got it," she said.

Eli and Bodhi worked tirelessly. Bodhi painted the chest piece and glued terrarium moss to the foam pads jutting from Eli's shoulders, and Eli detailed their headpiece, stringing cotton around the horns to look like cobwebs, dusting glitter onto flower petals, and pressing acrylic gemstones into empty pockets in the foam.

A volunteer shouted, "Two minutes, finalists!"

Genevieve pointed zir camera at Eli, then swooped around their chair and walked toward Zach. Eli tried to keep going, to get as much done as they possibly could, but they couldn't help stealing a glance. Their heartbeat stampeded at the sight of his massive wings, intricate foam pieces, and perfect costuming. He looked amazing.

"All right, contestants! Brushes down! Please gather your touch-up bag and cosplay props and make your way backstage for last looks," the other volunteer said.

Eli took a deep breath, staring at their nautical-blue eyes in the mirror. Their contact lenses were tucked away in their bag, and their handmade staff was in the bag, too. Bodhi had the rest of their outfit hidden inside a zipped garment case, and their very last prosthetic application—two sleek goatlike eyeballs—would be glued into the divots on their silicone cheekbone pieces. *Okay, yes, I got this*, they thought, and desperately tried to ignore the subtle tug at their hairline. *Don't slip, don't slip, don't—*

"You ready?" Zach asked, sidestepping through the doorway.

"Yeah," Eli said. They smiled, trailing their gaze from Zach's immaculate headpiece to his harshly painted rib cage and frayed skirt. "You?"

"Almost, I think." He glanced down at himself.

Eli supported their headpiece with one hand as they followed the Makeup Wars volunteers through a hallway that led from the green room to the left-wing backstage. They heard the crowded theater roar with applause. The resident DJ entertained the eager audience with Top 40 remixes and fandom theme songs. When the volunteer announced the beginning of last looks, Eli lost themself in the daunting fine details. They put in their contact lenses, glued the handcrafted eyeballs into place, brushed shaved Styrofoam over their horns to look like fallen snow, and . . . stopped. Almost immediately. Their attention landed on Zach—his paint, specifically—and they halted in their tracks.

It's flat, they thought.

They could stay quiet and let him bypass the mistake. They could keep the tiny overlooked detail to themself and hope the judges deducted points. Eli swallowed, considering, and shook their head.

"Cassie," they said, and held out a short-tipped bristle brush. Cassie and Zach glanced at each other, then turned toward them. Eli bounced the brush in the air. "Speckle paint him. Trust me."

"What, why?" Cassie asked. "It's fine."

Bodhi narrowed her eyes, tugging Eli's moss-covered pants and stilts out of the garment case. "Eli, what're you—"

Eli walked over to Zach and smashed their brush into a glob of brown paint puddled on his station, diluting the color with a splash of water. They met his eyes, waited for him to nod, and flicked their thumb over the bristles, sending pinprick dots onto his prosthesis. "It looks great up close, but as soon as you give it some distance, the paint flattens a little. You need more depth to create the illusion of skin tone. I know you layered in different shades, but it's still . . ." They gestured wildly to Zach's torso. "Really muted. This'll blend everything. You know what I mean, yeah?"

Cassie took four big steps backward and tilted her head. She flicked her eyebrows and gave a curt nod. "Now I do, yeah." She switched her attention to Zach. "They're right."

"Thank you," Zach said, studying their horns. "Try to keep your head tipped toward the floor. It'll help distribute the weight on your seam." He gestured to their hairline with his pinkie finger. "Move slowly. Chin down, not up."

They adjusted their stance, pointing their chin toward their chest.

"Feel better?" he asked.

The pressure pulling near their temples lessened. "Yeah, much. Thanks."

Zach smiled. Eli smiled, too. For a moment, their nerves died, and the noise faded. Zach looked at Eli, and Eli looked back, and suddenly they were fifteen, splattering discount liquid latex from a Halloween store on each other's cheeks, and then they were sixteen, holding hands, cosplaying Usagi Tsukino and Mamoru Chiba, and then they were seventeen, laughing and kissing in a bookstore, shielding their faces with a copy of *Evangelion*. The two of them had spent years falling in love, and Makeup Wars was just another memory they'd get to keep.

"I'd kiss you, but . . ." Eli pointed at Zach's painted mouth and waved their hand in front of their foam-covered face.

Zach winked. "Kiss me after I win."

Eli flashed a grin and sped back to their station, nodding at Bodhi. "Five minutes," they said.

"Five minutes," she echoed, and held the short, curved stilts she'd rented from her indie zombie gig out to them. "Ready for these?"

"I better be," they said, masking a cringe with a pained smile.

Bodhi clipped the mossy pelvis piece around Eli's waist, fastening the hidden buttons beneath brown fabric. She guided their feet into the boot apparatuses attached to the stilts and fit the fabric covering them around Eli's thighs, knees, and shins. The stilts were secured by hoof-shaped heels adorned with roots and vines. Eli steadied themself on her shoulders, mouth pulled into a hard grimace as they tested their weight, stepping left, right, forward, backward.

A volunteer shouted, "One minute!"

"I'm gonna let you go," Bodhi said.

"Can we not?"

"Holding on to me isn't really an option."

"Okay, just . . ." They trailed off and righted themself, easing their hands away. They took a step backward and stared at their reflection in the mirror.

Bodhi kept her arms outstretched, ready to catch them. "Got it?"

"Yeah, I sure fuckin' . . ." They wobbled but stayed upright. ". . . hope so."

They assessed their reflection. Sclera lenses stretched their pupils into rectangles. Ram-like horns curled away from roots, moss, flowers, and spiderwebs. They stood taller than they ever had. For the first time, they thought, *I'm set ready*, and blinked, taken aback. *I did it.*

Bodhi handed them their gnarled, woodsy staff. "Holy shit, Eli. You look—"

"Incredible," Zach said, adjusting a ratty cape over his half-moon forehead prosthesis.

Before Eli could respond, a volunteer clapped. "Time is up! Brushes down! Assistants, please take your leave. Zachary and Eli, stand between your stations."

You got this, Bodhi mouthed, and smiled over her shoulder, walking beside Cassie toward the hallway.

Eli tried not to tremble. They wanted to wring their hands or fiddle with their cuticles, but their knuckles were covered in prostheses, elongated into thin, knobby digits, and they couldn't do anything except drum them awkwardly at their sides.

"You look incredible, too," Eli said.

Zach hummed. "It's the wings, huh?"

"Definitely."

Stilettos click-clacked on the floor. Eli squared their shoulders. They wanted to close the small space between the two of them and take Zach's hand, hold on to him and feel his thumb on their pulse point. But they stayed still, dazed and overwhelmed and maybe, finally, *ready*.

Theresa, Scott, and the final guest judge, Nichole Stevenson, approached Zach and Eli. Theresa's high-collared crimson cloak billowed around her, and her short platinum hair was worn in a pompadour. She raised her glittery eyebrows, angling a comment at Scott, who nodded in agreement and grinned.

Nichole Stevenson, a famous key makeup artist for several Oscar-winning fantasy films, gave Eli a slow once-over. Her black-painted lips curved. "Saint Harlow," she said, tipping her head politely, and turned toward Zach, "and the Angel of Death."

"You two certainly didn't hold back," Scott said. He folded his arms, glancing between Theresa and Nichole. "Shall we?"

The judges circled Zach first, pointing at certain places, nodding, smiling, trading comments and compliments. Theresa gestured to a few visible edges on his temple, and Eli's heart tumbled into their stomach. They were excited. They were devastated. They were *so* many things at once. Their blood raced, dimming the sound of Zach's voice as he answered questions. Still, his raspy laughter brought a smile to their face.

"Eli Peterson," Nichole said, stepping before them. Her ocher skin was flecked with white hand-painted freckles, and her brunette curls bunched above her shoulders. She trailed her dainty finger down the side of their face, barely tracing their foam forehead prosthesis. "Rumor has it you utilized chopsticks during the construction of this makeup. What inspired a choice like that?"

Eli almost choked. They swallowed around the lump growing in their throat and thought of lying, of making something up and weaseling their way out of an embarrassing situation. But *why*? They'd done something they'd never thought they could do, and damn, they were proud. "When you're a poor kid living in a rich city, you learn how to adjust," they said, and shrugged. "I needed to strengthen my headpiece, so I used the tools I had available. Improvisation is a part of my brand."

The judges surrounded them, humming and nodding and jotting notes on individual clipboards.

"Improvisation?" Theresa shook her head, darting her gaze from Eli's stilted hooves to their decorative horns. "I'd call it innovation," she said, and nodded slowly. "*That's* your brand. Nicely done, Peterson."

They swallowed the urge to joyfully shout and simply said, "Thank you."

"Let's see how you two look on the runway," Scott said.

"Good luck to you both," Nichole said, and followed Theresa and Scott onstage.

The theater shook with cheering and applause.

A volunteer shone a flashlight on the ground, illuminating a path to the stage. "Finalists, let's queue up!"

Keep breathing.

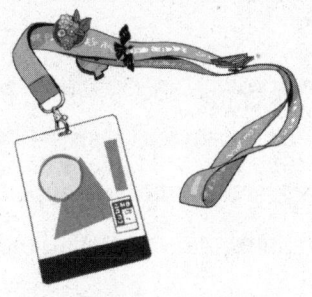

CHAPTER TWENTY-FOUR

Seattle-Sea City Comic Con

ZACH WALKED FIRST.

Eli stayed in the stage wing, watching fog machines spit mist across the stage. The Angel of Death from Hellboy spoke in otherworldly tones, and her eerie voice came creeping through the speakers. *At last. I have been waiting for you both.* Zach rose from a kneeling position at the base of a skinny runway and pushed the torn veil away from his face, revealing his extravagant facial prostheses. The crescent headpiece arched away from his forehead, cracked like porcelain where he'd dug the foam away, creating lifelike scars. *So, child, make the choice. The world or him?*

Eli mouthed the next word from the film's script. *Him.*

A spotlight illuminated Zach. He moved carefully, swiping the air with his long fingers, snapping his teeth at the audience, and took a bow. His dual black-feathered wings sent shadows darting along the runway, and his pale, sallow paint job shone beautifully under the bright stage lights.

I'm so proud of you. They clutched the metal scaffolding behind the folded curtain and resisted the urge to clap with everyone else as he exited into the opposing wing, following the route the Makeup Wars crew had indicated.

The lights dimmed. Eli braced on their cosplay staff, reinforced by a metal pool-net stick beneath fake branches. *One foot in front of the other,* they thought. Beyond was right there, hovering at their fingertips, and all they had left to do was walk onstage, remind the audience and the judges that Eli Peterson was a makeup artist to remember, and seize their dreams. They were the best of the best. They'd become the face of an ever-changing, always evolving industry— the future.

"Okay, Eli." A Makeup Wars volunteer melted from the darkness, beckoning them forward with a flashlight. "In three ... two ..."

Scott Brant spoke into the microphone, his voice echoing powerfully. "Please welcome to the stage Makeup Wars finalist Eli Peterson!"

The volunteer nodded and waved the flashlight back and forth.

Eli steadied themself and walked onstage. Their introduction music played: whistling wind, chirping birds, and a recording from the live tabletop session where Saint Harlow, the enchanting wizard from *Chaos Reign*, first entered the campaign. The dungeon master's voice filled the amphitheater—*You see a great faun who wears the forest as his armor, holding a staff cut from the Memory Tree*—followed by excited cheering and heavy applause. Neon-green lasers shot from side to side, and a spotlight blinked to life, bathing Eli in light as they took their place at center stage, staring out at the audience.

Every seat was taken. People shouted and clapped and pointed. Eli smacked their staff against the ground in time with the recording, capturing the point in the tabletop session when Saint Harlow walked from his grove. The faun's voice filled the room: *Hello, adventurers, how may I be of assistance?*

Eli breathed, took a step, and forced their legs to stop quivering, using their staff to stay balanced. They scanned the crowd, hyperfocused on lifting their feet, placing the stilts firmly on the ground, and doing their makeup justice. When they reached the end of the runway, they stood proudly, turning toward one half of the room, then winding their neck toward the other, careful to keep their chin tipped downward. In their fuzzy peripheral vision, they caught a familiar smile.

Bodhi waved her arms, pointing dramatically to the people beside her.

Eli almost faltered. Their mom and dad clapped, craning as far from their seats as they possibly could to get a good look at Eli. Claire grinned and Gary cupped his hands around his mouth, sending a cheer into the air. Stella, who stood a foot taller than their mother, pointed at Eli and spoke close to Claire's ear. Bodhi nudged Gary with her elbow, laughing and clapping. *They see me.* Eli jumped back into character and waved their staff across the crowd. For the first time, their parents were truly seeing what Eli could do with foam and paint, latex and silicone, and a lucky pair of chopsticks, and they knew only one person could be responsible for making that happen.

They eased down the runway, bowed before the judges, and took one last look at the theater before walking into the stage wing where Zach stood, wings already stripped from his back, smiling at Eli.

"Need help?" Zach asked. His voice didn't match the Angel's hidden eyes and skeletal face. He held his arm out for Eli to clutch, bracing them as they reached for the buttons on their hoof covers and stepped out of their stilts.

"Did you fly my parents out here?" Eli blurted. They flexed their feet, grateful to be flat on the ground again.

Zach glanced over his shoulder, then faced Eli again. They couldn't see his expression, couldn't read his eyes or the set of his mouth. He nodded, though, and cleared his throat. "I asked the airline to put the credit for the two canceled flights onto a gift card. I didn't, like, *pay* for their flights—I mean, I *did*—but I couldn't get a cash refund, and your parents actually *wanted* to be here." He shrugged, bumping his foam-covered fingers against Eli's hand. "I've known your family for years, Liz. They've been good to me."

Eli blinked. Their heart pushed hard against their ribs and *reached*.

"I didn't mean to overstep," Zach said. "I just, I know you wanted them here and—"

"Thank you," Eli said, sighing through a laugh. They wanted to throw their arms around him, but they might've torn their foam chest piece or ruined his paint job if they did. "I'd kiss you if we weren't covered in latex."

Zach's lips twitched into a relieved smile, and he took their hand, gripping gently. The foam prostheses bent and squished between their laced knuckles, but Eli didn't mind. They held on to the boy they'd loved and lost and vowed to never let him go again. Even with the results of the competition looming, even with anxiety bouncing around inside them, Eli knew they had *him*. Zachary Miller. And together, they could do anything.

"Liz!" Claire shouted, and hurried toward them, guided by Bodhi and Stella. She went in for a hug and stopped abruptly, shaking out her cheap French manicure. "Oh, sorry, sorry. I don't want to hurt any of the—" She glided her palms in front of them. "Foam? It's foam, right?"

"Mostly," Eli said. They let go of Zach's hand and reached for their mom, squeezing her wrist. "I can't believe you're here . . ." They turned toward Gary as he approached. "Hey, Dad, you made it."

"Zach got us on a last-minute flight," Gary said. He glanced from Eli's horns to their socked feet. "I've seen your makeup stuff before, you know. Always knew you were talented, but," he trailed off, sucked in air, filling his cheeks, and puffed out a breath. "This is a whole other level, kid."

"Yeah, it's been a long time comin'," Eli said.

Claire shook her head in disbelief, still assessing their makeup. "I saw pictures, and, and I mean, I've seen your Weblog channel, but I never, *wow*, honey. I never realized you taught yourself how to do *this*."

Eli tried to smile. They didn't know what to say to something like that. "I'm glad you're here," they said, fiddling nervously with their hand prostheses.

Bodhi lifted a brow and stepped into Eli's space, taking them by the elbow. Somehow, she could always sense when they needed to decompress. Despite the excitement crowding their chest, Eli knew they should take a breath. Be alone—well, not *alone*—and strip the glue from their skin, make room for the person they'd been before Makeup Wars, and sink into the self they'd become at Beyond.

Hopefully.

"Let's get you cleaned up," Bodhi said.

Eli sighed. "We'll grab dinner after the announcement, yeah?"

"Yeah, of course," Claire cooed.

"Cassie's waiting for me in the green room," Zach said. "You headin' that way, too?"

They nodded and released their mom's wrist. "Wish me luck," they said.

Claire and Gary both grinned. Claire glanced at Zach and raised her brows. "No offense to you, sweetheart, but"— she flicked her gaze to Eli—"you don't need it," she said, and blew Eli a kiss.

Eli clutched their stilts, and Zach carried his wings. The pair trudged behind the stage, through the hallway that led to the left wing, and walked into the green room. Eli held the door for Bodhi and Stella with their staff. They flapped their lips once the lock clicked.

"You two killed it out there. I'm not even kidding. Like, straight-up murdered the runway," Cassie said. She took the wings from Zach and hung them carefully on the wall.

Eli practically fell into the studio chair in front of their station. "I'm kinda glad it's over. Is that weird? Not, like, *overjoyed*, just, I don't know. Relieved, I guess."

"Not weird," Zach said, coughing out laughter. "I'm *extremely* ready to go back to being *Zach-who's-sorta-cool-on-Instagram* and stop being *Zachary-Miller-Makeup-Wars-finalist.*"

"I think you're stuck with the finalist title," Stella said. She worked makeup remover and alcohol underneath Eli's prostheses, easing the latex away from their irritated skin. "At least until they announce Makeup Wars season two."

"Damn, you think they'll do another contest?" Cassie asked.

Stella shrugged. "With how successful this one was? I don't see why not."

Eli pawed at their face, scrubbed stubborn latex from their cheeks, peeled the chopsticks away, worked Pros-Aide off their hairline, and rinsed their face in the temporary sink. Globs of foam and latex clung to their jaw and ears, but their Saint Harlow makeup came off more easily than it had gone on, leaving their flesh blotchy and naked. It felt like hours before anyone spoke. Bodhi moved between stations, assisting Cassie with Zach's makeup removal, then helping Stella with Eli. Once the sticky mess was gone, Eli unwrapped the bandage from around their torso and wanted, desperately, to get out of their binder.

They braved a glance at their Instagram messages and cracked a smile.

BeverlyBelle_BB: YOU DID SO AMAZING!!!

On the Makeup Wars account, two red bars inched away from circular headshots of Zach and Eli, showcasing the social media vote. The countdown—02:34 *Until Voting Closes*—flashed in bold letters. The two of them were *so* close. Eli slid their phone into their pocket. They wanted to sit on the floor. Scream, maybe. Unscrew the valve on their anxiety and let it drain.

"Brandon's waiting for me. We're grabbing a snack from the sushi truck parked outside the convention. Anyone want anything before we go back for the boss fight?" Cassie pointed behind her with her thumb, gesturing to the theater.

"I'll go," Stella said. She tied her hair into a ponytail. "I could use a soda or something."

Bodhi glanced between Eli and Zach, who watched each other from opposite sides of the room. "Yeah, I'll join you," she said. "You two stayin' here?"

"Yeah, I shouldn't eat," Eli said. The thought made their stomach turn. "Not until after we get the results, at least."

"Zach?"

"I'm good," Zach said.

"Okay," Bodhi said cautiously. She left with Stella and Cassie, throwing a last-minute smile over her shoulder.

The door closed and Eli let their shoulders go heavy. Their eyes softened, and they swayed on their feet, dragging themself across the room to sink against Zach's chest. "Help me get this thing off," they whined, plucking at the edges of their binder. "I know I'm tired, but I'm too nervous to *feel* tired, and I know I'm hungry, but I'm scared I'll puke in front of Theresa if I eat."

Laughter punched out of Zach. He ran his palm along their nape, scooping his hand around the back of their head. "We're almost done."

Eli made a pathetic noise and hiked their thigh around his waist, hands braced on his shoulders.

"Oh, my God, you gigantic baby," Zach mumbled, and hoisted them into his arms. "I can't help with your binder if we stand here like this."

"Fine, that's fair." They lowered their feet to the carpeted floor and tugged at their binder, folding the material around their arms.

Zach pulled the binder over their head and flipped it right side out.

Eli immediately grabbed at their chest, massaging sore places and rubbing their ribs. They took a full breath and exhaled slowly, letting air come and go in hungry gulps. Zach draped their binder over the back of his studio chair and flattened his hands above their breasts, kneading at their collarbones and the soft pouch beneath their armpits.

"Bet you're excited to get rid of that sometime soon," Zach said, nodding toward their binder.

"*Hopefully* sometime soon," they corrected. "But yeah, I am. I *really* am."

"Feelin' better, at least?" he asked, massaging soreness out of their ribs.

Eli nodded, lashes fluttering. Exhaustion and relief battled just beneath their skin. "Yeah, much." They crossed the room and retrieved their sports bra. Fingered through their stage outfit—black high-necked tank, torn denim, and sequined sneakers—and glanced at their reflection. *This is it.* Zach met their eyes in the mirror. *This is the end.* They stayed there, Eli watching him, Zach watching them.

"I love you," Zach said tenderly, honestly.

"I know," Eli said. Their lips curved. "I love you, too."

Zach laughed under his breath. "Yeah, I know."

Harsh light streaked the stage in the theater.

Eli stared at an empty seat in the very back row, narrowing their focus onto something immovable and unchanging. Something silent. Around them, the audience chattered and whispered, watching from the shadowed area beyond the stage lights. Zach stood beside them, stoic and handsome in his black denim and crisp button-down shirt. Music roared, flatscreens flashed, and Eli wanted to hold his hand.

They didn't dare move, though.

Colorful neon striped the stage, illuminating the table where Theresa Jenkins, Scott Brant, and Nichole Stevenson sat. Eli wanted someone to speak. Wanted the world to turn faster. They wanted to know—*finally*—whether they'd done enough, shown enough, proven enough to earn their place at Beyond. They knew their parents were somewhere in the crowd, sitting with Bodhi, Stella, Cassie, and Brandon, but they hadn't looked for them. *Couldn't* look for them, afraid their knees would give out or they'd start to cry the second their mom met their eyes.

"You okay?" Zach whispered.

Eli tipped their chin toward him. "Absolutely not."

Zach looped his finger around their pinkie.

Finally, Scott Brant brought the microphone to his mouth. "It's been a long road for our two finalists. From an immortal dragon to a reinvented beast, a well-dressed symbiote to the big bad wolf, Eli and Zach, you've shown us just how creative, innovative, and downright badass makeup artists can be."

"Both of you have created stunning cosplays," Nichole said. She leaned forward, hands knitted on the table, and flashed a smile. "Zachary, your mastery of overall design construction makes you a force to be reckoned with. Not only can you build a head-to-toe makeup, but you have an eye for movement, profile, stature, and texture that most experienced professionals still have trouble rendering. At this point, I have a hard time calling you an amateur." The audience whooped and clapped. Zach accepted the compliments with a smile and followed Nichole's attention as she switched her gaze to Eli. "And Eli, your creativity is bold and fresh," she said, furrowing her brow in concentration. "You display gorgeous, innovative technique that could shake up the industry, and you inject bravery into your work that speaks volumes up close and onstage. At your caliber, you'll be giving me a run for my money soon."

Eli nodded, because they didn't know what else to do, and they didn't know if they could speak, and they were scared that if they opened their mouth, they'd hiccup or sob or anxiously laugh.

"But there can only be one winner," Nichole said.

The lights dimmed.

Eli reached for Zach. Snatched his hand and squeezed. Breathed a little easier when he squeezed back.

Theresa stood and swept her slender arm toward the crowd. "All right, Sea City. Are you ready to find out who will win a twelve-month scholarship to Beyond and take home the first annual Makeup Wars crown?"

The theater erupted into cheers and shouts.

"Keep holding on to me," Zach whispered.

Eli squeezed his hand harder.

The flatscreens above the stage came to life. Clips from past runways played. Eli walking as Shenron and Zach baring his fangs at the camera. Beverly flashing a peace sign, kissing Eli's cheek. Sound played over the speakers—music, laughter, applause, memories—muting the sound of Eli's heartbeat. Rhonda Riot winked at the screen and said, "I vote Zach."

Next, Cassie Anne Montgomery fluttered her falsies, covered in glitter and pastel powder. She waggled her finger at the camera. "*Choose?* Between Zach and Eli? No way!"

Beverly Belle fluffed her powder brush at the screen and said, "I vote Eli, baby!"

Selfies came and went, still shots from judging panels, photographs from Oakland and San Francisco, San Diego and Portland. The last two shots sat side by side: Zach's entry video, his demonic horns and silicone sigil work, and Eli's entry video, their beautiful Annihilation makeup crowned with flowery antlers.

"And the winner is . . ."

Eli shut their eyes.

They squeezed Zach so tightly that their hand shook in his. Set their teeth hard and braced for *Zachary Miller* to echo through the theater. Rallied the courage to be happy, to smile and nod and be thankful. Underneath it all, they *hoped*. They clung to hope until it hurt, until hope filled their body, until hope was the only thing keeping them standing.

This is it. Be okay with it. I did it. I might not've done it. Be happy for him. Smile. This is it. Don't cry. Just smile. This is it. This is—

Theresa shouted, "Eli Peterson!"

Eli opened their eyes and whirled toward the oversized television. Their face filled the screen, and *Eli Peterson* scrolled across the frame. *I did it.* Their lungs emptied. They gasped, locking their knees to prevent a catastrophic crash, and stared at the impossible. All those excruciating double shifts, bargain hunting at the grocery store, haggling for bottom-shelf weed, saving every penny for top surgery. Coupon clipping for beauty supplies, skipping college debt to chase a wild dream, competing against the best and winning.

And winning.

"You did it, babe," Zach said, and brought Eli's knuckles to his lips.

Eli threw their arms around him. *Let the world see us,* they thought. *Let them see me.* They clung to him, laughing joyfully and frantically against his neck, and kissed him firmly on the mouth. Around them, the theater exploded into applause.

I did it. We did it. I made it.

Los Angeles-Beyond

"SEA SPONGES ARE GREAT TOOLS. I KEEP AN EMERGENCY one in my kit in case I need it on set," Theresa said, standing tall and poised in front of Eli's station. She dabbed a pockmarked yellow sponge on Eli's modeling clay and nodded curtly. "There we go. . . . Is that the look you were after?"

Eli assessed the tiny dents left in the clay, creating the illusion of scales. "Yeah, that's exactly it. Do you think I can deepen this kind of design with a spatula, too? Like, dig the holes out more?"

She tipped her head from side to side, considering. "You could. Be careful, though. Once you bake the clay and run your foam, it'll tear pretty easily. Make sure you're giving the prosthesis room to stretch."

"Right, got it." They flashed a smile as Theresa nodded and moved on.

Around them, other students carved clay into fantastical shapes—fins, eyes, feathers, horns—chatting with each other about creature design, internships, and the competitive job market in Hollywood. It had been three months since the fall semester had started at Beyond, and Eli still couldn't believe they'd made it. The curriculum was extensive, covering topics like character creation, full-face execution, running foam, working with silicone, and full-body application. They'd finished the first segment of character creation in November, and now they were working on the foam pieces for their final project before winter break. Of course they'd picked a serpentlike warrior from *Chaos Reign* to create. *Ridiculously difficult to pull off* was kind of their brand now.

Go big or go home, right?

They followed Theresa's advice and continued to blot the sea sponge over the gray clay smoothed onto their face-casting—basically a stone mannequin—and nodded as the scales took shape. *There.* They stepped back and gave the face-cast a once-over. Of course, Theresa was spot-on, and the sea sponge provided just enough texture to transform the plain piece into something feral and reptilian.

Sometimes they couldn't believe Beyond was real. They took a moment and listened to Theresa's stilettos click-clack onto the smooth floor as she made her rounds. The artist beside them, an exchange student named Francesca, sang along to the French hip-hop playing from her mobile speaker. The air smelled like latex, paint, and wet clay, and when they glanced through the open classroom door, they saw someone squeal and startle as they were splattered with corn syrup in the adjacent room. Mixed in between the film posters and inventive pieces of art, informative posters were pinned around the whiteboard, pointing out different face shapes, sensitive materials, and safety practices.

Another student patted Eli's shoulder as he walked by, rolling his makeup kit behind him. "See you tomorrow, Eli," Todd said, gesturing to their sculpted clay and grinning. "Looks sick, man! Can't wait to see it in color."

"Oh, thanks," they responded. "Fingers crossed it turns out okay."

They checked the time on their phone as more of their classmates started packing up and cleaning their stations. Most were going home, heading out for drinks, or trudging to an evening shift at whatever day job paid the bills, but Eli had a night off from the diner. So they took their time draping the mannequin in plastic wrap to keep the clay from drying out and tucked each tool into their brush belt, enjoying the growing quiet while the other students left.

Their phone buzzed, but before they could open the message, a voice sounded from across the room, and they turned.

"You're doing well, by the way," Theresa said, leaning against an empty station. "I knew you would, but . . ." She shrugged and adjusted her glittery cardigan. "You're an even happier surprise than I anticipated."

Eli had been enrolled for a few months, but they'd never talked to Theresa alone. Not like this, at least, one on one; totally casual. Sometimes they still felt like they were walking with giants. "Thank you. I'm . . . I'm still finding my sea legs, I think."

Theresa barked out a laugh. "You've found 'em," she assured them, and walked through the open door. "See you in the morning!"

"Yeah, bye—see you tomorrow," they called, kicking themself for sounding like a starstruck fanboy. *She's still Theresa fucking Jenkins, though.* They blew out a sigh and glanced at their phone. First, they flicked through their email, checking the confirmation for their next appointment with Dr. Tamura. *January 16. Presurgical screening.* Eli grinned at their phone and opened their text messages.

> **Zach ♡:** I'm downstairs
> **Eli Peterson:** sorry—got held up. omw.

Beyond shared a building with a vintage theater and a Euro-themed café. Framed photographs of graduates and famous designs lined the hall, showcasing major success stories like Ve Neill, Rick Baker, and Kazuhiro Tsuji. *I'll be up there one day.* Their heart revved at the thought. They waved to a few classmates loitering in the break area and said goodbye to the receptionist at the front desk. In the elevator, they checked their notifications on Instagram and TikTok. Ever since winning Makeup Wars, they'd been swamped with comments, likes, and requests for trades and features. Sponsorships had flooded their email, and they'd invested in a PO box to handle the influx of product being thrown their way. It was everything they'd hoped for: the high-end brands, the paychecks, Beyond . . .

Everything and more, actually.

Eli stepped out of the elevator, pushed through the door, and was greeted by Zach leaning against the side of his truck. He looked at Eli over the top of his black sunglasses and smiled, uncrossing his arms to reach for them.

"Good day?" he asked.

Eli found purchase on his waist and kissed him. "Great day," they mumbled against his lips. "Did you finish it?"

He made an uncertain noise. "Sort of. Maybe."

"C'mon, did you launch or not?"

Cars whizzed by and people crowded the sidewalk, but Eli ignored it all. They set their train case between their feet and leaned into Zach, watching him expectantly. Being with him again, after everything they'd been through together, felt like a new chapter in Eli's weird, fast life. *We were always supposed to get here*, they thought, and tilted their head, meeting his steady gaze. *We were always meant to be this.*

"Launched this morning, and I'm twenty percent funded," Zach said sheepishly. His smile stretched into a grin. "Guess people like my graphic novel after all."

"Told you," Eli whispered. They kissed him again—cheek, neck, lips, nose, lips again—and laughed. "Told you, told you, told you—"

"I know, I know—"

"Say it."

"You were *right*," Zach admitted, heaving a sigh. He bumped his nose against their own. "Thank you."

"For what?"

"Believing in me."

Eli smirked to shield the powerful, visceral emotion swelling inside them. Love and something else. Pride, maybe. Hope. "Yeah, always."

Zach pecked them on the lips. "Ready? Pretty sure Bodhi'll kill us if we're late."

Bodhi had insisted on dinner at a new sushi place in West Hollywood, Zach had finally started chasing the career he'd always wanted, and Eli was standing on the edge of something huge, and promising, and attainable.

We made it, they thought, and squeezed Zach's hand. "Yeah, let's go."

ACKNOWLEDGMENTS

This book wouldn't exist without the phenomenal influencers showcasing their skills on social media. A big thank-you to every homegrown, self-taught cosplayer, makeup artist, and designer—your artistry inspired me to write an entire book! Like, a whole book! My writing journey started on a whim and wouldn't have been possible without my agent, Haley Casey, who championed my work from the very first page, or my editor, Britny Brooks, who shares my love for everything nerdy, geeky, and romantic. I'm grateful for the team at Running Press for their incredible enthusiasm. To my family, thank you for having my back. To my pets, thank you for always making me smile.